CROSSROADS

JAYNE GRANT

To order additional copies of this book, contact:
Bookwhip
1-855-339-3589
https://www.bookwhip.com

CHAPTER 1

In the early morning hours just as the sun came up, Bond was running on the beach. Chris watched him from the patio. Bond ran to Chris breathing deeply tired from his run. What got you to be the athlete this morning? I need, he bent over breathing deeply. I need to get back to the way things were. Chris stood back looking puzzled at what he just heard. Everything is still the same. Where is your, wife? Jane, she is sleeping at least she was when I left the room. Good. What do you mean by that? Nothing, I'm going to go shower and leave. Leave for what? An appointment. With who? Just an appointment,

Chris watched Bond quickly leave and wondered on what he just heard him say and act. I'm going to get some coffee, I think that he has already had too much, too much of something, anyway. Good thing that I canceled my appointment this morning, I really need the time with her. In the kitchen after swallowing his first sip of coffee-nothing like dad's coffee. In turning he smiled when he saw his father sitting there at the table. I like what I just heard. He nodded then poured Vincent a cup and sat there with him enjoying the morning brew. He told Vincent the behavior of his brother. Vincent nodded, said that he noticed it too.

The morning silence was broken by the sound of a car engine racing to the side of the house. Chris looked out the side door of the kitchen and saw a Ferrari racing out the open gate of the estate. What has gotten into him? Hopefully it won't last too long. Where is your wife? She is upstairs sleeping; I think otherwise she'd be here. How about some breakfast dad, you always did like my eggs? Vincent nodded. Chris went on to cook breakfast then Jane came in looking very happy Chris instantly smiled to her. I'd hug you put my hands are full. She told him it was okay and poured herself a cup of coffee then sat down to a plate of food in front of her. They then all said grace and began breakfast. How'd you know that I'd be here when I did? We're married, aren't we? She snickered.

Bond drove, breathing out he made a sour face then lowered his speed. He turned on some music, a Meatloaf song played, 'All Dressed Up and nowhere to go'. Bond thought how fitting. He slowed down even more as he passed the boarded-up coffee shop with a for sale sign on it. He made a solemn face then sped up to merge on to the freeway. Parking at the medical complex was easier than he anticipated. A car pulled out in the front row, right as he drove there, he waited then took it. Alone walking in the building, he felt his nerves race through his body, He stopped holding the doorknob to the physician's office then held it hard and turned pushing it open. He was meet by a nurse sitting behind the counter, almost as if she was waiting for him. He registered then sat for only a minute until he was called in to see the physician. They smiled to each other then he took a seat opposite her desk. She asked him is that was okay or they could move to the couch. He told her that it was fine. What should I call you? Dr. Stone, will be fine, unless you have a problem with that. He shook his head, no.

Good thing that I had a cancelation this morning because on the phone you sounded like this was a most urgent matter of great importance. He moved back in the chair then sunk lower in it. That or this is, I mean it has been a certain way for years and now I question everything and don't feel like I am of. He stopped then breathed out. The doctor asked him to slow up and take the time to explain each thing that he said. He was quiet, she took over the conversation. When you say a certain way for years, what are you talking about? He sighed and remained quiet. Is it your marriage? He burst into speaking in a loud voice, NO that is just it, I am not married, but he is and his wife wants me. Slow down, when you say he, who is he? He is my brother. Does your brother have a name? Yes, it is Chris, and his wife is Jane.

And his wife Jane wants you, how so? Well. We had a sort of affair. When you say sort of, do you mean physically? I had to look after her and the closeness and we almost. But you didn't? Right, we didn't. Well then there is not a worry there. Why were you watching her? He stopped then pressed in at his inner thighs very firmly. He was away at work and she was staying at the house while he was away and needed protection and I was it. We were great friends and talked all the time and then I guess one thing just LED to another. Wait, wait, when you say needed protection, from what or who, was someone after her? I, I, I … have said to much. He got up from the chair and moved his body standing in place. You can stay or you can go, but what you say to me is purely confidential, I cannot say anything about it. I am merely here to help you and I do see that you are struggling with a lot right now. You made the correct first step in being here. Now, just stay here and follow through with it, so that it will not be a waste of either one of our times.

He sat back down and went on to explain most of the entire situation to her. She did have to interrupt him only to tell him that they were out of time. The foremost thing for him to do right now was continue on with appointments with her. He felt so much better in being able to release with her and not worry about backlash from saying the wrong thing to the wrong person. On his way out he scheduled another appointment, luckily one was available the following week. She told him that the most important thing for him to do was stay calm, and if he had a hobby to fully embrace himself in it for calmness.

He backed out of the parking lot feeling that a giant weight was just released from his shoulders. In viewing people walking up and down the streets, he saw that they were all wearing facial masks. He thought that was good then thought of the plague embracing society at that time then lowered himself back to feeling sad. He then thought that he didn't wear the mask in her office. She probably needed to see his facial expression and there was a distance between them in her large desk.

Now on the road with traffic he thought of anything to do. Basically, life had stopped with the virus. Solitude circled around him. "Well, I can drive by and just watch everything. Hobbies, what are my hobbies? Chasing enemies, thwarting crime…No Batman already has that job. And he has

Robin-sorry Batman, but I can't help you." He then laughed to himself thinking of a grown man dressed in leotards flying through the air to capture someone dressed as a Penguin.

He closed his side window and turned on the air conditioning, feeling the utmost still heat of the day. Nothing moved, not a tree branch, leaf, nothing moved-it was like the camera of life just stopped and froze in a locked frame. He thought it very odd being the ocean so close- but then the entire world was different at this moment in time. Watching everything-looking at the entire scope of his surroundings, he noticed a large sign to his right, it was advertising a sale at a local sports shop-golf clubs were on sale. He then perked up and moved his head to the side. "I haven't golfed in so long that I can't even remember. Go to the driving range a hit a bucket of balls. My clubs, I don't even know where to look for them and no help any more to have them go look for them. Well, it'll give me something to do. Back to the estate." He turned to his right and headed home.

Back at the estate, Chris walked the grounds and occasionally practiced karate moves, looking more than uptight being the lack of a goal to accomplish. And still lost in thinking of the illegal organ transplant operation and how that had been set up. Trying to clear his mind from this atrocity he thought of Lauren, his daughter. He was so proud that she was in college now, but then felt bad on the fact that he didn't even know what her major even was. "I can ask her in conversation sometime. Like that will ever happen, her sly wit and always wanting to get one up on the conversation. And Bond, he is my brother but the only things that we basically have ever done together is fight crime or have dinner together at the family table. What happened to life? There was never a question about it until right now.

Bond drove in the estate and the first thing that he saw was his brother, Chris. He saw Chris look to him as a stranger would look to someone in a parking lot, he then walked around the side of the house, and out of view. Now of the SUV, he turned to the gate hearing a car horn honk. He reached to the back of his pants only to find that his gun wasn't there, and he turned back to the direction in which he did see his brother and he was gone. Now his only choice was to apprehensively walk closer. His cell phone rang, instead of ignoring it being in action he stopped and answered it. It was a welcome voice to hear. He then ran to the gate and pressed it open for the white fiat to enter. He stepped back to make room for this man to get out. It was Jonathan. They each held their hands out to the other showing a welcoming. And exchanged that it was good to see each other.

"It is sure good to see you, Jonathan, have you recovered from Vegas?" He stepped back then straightened his posture and replied yes. "Vincent, will sure be glad to see you." He again stepped back then looked a bit nervous. Bond tilted his head in question. He spoke in a softer voice then before. "How, is you dad, ah father doing? I haven't heard anything one way or the other, so I am a bit nervous on how to behave." Bond sighed in relief, no fear in the question. He breathed in then straightened his stance. "My father, ah our father, is doing good considering what he has been through. Bond then stepped back. "Well that is good to hear. Ah," "What is it Jonathan?" "I am just going to ask you, are you okay, you seem a bit bothered by something." He thought, how could he tell, was it that transparent. Bond smiled and then said he was probably still experiencing jet lag. They both knew that this wasn't true, but it passed for the interim.

Jonathan then got back in his car and drove to the front of the house. Bond took his bags and welcomed inside the house. Maggie hearing the noise came out to greet them. She explained that Vincent was in his office and see would go and tell him that he was here. Jonathan waved his hands up, "No, don't bother him. I would just like to go and freshen up first anyway. Bond then took the bags up the stairs and Jonathan followed. Chris looked in the wall window watching this, he did nothing in regards to the new guest being there, he just stayed outside, quiet.

In walking down, the stairs, Bond more than felt that he was the new servant and guard. He thought to himself that Jonathan being there would be good for his father. They could tell old war stories or whatever, just most importantly especially at this moment-company for each other. Although after seeing Jonathan's actions in Vegas, he was still a very fit agile and intelligent man. Bond more than above anything else wanted to go outside to the beach and just take a walk and get his feelings in order, but then there was this mysterious behavior from his brother. He stood in place at the bottom of the stairs and just thought, why this "new" feeling toward him? All through life they had literally walked in each other's footprints. He then thought, maybe that was it, what was he looking for? Was, Chris looking for also- identity. But, why now? He breathed in and then exclaimed to himself, the virus was wreaking havoc with everything, this could be the explanation.

He went in the kitchen grabbed a bottle of water then went to the back deck and looked at the ocean. Not feeling the presence of his brother, he kicked off his shoes and went for walk on the beach. It literally felt like he was breathing in life to his body, he was very thankful for this feeling. Then in a quick flash he heard the sound of gunfire. He dropped and rolled on the loose sand of the beach and shivered in fear. Chris ran to him faster than could be seen. He lifted his wrist and felt for a pulse. Bond opened his eyes in fear as to who he was going to see. He was shocked when he saw that it was Chris. "Come on, let me help you up." Bond stumbled up from the sand. Feeling at risk at being in is brothers' arms. After a short walk to the patio, he placed him on a patio chair the stood back seeing the expression on Bond's face. "After everything, you saved me." Chris looked skeptical, "Saved, you from what?" "The shot." "Bond, there was no shot, no noise of any kind. Were you up late watching horror movies or something? There is nothing and nobody out there, I assure you. This is what I have been doing all day, guarding us." Chris then took Bond's tired body to his room and put him down to rest on his bed. As he closed the door, he heard Bond whisper "Thank You."

Especially after what just happened, Chris felt all the more need to patrol the grounds of the estate, but this behavior from his brother more than alarmed him. There was now an apparent need to talk to his father and if Jonathan was there, all the better. He made a quick stop from going directly to his father to see and check on Jane. She was in their bedroom and painting, when she saw whim see smiled to him then returned to her work. He smiled back to her then left the room.

He paused at the closed door to the office and heard only silence. This alarmed him. He returned to the front of the house and opened a bureau drawer then took out a 45 and checked the chamber, it was loaded. He then went back to the office; he knocked gently on the door and heard no answer. He held the knob tightly and swung it open instantly jumping to the side of the door jam. All was still quiet. Apprehensively with the gun cocked then he jumped into full view of the room. There it was or he was, his father was asleep sitting at his desk chair. Chris relaxed lowered his body and lowered the hand gun. He heard the sounds of a person walking toward him down the hallway to the office, he jumped to the side to see this anomaly- it was Jonathan who was composed and questioned his actions.

Everything is fine, father has just drifted off to sleep. "Oh, should I come back then?" He moved back leaving the doorway clear. "No, I know that he will want to see you, I will just wake him up." He gently walked to him then tapped his shoulder. He opened his eyes Chris smiled to him then pointed to Jonathan. Smiles and laughter then filled the air of the office. Chris then left, closing the door behind him.

Leaving the office, he naturally headed to his brothers' room. He gently opened the door and saw Bond lying on the bed and moving his body mumbling words that he could not understand. Then thinking of his behavior on the beach, he thought of whether to go or stay. He checked the room for weapons, there was a handgun at the side night stand drawer. Chris softly took it out then checked the bathroom. He came out with his razor and extra blades. He looked to him again and debated on whether to leave or stay. He then immediately thought of how this happened in Vegas only the situation reversed. The question entered his mind was he now an alcoholic again? The wrong drugs? So much had just happened and they each did not have the youth factor any more. He stayed in his room to observe him. A gentle snore was the first thing that he heard. "Maybe he is just exhausted and indeed sleep is the answer, hopefully this is the case." After 10 minutes of watching him sleep, he left and returned to patrolling the estate.

An hour later, Bond did wake up. He looked confused as to where he was and why he was there. "Was there trouble?" He went to the bathroom and took a long steamy shower he got out and tied a white plush cotton bath towel around his waist. He wiped the steam from the mirror and looked to the image in the mirror in question. I have aged and it shows. I have always been the calm one and I am alone. The future is here, I was going to be the one running the operation and now, Chris is here. It's a whole new spinning wheel, my life that has been planned out like a peg on a game board. Right now, I do not want to face life. So, what else is there to do? He breathed out and closed his eyes then got up from the bed and dressed for the day, walking out of the bedroom door he put on smiling shield over his face.

He opened the office door and was surprised in not seeing his father there, the living room was also empty and no sign of his brother. He went to kitchen; they were all there. "Ah, Bond, are you going to join us for lunch?" "Is it that time already? What day is it?" "It is Tuesday." "Well, that explains it, it is Tuesday with nowhere to go." A slight laugh centered the room. He looked to see what they were eating, fresh cut fruits and vegetables, He at first grimaced at what he saw then thought of the healthiness of the meal and pulled out a chair to join in. The talk was nothing more than each stating their own opinion on what was the best movie of all time. Maggie asked Bond on his favorite. "Well, of course, The Godfather" Laughter again filled the room. He did make note that Jane only looked over to him twice. Was it something that someone said to her or was this really her new feeling toward him? He was both relived and a bit hurt by her sudden loss of interest. Maybe it was just because everyone was there.

Jonathan thanked Vincent for that meal. "I appreciate that you made note of my diet now, on greens vegetables, fruits and limiting meats and sugars." Vincent, nodded in thanks. He then thought of all of the starch in their diets and how a change to eating like this will be beneficial to them all. The doorbell rang. They all looked to each other. Chris was not there, he must know and let whoever was there be there. Bond went to the door with Jonathan just a foot length behind him. Bond had to sign for the box. It was 24 by 24 inches and it had air holes in it. His first thought was someone sent them a plant, it seemed logical as his father was recovering. He picked it up and found it to be heavy he moaned. Jonathan then tapped him and told him to put it down. In doing this he noticed that all of them were at the door watching him. He ripped the heavy tape closure on top of the box then moved each side open. "I don't believe it, I mean I said it the other day, but really!" He smiled from ear to ear then picked it up tail wagging and all. A German Shephard puppy, black in color with a tan chest and face. He hugged it, it at first whimpered then licked his face. He put it down as it started peeing. They all laughed. "What are you going to name it?" He again picked it up and checked the plumbing. "It is male." The whole group responded "well." He saw that Chris was watching from the side of the house with a smile. "What am I going to name this little guy? Why James of course." Chris walked closer as he said this. "Perfect choice, Bond."

The next few days went on as the newly formed life as usual. Bond introduced James to the beach- at first water was the enemy to be barked at. Bond had to go and save James from being swept back out in the ocean water, he thought it better to wait a few months before having him comb the beach. He introduced the puppy to the water in the swimming pool, and was surprised at how instantly he was able to swim, the dog paddle of course. The one thing that Bond did not like in raising this puppy was the accidents in the house and on occasion stepping on little piles.

Chris looked down the hallway to Bond's bedroom and saw the entire hallway covered in training mats. He walked to Bond's bedroom and then saw it covered as well. He snickered- "Well I won't be cleaning it up any way." Bond more than enjoyed the puppy but still he felt a loss for something. He started viewing on line more, before he only went on line when something pertained to work. He answered an advertisement where it asked you questions and then gave uplifting feel-good responses. He seemed to be captivated by it and even ignored the puppy's whines while he viewed it. He felt satisfaction and encouragement from it. It was a website for spiritual intervention. He wrote down the meeting spot and time of the meeting. He felt happiness return to his body.

He took out his cell phone and found the address of this meeting place, it was that evening. He then looked down to James and sure enough he whined for a reason. A small pile was on the floor. Bond didn't get angry because he thought it his fault for ignoring him, he cleaned it up then bagged it and left the room with the puppy to throw it outside in the trash. James enjoyed the walk. Back inside in the kitchen he saw that Jane was preparing dinner. She smiled to him and he smiled back. He asked her if she would watch James that night because he was going out. She nodded her head then returned to give her full attention to cooking. He felt surprised that she did not ask him where or what he was going to do- but then the thought of the whole new behavior from her. He thanked her then left.

Chris was very happy that the moment of uncontrollable fear never returned or he saw it return to Bond. He still reserved a speculation of doubt that everything was truly "okay", with Bond. Chris noticed Bond leaving in the black SUV and was concerned as to where he was going and why he didn't saw that he was going anywhere. He took out his cell and dialed Bond's number, he waited, no answer, "All the more reason to worry, His strange behavior and now this." He paced back around the garage then instead of walking to the back of the house at the beach he returned to the front of the house and made sure that the gate was closed then went inside through the front door.

He stopped in his tracks walking to the office to speak with his father. He thought as he stood rigid in the middle of the hallway- father is not the man he used to be- no insult intended; it is just age. Jonathan is good but do I overshadow my father questioning my brother? He turned around and walked back to the front of the house. "Maybe, he just went to 7-11 to get a Slurpee." He laughed to himself, yeah right, cherry flavor yet," He turned back around and went to the end of the hallway and stopped at his brother's door. He thought no he'd be invading his privacy, but the onset worries and his recent behavior. He turned the knob and pushed the door wide open.

He walked to a desktop on a small table, this was new to his room. To the right of the computer were a stack of 8" by 11" papers. He picked one up and read it. "A Religious social for those in question." Oh, Bond, no- you did jump off the deep end. I mean religion yes, but these things are just giant brainwashing scams usually for all of a person's money or holdings." He held his hand to his mouth then breathed out and punched the air of the room. The puppy, James he barked as he entered, the room. Chris bent down and picked him up then pet its head. You, James, why did you let him do this?" The puppy whined.

"Maybe. He'll come back realizing what an idiot. Could it be that maybe he has a reason that he went there other then? Salvation, I mean you get that in church, not one of these." He held his forehead and shook his head. All that we have to deal with and now this?" He walked out asking God to help his brother work through this. "I had better to get to the kitchen and see Jane. I am glad that she is doing better. Love is the answer, I am so glad that I have her. God has blessed me."

Now in the kitchen he walked toward her she was at the stove and she just dropped a stirring spoon. He heard her mumble out words silently as she could, he picked it up before it hit the floor and handed it to her. She looked embarrassed then thanked him he smiled back to her.

Minutes later, father, Jonathan and the two of the sat at the kitchen table for diner. Vincent said grace then they all served themselves homemade vegetable soup and corn on the cob, she did place a bottle of Coppola Chardonnay on the table and was happy to see that all had some. The talk of the evening was nothing to even remember just happiness. The meal was finished with fresh peaches. They laughed as they each peeled their own then tried to eat them without the juice pouring over themselves.

Chris went to help Jane with the dishes, she thanked him but told him to go and relax, for he must be exhausted from patrolling all day. He thanked her then went outside to the patio and sat down looking at noting put the moonlit sky. It was very relaxing; he felt a gentle breeze wisp by him. He showed a look of concern over his relaxed body. "Am I, my new father now? Oh, I guess that I always knew that the time would come it is just that it happened so soon. And what about Bond? I have to have someone else, someone that I can talk to and someone who will listen. A hand laid over his shoulder, "That is me." He turned thinking it to be his wife Jane, and tell her no, it would be too dangerous for her. He saw who it was then stood up and hugged him, it was Troy."

They released from the hug and sat back down at the patio table. "It seems that Jonathan called me and told me of how…Well of how things are really messed up here. Thomas, well he is now doing another one of those sexy series and he doesn't need me for the next year, so I am here. Have you got any place for me to stay here?" "I'll make space and even build a space overnight so you can stay here. That room hasn't been used I so long. I'll have to vacuum and change the bedsheets." "I'll change the sheets but you vacuum, I hate that. Say, before you or we do that, have you got a beer?" Chris got up and told him that he'd be right back.

He was back in only a what seemed like a minute with 2 bottles of Stella. They relaxed drank the beers and talked of old times in Vegas. Chris informed Troy of Bond's recent activity. Troy responded relaxed "Things like this happen all the time to people, the main thing for you or us to do is show rationality and maybe as you say, he might just be checking up on somebody or something-the main thing for you and me to do is just stay calm as you have always been. I am surprised that this has worked you up so. I mean this is not like you Chris." Chris thought of what he just heard and agreed. Then twisted his empty beer bottle. Troy saw this then responded back, "Let's go and fix the room." Chris smiled and they both left to the house.

The next morning all but Bond were having breakfast, the mood was happy. Bond came then stood unamused looking to them and the table. Chris tilted his head to him, first being surprised that he did not say anything and wondered of his state of mind. He stood up, "Bond, look who it is, Troy, from Las Vegas, remember?" Bond smiled but showed no look of distinction, "Jane, can you pour me a cup of coffee?" She did then, handed it to him. Vincent thought it odd, Bond would never ask someone else to do such a trivial thing for him. He thanked her then said that he had to go. Chris very alert to this, "Where do you have to go at such an early hour?" He already turned from the table and was walking away;" I am playing golf. Bye." The front door then was heard close very loudly.

Jonathan remarked with a dry English voice, "He is going somewhere but, I doubt that it is golf." Chris thought, another excuse. Bond went to the same lot that he had parked at before and went right to the same parking space, it was taken, He mumbled, then circled the lot finding a space in the back middle. He wore his mask then checked in at the desk and sat down feeling upset that he had to wait and wasn't instantly called in as last time.

Dr. Stone sat back in her chair then nodded as he nervously sat down. "What is wrong" He scratched the side of his head and adjusted then readjusted his body in the chair looking as nervous as a guilty party being called to the witness stand. "Why, do you ask that?" "From just observing you. Is anything different?" "How do you mean?" "Come on and answer me, I do not feel like playing twenty questions with you, although it is your dollar." "I am different." "How have you noticed that you are different? Did you just now notice this?" He raised his hand to his mouth then stroked down over his lips stopping at his chin then immediately took his clenched fists to his thighs and pressed against them holding still for a moment then in a quick flask released them still at his sides. She observed this and made note of it remembering how the first time that he did this signifying that he was nervous at the situation.

"It is just you and me here, there is nothing to be afraid of." She waited and no words came from his mouth. "Obviously this is something that you are having a problem either accepting or admitting to." He remained silent. "If you do not feel that you can open up about this to me right now, let's talk of something else, shall we. Last time that we spoke I remember that I told you to yourself involved in something, have you?" "I was going to; I was going to start to…" "Well, this is good you were going to start doing what?" "I." The doctor raised her eyebrows, "Remember I told you to just be calm and be yourself. I am not going to judge you." "I am getting involved in a group." "This is good, is there a theme to this group?" "It is a, a Religious, spiritual awakening group." As soon as she heard this, she jotted down on her notebook." "Did a friend tell you of this?" "No," "How did you find out about this group?" "The internet," She opened her mouth and breathed out loudly. He retracted his body to her then asked her if there was something wrong. "All, that I will say is be careful, as you would with anything new to you, I mean you just don't sit behind the wheel of a new car for the very first time and be expected to know how to drive it, if you have never been in a car before. Do you understand what I am trying to tell you?"

He took his hand to his lips clenched them together then slid his hand down his chest saying nothing to her. She waited thinking maybe he was absorbing what she just told him. He closed his eyes and relaxed his body for the first time since he had been there. He jumped up turned from her then walked away telling her that he had to go. "Come back we are not finished yet; you have more time." He ran outside to the parking lot like he was at the Olympics. In quickly getting in his car he hit the door corner on his knee, it hurt worse than could bare, but he did not stop for the pain. Getting out of there was the only thing on his mind. He backed out without even looking and just barely missed hitting another car waiting for this space. He heard the car horn but paid no attention to it.

Now driving down the three-lane road he looked to each side of him. Seeing fast food stops he felt the hunger in his body. He stopped in back of parking lot of a In and Out' knowing that he could get a good burger there. The parked then left the car, stopping six feet away from it to snap his key lock. In taking three more steps to the building, he realized that he wasn't wearing his face mask, he ran back to the car and got it and put it on. Wearing it as he walked to the store, he felt like a burglar wearing a mask to cancel his identity. He waited in a short line, now in front of the counter, he knew what he wanted, but he was just having trouble saying it. He heard suggestions from the cashier in the end he ordered it just the way he liked it, a double burger, no cheese, sauce only, and a cola. In paying he felt that he was given a snide look by the server, by him having to state everything they had when he already knew what he wanted. He picked up his order at the end of the counter with a smile. In turning around and seeing that all of the tables and chairs were roped off due to the pandemic, he went outside and leaned on the side of his car to eat. Just in taking the first bite he took another even though there was still food in his mouth, it just tasted so very, very good.

He grabbed hold of the soda but didn't have a good grip on it and it started rolling off the car, he was able to catch it, he did lose about two inches of it. He snapped the lid back on and then saw that a woman standing by her car was watching him. Instead of taking the opportunity to flirt with her, he felt overwhelming fear. Either she was going to fire at him or she had a back-up that would take him down. He left the burger and the soda on the car then quickly got in and had the engine started before even closing the door. He swept around the cars waiting in the drive-thru line and raced onto the street driving down the road so fast that he didn't even know where he was going. It was miraculous that he didn't hit anybody or another car. The only place that he could think of to go to was the estate and he went there. Inside in front of the garage he could see Chris watching him and he didn't feel like taking to him, he closed the door of the garage with the remote and then just stayed there sitting in his car, so as not to have to face him or anybody, Chris waited seeing the door closed, then left walking around the back of the house getting that feeling of Bond wanting to be alone, He wondered of his brother and what feelings that he must be going through, then thought it best to leave him alone.

Right before Chris opened the front door of the house, he heard a peep from, his cell phone. He picked it up from his pocket and still went inside, not knowing the whereabouts of Bond. Inside he didn't look to see where anyone was, he just showed concern after seeing that it was from a Dr. Stone. He knew of her as he himself had seen her before. He thought he was doing good and under the medicine protocol. He read then called her back. "Yes, Dr, Stone this is Chris, I am doing good and under the medicine." He listened, she was concerned about this brother, Bond." He looked puzzled, "My brother, what does he have to do in all of this." "Well, your brother, he too is seeing me. And I cannot tell you anything of our discussions, I am calling you because I am worried about, he showed any signs, of shall I say ending it?" Chris dropped his body still holding the phone, "Ending it, what do you mean? His latest behavior has been odd, but he seems happy." "When you say odd, how?" "I don't know quite how to explain it, just a polar opposite of his usual behavior." "Now, this is going beyond what I should be saying to you, but do you in any way see that he is experiencing, fear? I am only asking because I am worried about his safety for himself." "Doctor, after you say that, this explains a lot-and I think that you are right." "I am going to text you over some more information regarding fear, his is just for you and see if you think that this applies to him" "Thank you, doctor."

He pressed the phone closed, put it back in his pocket, in turning, he saw that his wife Jane was standing there only feet from him, "Chris, is everything okay, was that your doctor?" "Jane everything is fine, she was doing a phone check on me and believe me everything is okay." "Okay, if you say so. I am kind of tired, do you mind if we just spend the night in front of the TV?" "That, sounds fine, by me." He followed her to their bedroom and they made themselves comfortable- kicking off their shoes and finding something on the tube that they would each enjoy. An old Odd couple episode, in only minutes they were laughing and momentarily forgetting about life. The Newhart show followed which brought relief and laughter and the stress of life. They most importantly felt the comfort in being together. He thought of saying what happened to the old times, then thought better of it, as he had not been there for most of the old times, but he was sure enjoying these times.

Troy had been and was now still guarding the back perimeter of the estate. At times he worried hearing sounds from beyond the back of the trees on each side of the perimeter, sheepishly walking to the noise, be found it to be just birds, "It is strange in the way that your conscious can play with you. That maybe was how Poe, got to be so very good at mystery, that and I think I heard he was a user of drugs." He laughed, "That'll do it." He walked back to the back patio of the house and thought that there had to be more of a reason that they sent for him. They surely could have gotten an unemployed security guard from somewhere, something more than just guard duty. Maybe I am in training, for what? He looked to each side of the empty beach then up to the moon. "Thomas, do an action flick again, please. Yes, this is paradise but I am already going a bit crazy. Like waiting for my turn to be on the roller-coaster."

Jonathan spook to Vincent in the confines of the office. He poured them each a shot of cognac. Vincent waves his glass to Vincent to toast. Vincent brought his glass only halfway to Jonathan's then stopped. Vincent breathed out and left his mouth open to speak. Seconds passed and only silence filled the air of the room. "Come on Vincent, I know that you want to say something. I mean you have brought us all here, and now; I see no moving obstacle before us, I and the others are wondering, what is it." "You know me too well." He stopped his speech and scratched the side of his forehead. "I have, (he breathed very heavy in speaking) he given everyone here a scare, with my recent hospital visit. Yes, I got better from the death that they, well at that time prescribed. I astounded everyone including myself." Jonathan spoke up saying that he did a great job. Vincent nodded. "I feel my body slowing down and I can't be surprised I am 79. There is going to be no warning flashed down from the sky, say you have only two weeks left." Jonathan raised his body up in the chair. "No, no need to console me, we all knew that this time would come. I was in the process of training Bond to takeover, but I can clearly see that he is not the choice.

Chris is married and I think that he should get his life back in order and I am proud he is doing that. But could you imagine his wife's reaction to him being…the Kingpin?" They both nodded and laughed. Jonathan, I know that you just recently had a scare and I commend you on the way that you handled everything. I am going to ask you a question now, and I think that you already know what I am going to ask you." He stopped and looked over to Jonathan's face, he could feel that he was shielding excitement. "Jonathan, will you take over my business and be Boss?" Before he even finished this last word that he spoke Jonathan replied yes, triumphantly. "This is good to hear, I was afraid that I was going to have to twist your arm and tie you up." He laughed then took hold of his glass of cognac and toasted the boss. His time Vincent fully reached to the glass and a gentle clang of crystal hitting crystal was heard.

Jonathan went outside to the back patio; Troy was already standing there watching him. "Relax, I just came out here to tell you that Vincent is in his office and he wants to talk with you." Troy crossed his hands to his chest and responded, "Me?" Jonathan ever so portrayed his calm self, "I think that you are the only Troy out here." Troy smiled to him then went to see Vincent. The door was already open, Troy looked to Vincent but had been acknowledged by him yet, he clears throat making a soft sound and Vincent did pick up on this and flagged him in to have a seat. Troy sat at the chair to the left. Vincent looked questionably to him. "Is there something wrong?" He reached to the top of his shirt and loosened up the collar then nervously put his hand back down. "No, it just is a little odd no one has ever sat on the chair at that side unless someone else was in the other." "I can move, if you want." "No, no, that's fine." "I know that you have probably been wondering why you were called down here." "Yes, I have. I mean I see no case that I am needed for but just patrolling."

"I know that there is no work in your regular job, and you have proved yourself to me, you are good." Troy nodded his head and grinned. "Bond, has chosen a different path." "Bond is giving this up?" "No, not exactly, he is just shall I say wrestling with other things right now, and I am looking at the long range for the future. I need someone who will be what he was." "What do you mean by that?" "Let me put this as simply as I can, Chris needs a partner and I want you to be it. Oh, do not worry there will be nice pay in it for you." "But what about my other job?" "You mean the job that you don't currently have with no pay?" "Yeah, it has gotten tight." "And no, you cannot think about it, I need an answer now." He lifted up this, eyes wide then sat back and crossed his feet. He clenched his fingers then raised his head up, "Yes. It's a good thing that I didn't get that dog that I was going to." Vincent smiled and chuckled, how about raising a puppy? There will be a dog," "Yeah, that sounds great. I'll just have to have my things sent here and stop the lease on my apartment." "Don't worry about that, I already took care of everything even selling your car." "Really, what if I'd oh said no?" No response came from Vincent.

He left the office happy returning to the back porch. Jonathan saw him then asked him if everything had gone alright. "Very good Vincent, we will be seeing a lot more of each other." "That's good, I do like you. Would you like me to take over your shift out here now? I have slept most of the day and you must need rest." Troy nodded his head and said thank you then retired to his room. He took a long hot shower then checked the messages on his cell phone. It's going to be a different life that is for sure. No more having to deal with the freeway traffic early in the morning, he laughed. No more of my regular hang outs, no seeing my friends any more, I mean it's not like I didn't have a life, I now just have to get used to a new one, and a puppy, I am really going to have to watch my step around here now.

Bond drove back inside that estate he got out of the SUV and ran to the front door. He fumbled with his keys then dropped them. Before picking them up he took a sweep of the view behind him then grabbed them then turned the lock and moved his body against the door while he went inside. Inside the room was lit only at the front door where he stood. He waited though he debated on what to do, then ran to the left to the hallway and his room. He pulled the door back so far that it the wall. He then pushed to closed and instantly locked it. The room was dark but he knew the footing. He side stepped to the bathroom then turned on the light and the shower. He even closed that door and locked it too. He viewed his face in the mirror and then on-coming facial lines that he didn't like seeing then pulled his hand to them trying to make them disappear. "If only." A heavy sigh overtook his persona then he undressed and got in the shower. The water was cold and he didn't even react to it. He just showered as usual then changed for bed. Now under the covers before reaching over to turn off the lamp, he exclaimed, "They are not going to knock and more."

CHAPTER 2

The next morning Maggie carried all of her belongings outside to her car. Vincent let her go- he thanked her paid her and she left with a smile and said good bye. Chris observed this then asked Vincent about it. "All I need right now is my family." "Father I have been meaning to talk to you about Bond, he has been acting differently lately and even." Vincent interrupted him. "I know son, and believe me and am doing something about this. Follow inside and we'll have breakfast." Chris just followed him.

In the kitchen, Jane smiled to them. She was cooking, she kissed Chris then they both sat down and were served scrambled eggs and bacon. Jane got up after hearing the toast pop then placed the slices on a plate to the table. "Bond has already left, and where he is going is concerning to me." Chris, looked dead-locked to Vincent thinking that he knew something and he wanted to know what it was. "Bond is working on something." Vincent stopped his speech taking a sip of coffee then bite of food. Chris grew too impatient to wait for the answer. "Are you having him do this? Whatever he is doing?" "No, I am not and I am trying to figure out what he is doing. He seems to be on a quest, his own journey so to speak and I have an idea of what it is. He more than anything wants acknowledgment right now." "His strange behavior? Dad you know something you always do." "Tell me what you know." He scratched his check then lowered his head. The doctor swore me to secrecy but I feel that you need to know." Jane instantly raised up her body in question, hoping that she would hear and not be sent out of the room, she sat there as quiet as she could.

It seems that somehow, we have both been seeing the same doctor without either one of us knowing that, a psychiatrist. She treated me, regarding PTSD and gave me the medication which has greatly helped. Vincent nodded his head signifying that he knew this. "She called me up and told me of how she had treated Bond." Jane interjected, "That is supposed to be confidential."

"Yes, she told me that and the reason for her call. To me is that she was afraid that he was going to try and off himself." "She said it like that?" "Well basically." Jane made a face, "Not Bond, I mean he has always been the quiet and composed one." "Chris, what do you think of this whole picture." "Fear." Jane jumped in the conversation, "He would be the last one to show fear." "At one time maybe, but this whole Vegas ordeal really got to him." Vincent sighed, "Yes, I saw that the very second that he returned, at first I thought that he started drinking again. I mean just look what this pandemic his done to people. I did have had Maggie check his room every day and she didn't find any bottles or casks of alcohol and no drugs other than the normal over-the -counter medicines that you can buy anywhere." "You had Maggie do that and not me?" "Jane, I have been aware of your soft feelings for Bond." "What do you mean she has soft feelings for Bond, what is going on?"

"Settle down son, they just became good friends, that is all." Jane felt like she swallowed her heart then was so relieved to hear him speak these words to Chris. "Well, what are your plans for him? Lock him down or what?" "Distance." "What do you mean distance?" Jane became very alert to this as Chris watched her actions and felt himself distancing from her-still wondering on the friendship accept. "He feels fear and in watching him, I see his actions on just being outside in the yard, he looks like he is fighting on the front line in combat."

"I know that we have been in the most precarious situations involving danger in our work and now with the uncertainty of the current pandemic, I guess I can see that. I am still having trouble absorbing this is he, well basically he is Bond." "Where are you going to put him, a ward in the hospital?" "Calm down Jane, I am not going to send him anywhere other than he wants to go." Both Chris and Jane looked apprehensively to Vincent. "Does Jonathan know of this? And what about Troy?" "Troy doesn't know yet, and believe me Jonathan knows everything." "Father why does he know everything and not me? This meeting or discussion has caused more questions than answers." "He is most vulnerable right now and he needs." He is interrupted from a voice at the back of the table before he can finish this sentence. Jonathan stood tall and composed "Me."

Chris relaxed his raised shoulders Jane looked even more confused and Vincent exposed a laid-back calm composure. "Dad always has a plan." He got up from the table said hello to Jonathan and left the room not even looking at Jane. After a moment of awkward silence, she got up and left the room. Jonathan poured himself a cup of coffee then sat down. "Trouble in paradise, I take it?" "They're young they will work it out, I hope." "So, tell me more of your plans? "Plans that involve you."

CHAPTER 3

Bond entered a parking lot at the public beach. There was a group of around forty people all sitting distanced in folding patio chairs. He went to a set up card table and signed in and was surprised when he had to show his driver's license for identity. This was more than surprising because he was always shielding his identity. He acted like all of these strangers were his family. And at that moment seemed to have lost his constant state of fear. He took a chair at the outside of the make-shift row.

A speaker stand in the front of the rows was set up, a red rug a microphone and two potted short four-foot palm trees where on each side of him. "I first of all want to welcome you all here today. This is the start of the right adventure for your life." He stopped his speech as the audience clapped. "We will help all and each one of you your true identity and maybe even some of you will find your true love in life here, today." The group again clapped. In the distant reaches of his mind, he thought, it's a set-up but then he more than quickly lost himself in the feeling of warmth in the meeting. "I want to remind all of you that this will be truly life changing intervention that you are entering into." A paper bulletin was then handed down the rows for each one of them. Bond took his and smiled in joy of acceptance.

The next hour went on with the speaker saying things with overwhelming applause to finish the meeting. Of course, he said before the meeting ended of their need of contributions to be able to keep these meetings going and to reach out to other people how desperately needed to follow the teachings of the group for enlightenment and help for all of mankind so that they will truly know the right path to follow in life. And most importantly do not let other people, friends, family tell you that this is wrong. It is the right thing to do and they have been led there for peace and harmony and love.

At the same table that they signed in at and even another table was placed to the side of that one was taking contributions, cash check or credit card transactions. Bond himself stood in line giving his name to these strangers then gave a $200.00 cash contribution, smiling every step of the way. The only thing that Bond did not notice was Troy standing in the parking lot watching everything. "This explains a lot right here." Troy put his sunglasses back on then stood to the side of a large tree shielding his view to Bond who looked at basically nothing to the side of him swelled by the meeting.

Back at the breakfast table, Jonathan took a plate of vegetables from the fridge and was eating those. "I do not know how this is going to work, Vincent, first of all him leaving the estate where he has always called home and living with me?" "I know that he likes you." "Yes, and I see friends at the grocery store that I like and they like me but not enough to live with them." "Here are the keys to a place that I found that I think will be prefect for you two." He reached for the keys finding trouble placing them in his hand. "Remember what happened to me at the last condo that I lived at? I do not want to end up dead at a storage unit. Why not here?" "Because he has to earn his place here. "" A lot of different things can be conveyed in that statement that you just made. Vincent, I will trust you and go along with this. I just hope that whatever it is that you are looking for to happen, happen quickly." "So, do I."

The buzzer to the front gate just rang. Vincent pressed a unit button on the side wall of the kitchen, and listening to the voice on the other end of the gate. Chris made an appearance in the kitchen at this time. Vincent looked up to him. "It seems that there is a delivery at the front gate for you." "Tell them that I will be right out there." Vincent did this and wondered what it was that Chris ordered and why he was in such a hurry to receive, he had never gone to the gate to get possession of anything, but a car that is. Did he order himself a car? He went to the front door Jonathan followed. They stood there looking to Chris that signed for a large package gave the clipboard back to the driver and waited for him to back out before he opened the gate a took hold of the large rectangular box. He at first had trouble balancing himself while carrying it. He went through the front door then out the back door to the patio to open it.

They followed them and watched Chris open this box. Jonathan turned around being surprised that Jane had not come to view, this maybe she already knew of it. It was a polished white, North surf board with navy blue down one end of it. He held it smiling -Vincent had make noise clearing his throat for attention. "Well dad, you said to take up a new hobby." "Surfing?" "You can't surf out here? Where then?" He received no answer. Jonathan raised his eyes to Vincent. "With your boys, you have your hands full."

Jonathan's cell then beeped, he walked to the side and viewed it, then texted back and walked to Vincent. "It seems that Troy found your other boy Bond, at the beach no less. Vincent, I think that we should go back in the office and plan some strategy." Vincent slowly proceeded back inside the house. They looked to each other while walking inside down the hallway, "It, never ends, does it?"

Jane stopped her painting then looked on the room for Chris, in not seeing him she went down the stairs and looked straight ahead to the living room. He wasn't in the kitchen. "Hum, he isn't here either. She then went to the backyard patio expecting to see him there, and viewed the surrounding area of the backyard, thinking he was on patrol. In not seeing him she went further down to the beach to find him. Hearing ruffling at the side by the trees, she dropped her shoulders and turned around to this direction smiling expecting to see his smiling face. It was barren, the beach the yard every visible area. She again heard this unexplainable noise. Against her better judgement she walked to the noise, then looked down to the sand and saw footprints that weren't hers. The air was then silent, she felt unnerved and scared, showing no fear she first stepped backwards a foot then circled around back to the beach looking at only the sky. Up the stairs of the patio, she heard a noise and looked up to it in fright. It was Bond. She relaxed her composure. "I haven't seen you around for a long time now. How are you?

You look a bit scared." She first felt the welcoming feeling that she had in seeing him, then remembered that things had changed.

"I can say the same about you." For that brief moment it seemed that he had reverted back to the old Bond. "I brought some food from the local deli it is on the patio table right behind us, would you like to join me?" "It seems like I just ate breakfast, I'll join you but for maybe just a soda." "Sounds good to me, come let's sit down." He took his paper wrapped sandwich out from the bag and handed her a large cold paper cup of iced tea, she took it feeling the cold, "It even feels nice." Then took a sip of the ice tea. As he unfolded his sandwich, she remarked on how very good that it smelled, he pushed another unwrapped one closer to her. She thanked him but still declined. "It is hot pastrami and melted swiss with that sauce that Marco's deli puts on it." "Yes, that is good, I am just not hungry right now. Thanks for the drink though." "You seem to be in a good mood, I am happy about that." "Since when has my mood ever affected you?" "Well, a, I guess never, I was really just making conversation." "Why?" "I guess because we are both sitting here and I wanted to just break the silence." "What is wrong with that?" "Nothing, really I didn't mean to offend you." He suddenly tightened up and entirely changed his demeanor.

"I brought you a sandwich are you going to eat it or are you just going to sit there and insult me?" His mood had quickly reverted. Feeling the utmost scared and not wanting to show it she took the sandwich sliding it gently over the table top then unfolded it and took half of it to her mouth. Chewing it she looked to him and nodded her head in thanks. Then he smiled to her. She realized in what a dangerous dilemma that she was in and wished more than anything that her husband would show up, where was he? Troy came to the table smiling to the both of them. At that very moment she looked to the sky thanking the Lord, for his presence. "Troy, it is good to see you." He smiled to her, "The same here. Bond nice to see you." Bond folded up the sandwich grabbed his drink then jolted from the table. Troy looked to Jane. "What did I say? Where you two in a conversation that I interrupted or something?" "No, no," She pushed the bag away from her. "That sure smells good do you mind if I eat the other half if you don't want it." "No, I mean yes, you can have at all, I never wanted it in the first place. I took it to make him happy and not to anger him. He just acted really nice then in a snap he did a 180." He stopped his chewing to wave his hand down to her, then swallowed and spoke. "Bond, doesn't mean anything against you he is just going through some emotional issues right now, believe Jane, it is not you at all. Don't worry. Thank you for the sandwich." "Thank you for being here." He smiled to her as he ate the sandwich. "Do you know where my husband is?" "He is out front. At least that is where I saw him when I came in." "Is he on patrol?" "He didn't appear to be. He was holding a board and looked very happy." "A board? I better go check this out." He placed his hand over hers on the table top, "It can wait, I like you company do you mind staying?" She sighed then smiled and stayed with him.

Bond made tracks to the garage instead of his room. Inside the garage he just sat in the SUV, looking at nothing put darkness as the overhead light turned off. "I feel safe here." He closed his eyes and drifted to sleep, sitting in the driver's seat. Troy finished his sandwich then went back inside the house and swore that he heard a puppy barking. He followed the noise to Bonds' room then still hearing the puppy bark even louder, he knocked waited a few seconds and opened the door. James, the puppy ran out the door. "Hey, wait a minute you. He squinted then held his hand over his nose. "That smell, he went inside then various puppy droppings and small wet spots were on the floor. "Oh! do I have to clean this up? No maid. I think that I'll leave this for Bond, wherever he is. It is his puppy. Speaking of that I had better go find him"

Troy circled the grounds and did not find Bond. He heard loud music coming from upstairs. He went up to the second floor then listened to see where the nose came from. It was from Jane and Chris's room. "I hope everything is alright, maybe they are just playing music loud to hide what they're doing? That doesn't sound like him though. "He knocked on the door, in a sweat Jane answered. He asked her if she was alright. She replied yes, oh and Chris is not here, nor do I want him to be. I just have the music on loud and I am dancing/singing. I am sorry if I'm bothering you." "No, you aren't I just wanted to make sure that everything was alright.

"The family that is here, though are far from each other. I just wish that I had some place to go. Right now, I think everyone wishes that they had somewhere to go." He walked downstairs while saying in his mind- I wish that I had somewhere to go. "Find the puppy" He lit up calling the puppy's name and searching the house for him. He found him on the couch in the living room. "How did you ever get up here?" Holding the squealing little ball of fluff was a joy. "Come on let's go outside and I'll run you or try to catch you, most likely. They went outside and James lit up in the warm air and sunshine, and he did run. Troy at first ran along side of him then breathing deeply he stopped. He just watched him and noticed that the puppy kept stopping and looking at him. He found, if he ignored him long enough, he would just take off any way. This was good to wear him out for the night.

He went in the kitchen with James. "I doubt that you have been fed. Let me see is there puppy food anywhere in here for you?" He opened cabinets and even looked under the sink, "Nothing, well I'll check the garage. I like you but I just don't trust you yet." He picked James up and carried him off to the garage to check for food. He opened the inside walk in door with a key, and immediately stepped back surprised from the darkness of it. He walked inside then turned on another light bringing light to the entire garage not just the side entrance.

He heard an instant ruffling noise and James started barking, he turned his head puzzled by this noise, then a car horn blasted piercing cries and screaming. He looked to the SUV where this noise came from and saw Bond behind the wheel crying in an utter panic. Fearful of what he saw he placed James on the floor and ran to the side of where Bond sat. "Bond, Bond, I am here, everything is alright-what is it?" He saw no change in his panicked behavior. He pulled out his cell phone and called the house, Jonathan answered, he told him what had happened and an ambulance was called.

Jonathan came to the garage and told Troy to just step back, in this rage that he was in he might hurt somebody and not even realize his actions. He opened the automatic door up behind the vehicle then Troy ran to the front gate to open it. Jane turned on the front light of the estate and looked wrapped in her bathrobe and slippers trying to see what was happening, she stayed at the front of the main house and didn't run to find out what the commotion was, something very surprising of her. Troy started to run to her to tell her what happened halfway to her he stopped and turned to the direction of the ambulance that was entering the gateway with its lights flashing.

Jane watched: seeing Bond wrapped on a stretcher and placed inside the ambulance. Jonathan talked with a paramedic from the ambulance and signed a paper. He spoke to Troy, "No, I'll go the puppy. Is right there at your feet. Take him over to her and tell her what happened, but do not by any means let her go to the hospital herself, you stay with her. Jonathan briefly went in the house just to get his car keys and followed the ambulance. Driving following the ambulance he was very surprised that Vincent was not there watching any of this. The only thing that he hoped for was possibly the medication that he was taking had him in a deep sleep. He thought also above Vincent not being there, where was Chris?

Holding the puppy Troy told Jane what had happened. She seemed unphased at what he just told her. He wondered if she heard him then debated on whether to repeat himself to her. He watched her as she went back in the house and up the stairs. He then yelled to her as she walked the stairs. "Have you seen Chris?" In a very even and low voice she replied back to him. "Don't know, don't care." He stood there unmoved holding the puppy, "That question was only half-way answered. I feel that I do not want to know any more about that one right now."

He stroked the puppy's head, then quickly realized he hadn't been fed yet. Instead of returning to the garage, he took the puppy to the kitchen and give him a bowl of cornflakes with milk. He watched as James ate, eating while wagging his tail. "Looks like you're going to be my dog for a while anyway." James briefly stopped his eating and barked then returned to finish the bowl of food. Troy smiled and laughed. "I need you right now to bring me some sense of sanity here. I hope Vincent is okay."

He wondered on the guarding of the state that night, he was more than tired but there was no one else there to take this duty. He took a can of Pepsi out of the refrigerator. I will use this, there must a little bit of caffeine in it. I mean I can't brew an entire pot of coffee for myself." "I'll do it." He turned to the nose and saw Jane already in the process of making it. He thought better than to talk to her and just put the soda back inside the refrigerator. "Good idea, I'll bring it out to you when it is ready." He took this as a clue to leave, holding the puppy.

Outside he turned on all of the outside lights and was surprised in seeing that the right side by the trees near the beach it was barely lit. "A lightbulb must have burned out, is all that I can think of." He stepped down to the side of the swimming pool. The puppy ran to the edge of the pool. Troy immediately picked him up. "I don't feel like going for a midnight swim with you, sorry." It whined. He thought of going down there but then thought of James and if he got out of his hold at the shoreline, he could be swept out to the ocean. "I think that I will just stay here near the house tonight." "Good Idea." This voice came from behind him, He walked back up the cement stairs to the patio and took the cup of coffee from Jane." "Do you, have a weapon?" He jerked back hearing this remark from her. From her other hand furthest from him she handed him a handgun. "Watch out, it's loaded." She turned and left him without another word. He held his coffee in one hand and the gun in the other then placed the coffee down to the table top. "I don't feel safe having this with you out here James." He left the coffee on the outside table then went back inside the house and put him in Bond's bedroom and filled its water bowl. Then went back to his coffee and gun. "No cream for the coffee, just gun for the coffee." He took a couple of sips then got up and looked to each side of the beach. "That area to the right of the sands still worries me, hopefully morning will be here soon and I'll see Vincent and hopefully somebody else."

CHAPTER 4

Jonathan waited inside the emergency room waiting area, pacing the floor. The room was full of people crying, something that he didn't welcome hearing at that moment. An empty chair had now become available he just didn't feel like he had the stomach to take it. The three medical staff members behind the glass wall check in aware all busy on phones and computers and talking to registering patients. He wanted desperately to ask on of them, of Bond's condition, but saw no option to do this. He paced the floor of the room, he started counting the circles, he was now up to 55, Thinking in his mind of why he wasn't dizzy from all of this circling, at just that moment he heard his name being called from behind a partially opened door to the side of check-in. He ran to it.

The white coated doctor motioned him inside a room, though he was surprised to see that Bind was not in it. He looked at the name on the doctor's lapel, then had to focus again to try and read it. The doctor saw this, then, said aloud, Dr. Gong. "Are you Bond Modella's father?" "No, his father is or has been recently released from the hospital and is on bed rest. I am, I am, a very close friend of the family. I called the paramedics ambulance and traveled alongside of them and brought him here, I need to know."

"Lucky for him that you found him in time. His blood alcohol level is .08, one the highest levels to be called drunk. "He gave that up years ago." "Maybe he did but he started up again. Also, in reviewing his medical records, he has recently gone under the care of a psychiatrist. Do you know anything about this?" "No, no I don't." "I have had him sent up to the 3rd floor ward." "Not the third floor." "Is there anything wrong with that floor?" Jonathan quickly remembered that he was in Hawaii and not Vegas were the medical ordeal had taken place. "No, no."

"Noted in his chart by the ambulance, they think he also has a case of extreme Paranoia." "What?" The doctor reads the file- "Cool clammy skin Pale Rapid pulse rapid breathing he was vomiting. Also enlarged pupils and he seemed extremely tired. Paranoia is a thought process called delusion- the they think that other people are out to get them. Again, I stated that I have had hi sent upstairs where trained psychiatrists will treat him. I have no idea if they will get you see him. You'll have to check it out." He thanked the doctor and left the room.

Chris drove in the open the gates puzzled as to them being open. He could see tires tracks in the drive. He parked under the portico, that never before being a place to park. He ran to the open garage seeing no one but feeling something. He then went into the house and was surprised at all the lights on inside as well, he called out and heard no response. He grabbed a gun from the front credenza then checked everything in guard mood. He went to the kitchen then saw his wife Jane sitting at the table with her hands over the bottom of a cup of coffee moving it from side to side but not drinking it.

He walked to her and started to place his hands on her shoulders leaving the gun on the counter. He more than felt her tension as his fingers grew closer to her. At three inches from her body she tensed up more and said aloud. "Don't." "What is wrong? What happened, why are you up, where is everybody?" She leaned back then dropped her hands to the top of her thighs. "Where were you? When all of this happened?" "All of what happened?" "Bond and Jonathan are in the hospital." "What?" She broke her locked state and sat up then stood. "Where, were you?" "Me, I mean why are they in the hospital, what happened?" She walked out from the room, before closing the door, "Don't bother coming upstairs tonight, there is no room for you on our bed."

He looked in a madden stare to only the air of the room. Pulling out his cell phone he called Bond's number, it rang 6 times and no answer. He then tried Jonathan's number no answer there either. He thought somebody has to be here. He went to the backyard patio and saw Troy and was surprised when Troy didn't smile back to him. He showed a look of being cold though not really showing any emotion. He walked to side of him standing 4 feet away then looked down hearing the puppy he started to reach for it, and Troy's hands swept it up to his chest holding it. "What happened here?" "Have you seen your wife?" He shakes his head yes. "Didn't she tell you?" "Tell me what? "Oh, there is lot to tell you and I think that you should hear this from your family." "What is so important that you cannot tell me? I mean why is she being so cold?" "Like I said, I do not want to get into this …" He stumbled for words then remained quiet.

He stood there and locked his eyes to Troy. "Do you know where Vincent my father is?" "Look I have not seen him; he is sleeping I imagine. Please talk to your wife." After what seemed like never-ending seconds of monotony, he left then tried calling each cell phone number again only to hear it ring until the line went dead. Seeing no other option, he went to his father's room and gently knocked on his door. He received no answer, debating whether to go or not, he turned and left the doorway. In one motion he retraced his steps then silently pushed the door open and left it open offering a limited amount of light to see where he was going. He saw his father lying flat on his back with his mouth open on the bed.

He's asleep. No father would have woken up, he is so keen to every little thing even at his age. He bent over then pulled his wrist up. His body was cold. He dropped his father's hand back to the bed. Then looked down to his complete stiff torso laid on the bed. For a moment he became locked in movement and couldn't breathe. No not now, not me, father please, please be okay. He knelt down to the floor at the side of the bed and put his ear to his father's heart. He started crying, "NO, NO God, why?" A cold rush ran down his spine. He clasped his hands together at his face crying. Then pushed each one tightly at each side of his face running them down over his neck and stopped at his chest. He moved his fingers together then swung his upper body back and forth. "GOD WHY?" He closed his eyes then reached over and kissed his father. "God, it is just too soon, why?"

CHAPTER 5

Hearing a noise, Troy went in the house and followed the cries, James afraid stayed at the living room couch. He stopped at the open-door seeing Chris knelt over crying to Vincent's lifeless body on the bed. He closed his eyes and reached for air then breathed in and let out heavily. He slowly went to Chris right as he approached his side, Chris's hand reached up to his and grabbed so tight he had to breath in and winch at the pressure. "I am here, Chris." He could not think of anything else to say to him and at that moment he wished for the intelligence and compassion of Jonathan more than anything. If Jane hadn't done it before this, how was he going to tell him of his brother. Panic desperation and fear controlled every movement of the room.

Troy helped Chris stand up, as he leaned to him crying. He closed then opened his tear-soaked eyes, "What are we going to do now? He was the boss, the boss of everything." The sound of sirens entering the estate then filled the air. Troy thought how? He looked to the opened door and saw Jane's shadow watching the room. He opened his eyes wider to her view and opened his mouth to talk to her and her shadow disappeared. The next thing he knew, he could hear sounds coming in the front door and people talking, movement was coming closer. That was it- she left to let the ambulance crew inside.

The next few minutes were chaotic to say the least. People were asking questions, moving Vincent out of bed and out of the room. A different person asked questions another talking on a phone, murmured cries from Chris, Jane watching in the background like she was hiding. The puppy whining- Troy more than anything felt like me was going to lose it. This was the time that Bond would have been there to silently hold everything together. Chris cried out Bond's name. Troy finished signing and hearing what was said to him, took his keys and led Chris out the door to travel with him to the hospital. There he would tell him of Bond and hopefully they could see him or at least find out more of his situation, and more importantly above everything, Jonathan would be there.

Walking to the emergency room, cries and conversation and an unknown crowd of people filled the air of the room. They looked lost on where to even go. Troy finally figured out just go to the counter, he had expected someone to come to him to give him instructions, on what to do next but that wasn't the case. He waited impatiently in line holding Chris's grief-stricken hand. He counted his place in line, one of the only things that he could do to pass the time and try to ignore the crying pleas for help. He felt a strong gentle hand over his, instantly thought Chris is doing better but then thought I am already holding his hand. Who took hold of the other, a doctor maybe? He turned to this man and smiled. Then widened his smile even more, seeing that it was Jonathan.

"Jonathan, how did you know? Chris tried calling you put there was no connection." "I know, I have been here busy with something else. Jane texted me." Troy at that point looked utterly lost at the words he just heard. "Oh, yes Bond." Chris's eyes lit up hearing his brother's name. "I already took care of this, come on, there is no need for you to be in this line, we'll go upstairs." "Upstairs. Why?"

Now on the third floor, he stopped at the closed door to a patient's room. A nurse just come out of this room. He caught her attention and explained that his brother and friend were there to see him. She explained that only 2 people could go in the room at a time and they would have to sign a paper stating that they did not have the corona virus. They waited, Chris, said "When can we see father?" Troy whispered to Jonathan, that he was out of it." Jonathan calmly nodded to this. The nurse brought the paper and he helped Chris sign his name.

Jonathan started to have the two of them go in. Troy shakes his head, no." Jonathan, you can do this better than, me." Softly Jonathan led Chris into the room where Bond was laid on a hospital bed with tubes running to his arm and a monitor for his vitals. Chris, followed him then looked down to Bond on the bed. "This is not father." "No Chris, it is Bond, your brother." "What is wrong- is this what Jane said happened to him?" In the way that he said these words and the uplifted composure of him at that moment, it was like he reverted back to his true emotional form, Chris being Chris. Jonathan was very happy to in seeing this.

Bond wavered his eyes open and closed, Jonathan looked to the monitors and saw one of the curved lines going higher. He then pushed the two of them further back form Bond. Bond opened his eyes then closed them. They both lowered their built-up hopes. After a brief minute he opened his eyes back up and blinked. "Chris, it's your turn." Both of them watched and heard Bond. They were both happy and surprised that he woke up and was already talking then wondered on the meaning of what he said. "Good to see you brother, but it is my turn for what?" "It's your turn to watch over everything, I am kind of indisposed right now." They laughed, it seemed that Bond had returned to being himself, for that moment any way. Jonathan worried for how long though and when it would be wise on how to break the news to him of his father's passing. But right now, it felt like a small victory had been accomplished.

The nurse stepped back in the room and told Jonathan that she needed to speak with him. At the open door as he walked out Troy entered. More happy laughter was heard as the door to room closed and Jonathan was brought to the side nurses station desk where the treating doctor waited to talk with Jonathan. He discussed the prognosis of Bond. "He had a blood alcohol level of .08 when he was brought in here." "What, he gave up drinking a long time ago, he went to AA and everything." "Well it seems that he started up again, the paramedics found an empty vodka bottle under his car seat." "We checked his room but not his car." "So, you were suspicious? of this?"

His recent behavior has changed, but he has recently gone through an emotional ordeal. The doctor shook his head. "Right now, I have prescribed a psychiatrist here at the hospital to evaluate him. "When can he go home?" "Right now, it is too early for me to tell you." "His father, just died tonight actually, he was, or his body was brought here just hours before or after he was." "Does he know of his father's passing yet?" "No, I didn't want to create any further trauma right now." "I do not want to order anything for him until I receive the." Jonathan interrupted him, "The report from the Psychiatrist" "I am sorry but I have to go now." Jonathan thanked him then stayed standing there. Searching for the next step which always before he already had planned out. He took the opportunity at that current moment to just go sit and rest his tired feet.

Sitting down at the side bench against the wall he hoped that they were enjoying this time together. It seemed that right now Bond had it all together. Could just alcohol have caused such an extreme change in behavior? He thought that maybe that was partially it, but there was something else. His phone beeped, he took from his pocket and read the text. It was from Jane, she asked him if there was anything that she could do. Most importantly in all caps she asked of Bond. He texted back that at that time he looked and sounded good. A smiley face instantly showed up on his phone. She then texted, Vincent? He texted back; in the morning he'd call his lawyer. Take care Jonathan, he typed, you too.

Is this all a charade now? I mean everything is just falling into place, sad events that led to this point- but I feel like there is a reemergence happening. And now I am the leader, some retirement. Tomorrow, do I dare leave the hospital? Putting my head on a pillow sure sounds nice. He looked at his wristwatch, tomorrow is in one hour. He closed his eyes and in minutes he was asleep sitting there at the chair bank. Chris and Troy left the room as a nurse informed them that Bond needed his rest. They left Troy instantly saw Jonathan asleep at the bench. Chris whispered to him. "Shall we wake him up?" Troy moved his head then waved for Chris to follow him. They went to his car and left the hospital and headed for the estate.

Arriving there, Chris was surprised to see that the front gate was open then commented to Troy about it. "Well remember the ambulance was here tonight- I guess in all the commotion it was just left open." "My wife, I hope she is okay." "She is." He looked to Troy questionably. Troy parked outside to the side of the portico, instead of the garage, he didn't want to have at that point explain anything else. Jane opened the front door, Chris instantly smiled to her she gave him a half-smile then looked to Troy. "How is everything?" "Good his brother woke up while we were there." "So, we are together tonight?" She nodded to Chris. Jane mouthed to Troy, "Does he know about Vincent?" Troy shakes his head no. "Have a good night Troy, see you in the morning." "Good night to the both of you."

As she entered the open bedroom door, she could her the shower running in the bathroom. She closed the door then closed the drapes of the room, put on music of The Goo Goo Dolls. Chris came out from the bathroom wrapped in his white bathrobe. She sat of the edge of the bed and pated the top side of it for him to sit, he did. "Chris, I love you." "Jane I am sorry for whatever, I don't even" She held his hand, "You don't need to say anything else, Chris. She opened her mouth and breathed in air. "We, I am not in trouble am I, I mean our relationship." "Chris, we are okay, you know that I cherish you and this is where we both belong. I hope that you are calm now because there is something important that I need to tell you." "We are okay then; it is not about us?"

No, it is not about us, I love you so very much and we, you and I will be together as long as there is a Moon in the sky. I repeat it is not about us. He relaxed. She moved her hand up over her mouth then clenched it as she lowered it back down to her side. "Honey, what is it?" She placed her around him then quietly spoke to him. "Are you going to be the head of this organization now that your father has passed." He became rigid. "He really did pass, I mean die?" "Remember you found him" "That was real, wasn't it?" He held her hand then raised her up from the bed then locked her in his arms holding her tightly. "It'll be alright as long as you are here with me." "Forever." He looked to her as she finished saying this then kissed her. "We really do need each other don't we." She brought him back to lay down on the bed and turned off the lights. The music C.D. ended playing with the last song being-John Reznik singing Better Days.

This there will be, he said as they touched each other than experienced a night romance and love for each other for first time in ages it had felt that way, overwhelming love.

The following morning Troy made coffee then had his normal tea. He played with James the puppy then took him outside to run him before he left for the hospital. He made a small cage for him outside at the side of the patio, he thought it a lot healthier for him then to be cooped up in a bedroom all day not knowing when he would be returning.

On the drove to the hospital, he listened to a local radio news channel. It seems that there was unrest and rioting all over the country and world. Rioting for Black social injustice and separate views on how to treat the current Coronavirus outbreak and what should happen to public schools. It will take more than just a magic want to fix all these problems right now I have enough of my own. Pulling in the look he drove around the valet entrance especially today he wasn't going to trust anybody, finally he found a place that offered a brisk morning long walk to the main hospital, He made a brief stop inside then went to find Jonathan on the 3rd floor.

A paper cup of hot coffee was placed under Jonathan's nose. He woke up from the smell then thanked him for it. "Any word on him?" "As you can see, I haven't heard anything yet."" Why don't you go home get showered and rested and I will take over, I mean it is not like they are going to do surgery on him or anything." He opened his mouth then collapsed down and stood up saying thank you and left. He looked to the chair bank then turned to the nurse's station instead and went there. He didn't recognize any of the workers from the day before he still asked what appeared to be the head nurse there on an update on Bond. He was going through a Psych exam at that current time and she had no news other than that.

He reluctantly sat down, still thinking that this was good that progress was being made. He then wondered on the burial plans for Vincent. He hoped that some arrangements were being made. Feeling a bit perturbed at all of the people walking by him coughing etc., he left the chair bank then stood to the side of the door of the room that Bond was in. He stood back hearing someone approach the back of the door. A balding tall heavy man wearing gold wire frame eyeglasses came out from this door and looked directly at him. Troy seized this opportunity to talk to him regarding Bond. "Ah, sir, I am his family and would like an update on his condition, you see his father just died and there will be a funeral being that he is his son, he'll want to be there." "I cannot tell you anything, I have to make a report to his attending physician and then you can find out from him."

He thanked him as he walked away and felt anger that he didn't find out anything. "The only thing can do now is go in there and see him." Inside the door he was all ready to talk to him and smile. Bond was sleeping still hooked up to machines. He sighed, no progress, this wouldn't have happened if Vincent were running the show, Vincent." He sat down in a bedside chair then tired of circling his eyes looking at everything in the room. He even started counting in his mind, when he reached 176 something, he just lost count, I am not going to go back to zero. He took the remote for the TV off the side nightstand, and turned it on, turning the volume off. Luckily it has closed captioning, Price is Right, it's entertaining any way. What ever happened to Bob Barker? A new host, hey that is the guy from that old sit-com that I don't even remember the name of.

He watched it all and now viewed a soap opera. He couldn't believe that he was watching a soap opera but then thought what was his other choice, in only minutes in to it he already chose a side on a marriage that was dissolving. Now a bar fight was starting he raised up his body in excitement to see who was going to win. The door opened and his attending physician looked to him He turned the TV off embarrassed at watching a soap opera. "Relax, I see this all of time. He yes did have alcohol in his system and that was our first assumption but after reading the Psychiatrist's report there is something more.

He currently needs CBT. Troy thought, "marijuana?" "No, CBT stands for Cognitive Behavioral Therapy. He suffers from panic and delusions. This might have been caused by a personal experience. It sounds like the source is something that he has just gone through." "Well is there a treatment for this? He seemed fine yesterday." "Yes, the therapy is a type-of talk therapy the principles of his behaviorism. His behavior can be controlled with meds. And theories of cognitive focusing on understanding how people think, feel and understand themselves in the world around them. Pairing positive and negative reinforcement with behaviors that a person wants to increase or decrease." As the doctor finished saying this, Troy looked and felt lost.

The doctor then told him that Bond's regular psychiatrist will be soon, and maybe she can explain more about this to him. "Excuse me, his regular psychiatrist?" "I presume that this means that you didn't know that he had one?" "I guess so?" "Well until she gets here, there are more soap operas to watch." He left the room. He got up and stood to the side of Bond looking down to his sleeping face. "I didn't know that you had it so bad. Bond, we need you, we are all here for you." He hoped that he would open his eyes hearing what he just told him, but here was no response verbally or physically. "I hope that I hear from Chris soon or your doctor soon."

He sat back down and commented to himself, this is a lot harder than being an extra in Hollywood.

After two soap operas were finished and hunger bangs for lunch hit him, anything could have overwhelmed him, the door flew open. "It was Bond's regular psych., Dr. Stone. She looked to Bond laid on the bed walking right past Troy without saying a word. She looked the monitors then pulled up Bond's wrist. There was a response, the sheets moved and his body whispered unknown words. "How long has he been like this?" Troy straightened his back on the chair. "Are you talking to me?" "Are you his brother?" "No, I am a very close friend of the family. And, I am here for them." "So, you are Troy?" "Yes, how did you know?" "He has spoken of you." "How long has he been seeing you?" "That is patient confidentiality, I am not breaking that." When has a psychiatrist from the hospital been here?"

"Ah, he was just here and explained CBT." "Yes, I know, I was briefed. Why don't you go and get yourself some lunch? I will be awhile with him." She looked at him waiting for him to leave. After thirty seconds he picked up on the clue to leave. Now that he was out the door, she said his name out loud over and over until it had become annoying. He moved his head appearing that he was waking from an all absorbing nightmare. "You are here? Why? Where is Chris, where's father?" "Chris is back at your house; everything is alright and your father is in Heaven." "What?" "Bond, you are doing better, but you are going to need my help regardless of whether you want it or not." "Your help for what?"

"I'm thirsty." She poured half a cup of water and gave it to him saying careful. He drank it then placed the cup back down on the night stand.

"What day is it; what time is it?" "Relax, you have nowhere to be and no plane to catch, everything is good. We just need to talk." "Why am I in the hospital? Is everyone else okay?" "This is something that we are going to talk about. Do you know how you got here?" "The last thing that I remember is that I was in my car, where was I going?" "Apparently here." "Why would I drive myself here?"

She pulled the chair closer to the side of him and sat down. "Do you remember anything on what you did yesterday?" His mind was in a haze, he said no words. "Bond we are, you and me are going to be working on something, something for your own good., you need it and you need me." "Where is Chris where is father?" She bit down on her lips then rolled them out looked down to the papers she was holding then back to his face. "I have already told you that your brother and his wife are fine and your friend Troy is also fine as well as Mr. Jonathan. They are all home and safe, well Troy is here, he is having lunch right now."

He breathed in and then looked like he was counting sheep closing his eyes then re-opening them. "I feel fine now, I have to go home." "Wait hold it, watch your movement, you need to rest that is why you are here." "Do they know that I am here?" "They all know except your father." "Why doesn't he know?" She leaned back, "Bond, relax breath in and out slowly," He did, she had him take these deep breathes four more times. "You are doing really good now. Stay relaxed and calm breathing. I have already told you." She knew that he heard her, it was just the regular action to avoid the truth hoping that it wasn't truly real. "Your dad came here, here to the hospital." He smiled, "Send him in I want to see him. He needs help walking though."

"Bond, you know that you father loved you very much. His time on this world became over, he came here just like you did on the same day and almost the same time" "Where is he?" "He lived a long life and he was very happy with you and all of his family." "What do mean, was?" "He passed; he is now in Heaven." He stopped movement of his body completely, held his mouth open and made no sound breathing. He slipped down in the bed to where his mouth was covered by the sheets and silently took a deep breath. "He I dead? Who killed him?" "He wasn't killed by anyone. His time here on Earth just ended, he lived a long and happy life, and he was proud of you, Bond."

He lowered the sheets that were covering his mouth. "His time came and I wasn't there. Why?" "Bond, you were there, you are always on his heart, he died in his peaceful sleep." He moved his head from side to side then shed tears, "But, I wasn't there. I wasn't there to hold him." "Relax, Bond, he knew that you were there." "He as alone then? All the worse." "He wasn't alone, your brother Chris was there." He swallowed hard and closed his eyes falling back down further in the bed. "Chris, was there and not me, that is only natural, I have always been back up. Even in the death of my father, I am back up. Chris, naturally. He covered his face in the sheets. Dr. Stone pushed the call button for the nurse, she ran in followed by the doctor.

She got up and collected her belongs in knowing that she could not work with him now or any time that day. Leaving down the hall she passed Troy. He looked to her expecting good news, and that hopefully he could take him home. She looked to his full hopeful eyes. "Not, today." She knew what he wanted to ask her. Though still standing he collapsed in his heart. Everything had been going so good to that point. He didn't want to go, but he force himself to go back home, all the while praying for the best on Bond's recovery.

Chris and Jane went downstairs to the kitchen, both were surprised and happy at seeing brewed coffee waiting for him. They sat down enjoying the brew and being together. The only other thing that they shared was sliced apple. He made a face then answered his cell phone, "Yes, I'll be there, when is the time again? Okay thank you." Jane looked to him expecting an answer from her inquisitive glare but none came forth. She asked him who was on the phone. "Dad's lawyer, I have to be there in an hour to hear father's wishes and make funeral arrangements. On the last part, the funeral, it is none too soon. We don't have time to mail out anything, it'll have to be e mails. She put forward her tongue then bit down on it. "Everything is just going so fast; I still feel that he is here." He got up put his cup in the sink and commented, "He'll always be here. I have to leave now." He bent down and kissed her forehead, "You take it easy here today, I'll be back when I can." "Okay, we still need to talk about where you where that night." "I know, babe, later."

At Vincent's lawyer's office Chris felt nervous though didn't show it walking in and sitting down at attorney's office. They each nodded to the other then sat down. Chris looked straight forward to the name plaque over his large mahogany desk. Attorney Randel, he was surprised that it wasn't an Italian last name. He did look Italian though, tall thin frame, tan skin starting to show facial lines and thick wavy black hair.

"As you are probably aware of, your father, Vincent wished to be buried at the Gate to Heaven cemetery right there on this island. His wife is buried there and the plot right next to hers will be his." Chris nodded his head. "Time is of the essence here. Vincent did make some minor changes to his will before his passing and I know that they are legitimate because he made them through me. And just as a precaution so that this will be valid a physician would have examined him at that time to make sure of his cognitive ability at that time. And this was done and notarized." "What you ARE saying is that this cannot be challenged." "Yes, not exactly in those words, but the answer to your question is yes." "When will those. (He paused breathing out and moving his head looking for the right words to say). "Everything is in effect as we speak." "I mean, how will I know what to do?"

He slightly titled his head and raised his eyebrows. "Right now, we have to or you have to pardon the bluntness but just get him buried at this location where he chose to be put. I can't make it any clearer than that. And at the reading, do you want your brother here or a legal copy be sent to him?" Chris's face became saddened, "Bond, my brother is now in the hospital, I do not know when he can or will be released…I would like him to be here, it is now the circumstances." The attorney but forth his hand for him to quiet. "That is all that I needed to hear. Money, and receiving it as in the passing of a loved one changes a lot of people believe me." Chris looked questioning what he just heard. The attorney instantly picked up on it. "I will just say this is off the record and between you and me. Men that you have loved, respected and looked up to become vultures, and not caring of other family members feelings or needs." Chris breathed out, thinking he was right. "Your father, Vincent told me that you put other's needs before your own and take care of your family, in just talking with you now, you have proved this to me." He stood up and then Chris took the clue to leave. He stopped at his secretary's desk and got the needed information for the funeral.

Inside his car in the parking lot, he looked through the list. Then went to needed places, the florist, and the church. The was thankful that the priest there had already been informed of the situation, that was a relief off of him. He last place that he went to was the cemetery, after speaking with all he needed to see there, to get everything together, the soonest was two days from today. In the parking lot near his car he choked and his eyes swelled, "I cannot cry, I have to be strong," A person getting into their car near him turned their head to him and sneered as he said this. "I can't leave yet." He unlocked his car then pulled out a bouquet of flowers, all white, roses being the foremost flower in the bunch. He walked to the outline of the plots some with raised headstones others flat on the ground. He didn't even look to where he was going. It was like he followed stepping stones that had been already laid out for him.

He stopped at a raised headstone. It had her engraved picture on it over a heart background of a darker color stone, there was another empty heart to the right side of it for another person to be buried there, a double burial plot. He remained silent looking to it. Silently crying he reached for a handkerchief from his pocket and wiped his tears. "I love you mom. You'll be receiving company soon, father, your husband will be coming to join you." He opened then closed his mouth shaking his head and wiping his tears. "Come on, I have to strong." He touched the top of the headstone-right above the picture of her face. "Bond loves you too, he just couldn't be here right now but you know that we are or you are always with us. The best mother in the world." He bent over kissed his hand then touched the headstone and placed the flowers down on top of her grave. Then walked slowly and solemnly back to his car.

CHAPTER 6

Bond sensing no one in his room opened his eyes, instead of feeling sad that no one is there with him, he welcomed it. He tried moving his arms and his legs, he could, he feared that they had locked him down. He said softly out loud, "I am free. I just have to plan." He stopped talking hearing foot prints approach. A nurse came in his room. He closed his eyes and became still. "I know that you are awake, I heard you say something, I don't know what but there was a sound that you made."

Seeing no other option, he opened his eyes though said nothing and acted to be in a very sleepy state. She handed him a cup of water, which he made the effort to take hold of. Then handed him a small paper cup with a pill capsule in it. "Take this and swallow it." He did, spilling into his mouth then acted out the trouble of swallowing the large pill. She asked him to open his mouth afterward, he did, she looked for the pill in this mouth, not seeing it, she left the room. He waited counting the seconds in his mind after she closed the door, then he took his index finger and thumb to the side of his mouth under his tongue and pulled it out. He carefully got up from the bed and rolled the monitors with him to the bathroom. Once inside he flushed the pill down the toilet. He briefly looked at himself in the mirror then left returning to bed.

He turned on the TV and viewed it silently with just the closed captioning. It was a news story on the passing of his father. "As usual, it was only half right in what they said about him. The service is the day after tomorrow, He heard voices in the hall then instantly turned off the TV and closed his eyes. The door half opened, then there was talk back and forth which he couldn't quite make out what was said, he just laid there as still as could be. The light then darkened from the door closing. He didn't know who or why but to stick to his new formed plans he had to be dormant and what appeared to them as under control.

The following morning, Dr. Stone came to his room at an early hour, maybe this was to see him before she saw her regularly scheduled patients at her office. She tried speaking to him. He acknowledged her put didn't respond back like he'd regained his full composure. He laughed to himself, he was making her seem needed by me.

She sat down in the room chair like she was sitting behind her desk at her office, she was professional. "Bond. I know that you can hear me, and you are a smart man, maybe you know too much." She only took her head up from the notepad in front of her long enough to see his response. There was no movement or response from his body. "You are coy. Well, I will get on with this, you need cognitive behavioral therapy, this is where I determine your state. Perhaps there are hidden messages in the things that you do and you overthink interactions." Again, she saw no response from him. Usually when she says these things to patients, they will spring up to conversation and agree with her words." Trust issues: Unrealistic or exaggerated distrust of a stranger or loved one." She looked for response, her eyes lit up seeing him move. He sneezed. "You are really going to make me work today aren't you. Well, I can see that there is really no point in me even coming here." She turned her body away from him. "It is your health, do what you want."

She gathered her belongings back up and holding the door open she commented to him before leaving, "I know that there is a rabbit looking out from that hole." He thought of her intelligence, she knew. He thought I have one more day to go. I am getting so tired of acting tired. Right now, I just want to run the beach, the beach, Jane. Her and Chris…I hope that they are taking care of James. I miss my puppy.

While Chris was gone, Jane decided to clean the garage. She finished straightening and sweeping with the automatic door up. She stood at the back of the SUV and noticed a little ping at the side of the back of it. She tilted her head and thought he must know of it. Maybe something just hit it, or with all of the commotion that night maybe something hit it then, he appears to be such a clean freak that he would have done something about it. She opened the passenger door and picked up a few dried tree leaves from the floor of it then noticed something shinny that came from under the driver's seat. She closed that door and went around to the other side and opened the driver door and reached under the seat. She pulled out an empty Vodka bottle. "Bond no, My God, no wonder, when did you start?" She breathed out and collapsed her body to the floor of the garage. She closed her eyes while holding the bottle of Kettle One, it is not even the brand that we have at the house, Grey Goose. Maybe that is it, nobody would notice any missing. Why, Bond? Why?'

She sat there on the floor holding the bottle. "Now I have my finger prints on it. Should I just throw it away? Or should I tell Chris?" She sat there locking her eyes shut. She raised up her body up then herself falling back down leaning to the back of the car. Then got up to stand, feeling that the uncertainty of what to do was weighing her down. She moved the bottle to the side of the garage on top of the side counter then reached for a bottle of cleaner and wiped the entire bottle, now maybe her fingerprints were not on the bottle, but she wiped his prints off of the bottle as well. Now, how could they tell that it was even his? "Now. I am guilty. She reached to her forehead and touched it deeply pressing in. "They know that he was drunk." She went to the kitchen and came back with a dishtowel and paper grocery store bag and a large trash can bag. Wearing dish gloves, she picked it up off of the counter wrapped the dish towel around it placed it the grocery store bag then the large garbage can bag. She did all of this movement without stopping once. She took it out of her hand and placed it back down on the counter, "I'll never sleep tonight if I do this, but I already have." She looked at it again then ran to the door control pushing it to close the open automatic door.

The overhead light went off, she stood in the darkness of guilt. "I can't turn back now." She felt for way to the door and left the garage. Instead of walking to the front door of the house the way that she got there, she turned around to the side of the house opened the trash can and dropped the bag in there then closed the lid. Walking back to the front door she felt like a glass of wine but then reminded herself of what she just did. She had a glass of ice water instead and prepared the puppy's dinner.

Chris came in, she didn't even hear him. He placed his hand on her shoulder, she jumped. He looked at her concerned and said he was sorry. "I just didn't hear you that's all." "So, relax, I was just talking to you what did you do today?" She retracted her body, tense, and asked him why he needed to know. "Again, I was just making conversation." She paused then thought of her actions, "I am sorry, it hasn't been a good day for me. I dropped a glass and then watched soap operas where there was nothing but fighting and…" He laughed, we have a lot of glasses so don't worry, and I agree with you on soap drama, maybe just watch comedies instead?" She shook her head, "Yes, I'll do that tomorrow., something different from today, that is for sure?"

"Did you get all of what you needed to do today done?" "Yeah, but I really do not want to talk about it right now, please." She nodded and said OKAY. "I want something but I do not even feel like a beer." At that moment she put a cold glass of water in front of him. He looked to it then at her and said thank you then drank it all. "Have you heard anything about Bond today?" "No, I haven't seen Jonathan or Troy either." He got up handed her the empty glass and said "No news, is good news, I am going to go take a shower. If you haven't got something planned out for dinner, how about just ordering a pizza, I feel like something simple tonight." She agreed with him then reached for the phone to order one.

Jonathan said good bye to the trade wind condominiums manager got in his car and headed for the estate. He turned off to get gas. After he finished filling the tank he pulled to the side, parked and called Troy who was still at the hospital for an update. "Nothing much new to report they just gave him more meds, to settle down for the night. I just heard from the nurse that his regular doctor and the Hospital Psychiatrist are both going to see him tomorrow. I have peeked in a few times and every time he appears to be asleep." He said thanks and good bye to Troy then felt more than suspicious.

Pulling to the gates of the estate he saw the pizza delivery car. He put on his mask and got out of his car signed for it then drove it to the house.

After parking he called Jane and told her that he was there with it. She opened the front door for him to come in. Smiling they went to the kitchen he placed it on the table as she got plates from the cabinet out. Chris came in wearing his sweats looking surprised then smiled seeing Jonathan. In unison they each said" after dinner", A laugh was exchanged, sausage pizza and Sprite wear enjoyed.

Jane cleared the table. Chris kissed her then told her that he and Jonathan were going to be in office. She nodded her head to him and replied back that her and James would be in the backyard patio area. She did take the puppy James to the back and she tried training him. The only command that she could get to follow was sit and she wasn't sure if he was actually obeying or if it was coincidence that he did it. It sure made her feel good to be with this precious play toy that he was. She could already see that the way he observed and acted to things that he was going to be a smart dog.

In the office Jonathan sat behind the desk where Vincent once sat, Chris wasn't fond of that but showed nothing of the way that he truly felt about it. Jonathan got a sense of this though. "Chris, what did the lawyer say?" Chris breathed out caught his brief then replied almost word for word what attorney Randell said to him at the office. Jonathan raised his eyebrows and put his head down, he looked at the empty desk top then told Chris that they had better get busy. "Get busy doing what?" "Busy sending out those e mails." Chris was relived hearing those words, then moved his chair closer to the desk to view the computer screen to do this.

It seemed like to was going to be an easy task but it took well, over two hours, deciding who to invite and who to casually omit. They then had to try and calculate who would actually show up. At such short notice the idea of a reception with food afterwards would be too hard to plan out. Instead, they opted for a get together there at the estate after the service and called a caterer that would be able to do this.

Four hours later they both breathed a sigh of relief. "The day after tomorrow-it looks like everything is set now." "There is one important factor missing though." Jonathan worried hearing this from Chris, "What is that, did I or we forget something, please no, I am just too tired." "Jonathan this is something that you cannot fix. It is Bond." Jonathan then looked remorseful, "It is a tragedy, but what can we do?" Chris slid his tongue over this lower lip then raised his eyebrows and made a long face. "I wish that I knew. Well thank you Jonathan, we had better try and get some sleep now." He got up from behind the desk and mumbled yes to himself, then followed Chris out of the room.

Upstairs he was very surprised to see that Jane was still awake. She was reading a novel, and took her eyes off of the page to see him walk in the room. He instantly walked to the bed and laid down. She looked to his tired body then turned off the lamp and reached over to his check and kissed him goodnight. He reached for her hand and held it tight though said nothing to her. There were many words that transpired in doing this and they both felt it.

CHAPTER 7

The next morning at the hospital, Troy was asleep or partially asleep at the same chair bank, someone tapped on his shoulder. He raised his eyes up in a startle through his body. That same hand placed his hand over his shoulder and then said, "Relax, here is some coffee, get up it is my turn now." It was Jonathan. Troy raised his back in the chair then took the lid off of the coffee and took a sip. "Just how I like it, with monk sugar, thank you." He took three more sips then got up and told Jonathan swaying his hand over the chair bank. "It's all yours." Jonathan lifted this head to him then looked at the exiting hallway for him to go down, which he did. He then saw Bonds' doctor and Hospital Psychiatrist enter Bond's room. He hoped for a good outcome.

Bond opened his eyes then raised his posture laying in the bed. "You have passed all of your tests. Blood pressure has greatly stabilized, your heart rhythm is good. Still your appetite, you have barely eaten anything." He looked to the Psychiatrist and asked him of his opinion. "It is my opinion that he is suffering from this pandemic. It has affected many different people in different ways and panic being the most prevalent. Let's get him up to walk move around the hospital supervised of course and track his actions. Mostly to see how he can interact with other people. A prescription to calm his nerves might be the solution. He listened to this saying nothing but his actions proved that he understood what was said.

Jonathan later observed Bond being led out of his room, still wearing hospital attire. A male nurse was to the side of him-tracking his behavior. Jonathan observed the smile towards him as Bond passed on the other side of the hallway. "I am hopeful and this would be a remarkable recovery, if in deed." As he finished the words of this last line that he said his voice soften at each syllable that he spoke. The male nurse made a full turn in middle of the intersection of hallways. The sound of something dropping made a crashing sound. "Bond, freaked, he clenched his fingers trembled his body and grabbed tightly to the shoulders of the male nurse at his side. As this happened another male staff member ran to them and held Bond from his raging moving panic, the two of them held each side of his body tightly and took him back to his room. He trembled even laying there in the safety of the hospital private room.

Jonathan's head collapsed as he saw then heard this action. "From the way that it looks now, he'll be flying solo here tomorrow. Oh well, pictures." He stopped his words, then remained in a headlock with his mouth still open only a quarter of an inch looking down to nothing but the present bad dream of reality. He whispered to himself, "I can't believe that everything has worked out this way, we were all so hopeful. What is the use of me even now being here?" He slowly got up from the chair bank and walked to Bond's room. Looking down to the door handle he pulled his lips in bit down looking at the floor where his feet were. "No, I do not want to cause anything." He turned from the door and walked down the hall to leave. "I am sure that they have given him something to keep him under. I feel so sad and sorry for him, right now of all times."

Driving out of the parking lot, now on the main roads to get home he cried a tear. "Vincent, I miss you so I feel you in my heart." Wanting to be lifted from this daunting feeling traveling through his body he turned the car radio on, he didn't even remember what song that he listened to or who sang it, at that time, it was an escape, a small sliver of escape. Pulling in he saw that he had to park at the large garage to the left on the main house, the right side of the property was set up for a gathering after the funeral, Long tables with folding chairs were there. Once parked he walked over and looked inside these boxes, there were white cotton table clothes and red runners. "It looks like everything is set to go, except Bond. He composed himself before going in the front door. In trying to turn it he was surprised that it was locked. He then thought if Jane is there by herself, this is good that she is looking out for herself safety wise. He opened it with his key.

Inside he was surprised seeing everyone sitting there in the living room, he felt like they were waiting for him. He said hello then took a minute to use the bathroom then went back to the silent room. Fearful of what they were going to say, he waited in not hearing anything back, he simply said "Hello" then sat down on the end of the couch. Chris asked him if he wanted a drink, he did but declined wanting to hear what had caused this desperation that he felt from them. Not being able to stand them not asking it he decided he had to. Jane asked, "Is Bond, okay?" That same feeing, he experienced earlier thinking about Vincent, absorbed his spine, he did flinch.

"Bond, is okay." He felt like breathing out and wiping his forehead but remained still to words he was going to hear. Troy spoke up, "A small cyclone is heading this way to the north shore of the island, where we are and it has intensified to a major hurricane. There is a probability that it will strike us, it might just roll off to the outside of the island, but the strong chance remains that it will hit us. There is a cellar in this house but nothing near big enough and not enough power to entertain all of these guests. We are baffled on what to now do."

He sat there unmoved breathing out now wishing for that drink." So, you are telling me that we need another option." All heads in the room nodded yes. Troy said that, "I feel like we are still in Vegas playing the odds." "No, no we are not, we'll just keep on with the plan of having it here and if, only if there is the need to tomorrow, we'll just postpone everything to a later date." "But, what about the burial for Vincent?" "They are a funeral home; they must have facilities inside. Their problem solved. Now what's for dinner?" The mood in the room more than lightened up.

Chris put on music from the stereo, Jane returned to the kitchen Troy set the rest of the table and Jonathan did now pour himself a drink, a Jameson on the rocks. The mood was light as they all sat around the dining table having this Lemon Chicken meal that Jane prepared, no one said anything about it they just ate. Jonathan sat back nodded his head to them and felt an overwhelming feeling of belonging.

After dinner was finished and the kitchen had been cleaned Chris started to go out to the front yard and take some folding the chairs etc. up and pack them away from the potential storm. Jonathan laid his hand over Chris's had on the doorknob, and said "No. let whatever happens, happen." He raised his face then retracted his steps then waited at the foot of the stairs for Jane and went upstairs saying goodnight. Troy said good night, then Jonathan went to the office sat behind the desk. Pulled the picture of Vincent's wife off of the side of it. Held it looking at it then turned it down, "This does not belong here anymore for you are going to see her Vincent, maybe you are there now."

He got up feeling that it was time for him to retire for the evening which he did. Before closing his eyes to sleep he prayed to the good Lord above for strength in tomorrow and for him to bless and take care of Vincent in Heaven above. In reaching over to turn off the side nightstand lamp, it burned out, he didn't even have to reach for it. "Thank you." He then closed his eyes to slumber. Falling asleep easier than he thought that he would. Troy had no problem in drifting off to sleep either.

Upstairs both in bed with their backs raised to pillows against the headboard, Jane asked Chris why he was away that night. "Oh, yes we never talked about that. The answer, is rather embarrassing." She looked to him not knowing to kiss him or send him out of the room. "Remember all of you told me that I should get a hobby. I did unpack that surfboard that I ordered in the mail. I spent the good part of the day and early evening driving around the Island. Looking at surfing spots. Right before I entered the freeway to come home, I got a flat tire, and discovered that there was no spare in the car. I had to wait for a tow truck to change it. He put one on, and said that you can only drive a few miles on. The I had to find an open shop with the right size tire to put on. He looked to her. "Oh, that's all, you didn't need to take so long to say it, goodnight." He looked at her after he turned off the light and thought, why do women always have to win? especially her." He then leaned over and kissed her check.

The sound of gushing winds decimated through the estate, a powerful force that would win no matter what, fear was the first thing to strike. With the shadow of sleep over each one of them they gathered at the entrance to the front door. "It is here." Chris spoke in loud strong words. They could hear the distant sound of a siren; this was to warn people of the hurricane. "The office or Bond's room they are the only 2 rooms of the house without windows. They opted for Bond's room, being there was a bathroom in it and they didn't know how long this lockdown would last.

Chris looked to Jonathan, "You stopped me from moving everything outside last night." Jonathan kept silent and strong then turned his head from Chris. They each sat on edges of the bed and counted the passing time with worry. Troy got up walked back in forth and said, "He doesn't have a TV, in here? He went to the computer desk-top and turned it on, just as the screen lit up the power went off. "Great collapsed his body in stance saying, "Great." Moans were then heard from the room. He opened the door of the hallway to bring in any light. After twenty minutes a beep came from Chris's cellphone. He read it, then got up from the bed. "It's over, we can go out now." Slowly feeling uncertain they left, returning to the living room. Chris opened the front door; everything is still there and appears to be okay, just tossed around.

Jane looked out the back widow then replied, water has splashed from the pool but the same here, things just need to be picked up and put back where they were. "Let's go turn on the TV and hear what the news says." They all went to the kitchen. Jane made coffee for all as they listened to the news. "The storm had passed and was now heading north, there is no other reported activity for the day. "Ha, you call that a storm?" As Jane handed Jonathan a cup of coffee, he heard Chris tell him, "I don't know how you knew, but it is over, we can have the gathering here today, maybe you are the best man to takeover father's role." Jonathan took a sip of coffee and remained silent.

Minutes later they were all outside moving things around and setting up for the day. Chris was happy to see that the catering truck had already come to set up. About and about an hour later they all meet back and the front door dressed for the funeral-basically in basic black. Jonathan nodded, "Black is color to show respect at a funeral." Troy remarked that he thought it was something like that. They nodded heads and left. Jonathan went with Troy and Chris and Jane went together, they met back up at the cemetery parking lot. Others that were invited were already there.

They all took seats at the outside service; the view of overhead clear skies was the backdrop. Chris looked to Jane and smiled. He sat at the second to the aisle seat at the left side of the service, she sat to the inside right of him. In all around 30 people showed up and were there. The soft mournful music stopped; the priest stepped to the podium to start the service. He started speaking, they listened in silence to his words. Chris could hear footsteps approaching him. He turned his head to the left where this sound came from. He smiled, a happy feeling that he could feel all through his body, it was Bond. He was dressed in a black suit for the funeral. He sat then whispered to Chris, "I am here." He reached out his hand to Chris's hand and squeezed it, then retracted it with a great feeling at this otherwise sad time.

After the funeral ended, they meet back at the estate for the reception. The food had been served and the champagne corked, they gathered around areas of the yard walking, talking and drinking to the beautiful day that it had become. Bond, his quiet self, walked mostly at the outside perimeter of the party. In boredom he sat down. People talked to him he answered politely but felt no interest in their words. He got back up holding a glass of ice water then walked to the other side of the tables.

Chris took his eyes from the crowd looking to his brother, who seemed and he sensed was faraway. He was more than concerned at him distancing himself and his safety. He nudged Jane and whispered to her. She smiled then left the group of people that she was talking to. He next thing that Bond knew, she was standing right in front of him, holding James. Bond said nothing as he quickly took ahold of James. James barked and licked his face. He whispered "Thank you" to Jane. Warmth had filled his lonely heart. Chris looked to this and smiled to him; Bond looked back with an appreciative face.

A little over an hour later, the crowd dwindled down to none. The caterers cleared everything to take away and left. Chris put his arm around Jane. "Well, the major part of the day is over." "I do not see Jonathan or your brother." "Jonathan told me that he was going to go rest, I am not sure of where Bond is, we had better go in the house and check.' Chris opened the door to Bond's bedroom both he and James were on Bond's bed. They were each asleep snoring. At seeing his he laughed holding his hand over his mouth then silently closed the door. He met Jane in the living room and told her what he saw. She smiled and replied, "What do we do now?"

"At this point, as far as I know, nothing." "There is some champagne left, would you like some?" "No, right now, I just want to go upstairs, shower change into my sweats and relax for the rest of the day. Or the rest of the night, now" "Sounds good to me." They both went up the stairs. He asked her why, Lauren had not been there." She breathed out slowly and sadly. "I know, I would have loved to have seen her and for her to have been here. But she had tests that she had to be there for today." He shakes his head, saying "Understandable" while turning on the shower. She looked out the window before closing the drapes, "It is now was now dark with clouds and raining. After they each showered, they laid and bed and instantly fell asleep.

CHAPTER 8

Seeing Bond outside at the patio area of the backyard he went out and said Good Morning, to Bond. Bond pulled up his head to him and said, "Good morning. Would you like some coffee?" The pot and coffee cups, cream and sugar where on a tray in the middle of the table. Chris sat and poured himself a cup. He took a sip and told Bond, good coffee. Looking over to the ground to the side of Bond, he saw the puppy chewing on a bowl of food, a water bowl was to the side of that. "James is eating before you are." "Well I can feed myself, he can't." "Father's will." "Yes, that will be next." He was surprised hearing this from Bond. He was so peaceful and composed at the words that he just said.

"The lawyer sent me a text this morning saying that he will not have any time open to meet with us regarding this until tomorrow afternoon." Bond poured more coffee in his cup then started peeling an orange. "Sounds good, financially are we okay right now?" "Us, or the company?" "Aren't they one and the same?" "This is one of the things that we'll be finding out from the attorney tomorrow, but I am sure that we are in good standing, I mean, father." He stopped peeling the orange. "He always took care of everything, I know." "Today, you can just rest" "Get back-used to everything, I know. Where is Lauren?" "She had tests that she had to be there for." He nodded. He stopped eating the orange leaving about a quarter of it on the table. He got up looked down to James who just finished his food and just finished drinking some water. Chris looked up to Bond. They started leaving going back inside the house. As he walked away, he said to Chris. "It is good to see you brother, your presence here, is home."

Chris swallowed hard, hearing these words and felt grateful. "Bond." Bond stopped holding the sliding door open to listen. "Thank you, and was your sudden shift in behavior just alcohol?" He sighed then in a straight voice replied back to him. "That and I took a pill that I should not have taken, no more about any of this, please." Chris put his head down then raised it up. Bond closed the door.

He wondered what he was going to do now, an empty feeling of loss prevailed in everyone at the house. A deep feeling of lose, the feeling of being trapped inside deep hole, looking around every side and seeing no way out. He thought also with the fear and containment of the Corona Virus Pandemic, making just living daily life all the harder. "At least my daughter, Laureen has school and I hope that she has made some friends. Friends to stay six-feet away from."

Jonathan went to the kitchen expecting to smell coffee. Seeing the pot missing, he wondered then went to living room only to find it empty. He looked out the window and saw Chris sitting alone looking forlorn with a half-empty pot on the table. He didn't want to face grief, so early in the morning. He opened the door then yelled out to him, "Bring that pot in and I'll make some fresh." Chris heard him then tried snapping himself in a better mood. Inside the kitchen they found Jane. "Well hello you two, I was wondering where the coffee pot was." She took it then made some fresh coffee.

Jonathan made a side glare to Chris. He wondered what it meant. "Jane, give us a few minutes, I'm taking your husband to the office for a small talk, don't worry everything is okay." She looked at him for only the time that he spoke and proceeded with her morning routine in the kitchen. Chris followed Jonathan to the office. Jonathan sat in on one of the two chairs opposite Vincent's chair. Chris looked to him surprised then sat at the neighboring chair. "I am sitting here, because we do not know, who will be taking your father's place. I do not want for you to be thinking that I expect to. I knew Vincent quite well and for many years, but that does not make me family. I truly do appreciate you and your family and I do love you all and feel for you. I do not want in any way to be in the way here."

Chris showed a look of surprise in what he said to him and took a minute to respond back. He adjusted his eyes and scratched his head. It appeared like he was reaching for time to find the right words at this time. "I don't know what to say. Jonathan you are most welcome here and I really." He stopped looked down to the floor and shakes his head. "Pardon me in saying this but I have put you in my father's place." "Is it my age?" "No, it is your power, how you control yourself, your knowledge, Jonathan you are a pro." He let out a laughing sigh," A pro? I don't even play golf. He paused, "I know what you mean."

"It is a difficult time right now for all of us." "Yes." "We had better get back in that kitchen before she brings us breakfast in here." They let out a smirk and returned to the kitchen. Looking out the front window, Chris saw a taxi, Bond got in it and it left out the open gate of the estate. He was very puzzled seeing this, then texted Bond as to why and where he was going. Bond texted back, the cemetery to see father's grave. Jane noticed Chris's look of loss over his face and asked him if he was alright. He smiled to her saying yes, then went to the table to share coffee and breakfast with them. The morning talk was of the dilemma of the virus and how tourism to Hawaii was now banned until October. "If only we could bring back yesterday." "I am sure that more people than one wish this right now, but then we would still have to deal with this in the future." "So, Jane what is the latest on the soap operas?" "Not much they are all repeats. Right now, I just start watching one that I haven' see before, but even this is getting old, fast. I feel like I have put one ten pounds in just staying home to monotony."

The taxi stopped at the funeral home of the cemetery; Bond waved the driver on to the area of his Father's resting place. It stopped to the cement side of the grass lot. He asked the driver to wait for him then closed the door. He stumbled once out from the car showing no embarrassment, he regained his footing and went directly there. He breathed in and swallowed hard looking like he was holding back tears. He placed his hand on top of the raised grave stone. A tear fell from his eye. He wiped it with his sleeve then blinked.

"Dad, I am here, I suppose that you know that anyway. I cannot tell you how sorry I am that I was not there for you in your final hour. This will haunt me all of my life. Oh, don't worry, I know that I will see you in heaven." He stopped talking, bit his lips hard and had trouble swallowing-now silent tears fell from both his eyes. He wiped his eyes with only his hand. "Father, Vincent, I never called you by your first name, you were either Dad or father, mostly father. You never had trouble with anything. Rest in peace, with mom. I love you." He bent over the head stone in tears.

He raised his head looking to the grave walking backwards feeling loss consume him. Fearing he'd lost his footing he turned around to find the taxi before he knew it, he was opening the door getting in. The driver handed him a tissue, He nodded, feeling grateful, then told the driver back home. He forgot loneliness, feeling a new found power he thought it must have come from father. Strength I have to remain strong.

The driver let him off by the opened gate. He went to the house looking at nothing but the door then went to his room. He changed into his sweats and went back outside to James and started training him. James already had the command 'sit' down. Lay down and stay were far from happening, he thought just keep working on it, hopefully something will happen. One time after giving the 'down' command the puppy laid down. Bond lifted his eyes in delight. Then James rolled over and wiggled, meaning that he wanted his tummy rubbed, which Bond did, then held him up in his arms and carried him to the beach for a walk.

Jonathan sat behind the office desk, readying himself for the takeover, it was almost sure he was and that would be tomorrow. He opened the computer putting in the written codes from the desk drawer, he found that he'd get halfway through any file and it would just stop. "Was this where he was when he passed?" He went to the financial file and was very surprised that he so easily was able to access it. He leaned back with desperation on his face. "We are not in good standing right now. I thought that there would be more. I remember he said that he sold the coffee distribution and was moving to automobile business ownerships. He just about came out even in selling the coffee businesses, but there are no recorded titles of any ownerships of anything pertaining to the automobile companies. Where did it go? Did you lose it? All the bills that will be coming in this month.

Maybe I do not want to be the head of this after all." He swiveled in the chair- "Yes, I do. And so, does Chris." "Sell some of the Ferrari's that we own?" He looked down to the desk top then walked out of the room and stopped at the large view from the living room window. He waked right to it and touched the glass. "I had better go back to the office, there has to be something that I am not seeing or doing, I just can't let on to this. Tomorrow will be take-over."

Chris was now outside to the side entrance of the kitchen, with his punching bag set-up. "Hopefully doing this will release some pressure." He, hit it hard and then had to jump back from the force of its return. He did this for an unknown period of time, dripping with sweat and hunched over in pain, still thinking of the possible out some of everything and still worried about Bond. "I am his family and the oldest-everything will be mine, fall into my hands, I am family."

The rest of the day went basically as it had from the start. Each involved their own private world distancing themselves further from each other. Bond looked to James now resting on the beach. "The world hasn't stopped spinning everything is still moving-it is just us. James, are we making more out of this then we need to?" James looked up to him and tilted his head." Everyone is wearing masks businesses have closed plexiglass between people, but it seems to be getting worse every day. James got up and started walking away from him. He caught up to him and picked him up still not knowing what he would do on approaching water from the beach.

He walked to the house, thinking what to do when inside, there was presently no plan: nothing to get involved in, there has to be something other than to just sit at home and age. Friends? It seems that I have many when I go out but here none, who do I have? No, I have to stop this and now. It's nearly lunch time or is it dinner, everything is just running together… I never have been a reader, maybe I should start now. Inside the house he went to the office to get a book from the wall book shelf. Opening the door, he was surprised at seeing Jonathan behind the desk. Jonathan said nothing to him just raised his eyebrows to him. He saw this and told Jonathan to relax, he just went in there to get a book to read. Jonathan still said nothing to him, he just watched his every move.

He more than felt unnerved then ending up just taking a book from the shelf to get out of there as quickly as he could. James followed him in his bedroom. He closed the door then turned on the desk light and opened the book. He closed it back up to see what he picked out. "Let's see here, 'October List' by Jeffery Deaver. I don't know anything about the book or the author, this out to be interesting." He looked at James then got up and gave him a rawhide bone to chew on. After sitting back down holding the book open, he looked back over to him and saw him fast at work, chewing. Now at page 13 he was trapped in suspense that reminded him of work, his work.

Reading it took him to dinner time. He took James back to the-beach area then put him in his outside cage and went to the dinner table fearing dinner conversation. Basically, knowing every step of this routine. They'll all silently check each other out, of course someone will tell her how great the dinner is. She'll ask if anyone wants seconds. Empty plates will be passed to center saying oh no, I'm full and one by one everyone will leave going their own ways.

The dinner hour proceeded just as he thought with one major exception, silence, either no one knew what to say or feared what to say. Leaving the table and thanking her, taking his plate to the sink and in leaving, he didn't even remember what he even ate, other than it was food. Now it was whether to return to the confines of his room or dare to go outside where someone, one of them would approach him and most probably start a conversation that he did not want to be involved in. He brought James in the house then went to his room locked the door and got in a warm steamy shower trying for that time to just forget the world.

Jonathan went back to the office and closed the door; Chris saw this and had an overwhelming feeling right now of contempt toward him. He circled back to the kitchen and looked to Jane. She saw him only this time she did not smile at seeing him as she usually always did. He motioned the way then asked her, to go upstairs. She dropped the dish towel to the counter. "No, no I don't, I just feel like being alone now. Maybe I'll go outside and just rest." He frowned to her and said nothing in response as he made his way up the stairs.

She poured herself a glass of Pinot Noir and went outside to the patio then took a chair from the outside table and carried it to the beach and set it down on the sand. Only far enough to escape the tide but still being able to feel the moisture of the on-coming flow. "This feels about right, close enough to danger to feel it but protected enough to escape from it. Kind of like what I feel about the reading at the lawyer's office tomorrow. Everyone here is just on edge the only thing saving us is fear of who will be the Victor." As she relaxed in the Moonlight, she thought the only thing missing is Bond. She then looked down hard feeling the tenacity of what she just said, Bond, not her husband, Chris. "Oh, there is trouble in paradise."

CHAPTER 9

- -

Everyone there at the estate followed their own paths readying for the day and only stopped at the breakfast table long enough to drink a cup of coffee and have a piece of toast. At the table Bond slid his hands up and down his thighs., a nervous habit. Jonathan wore his reading glasses half-way down his nose looking to same page of Newspaper over and over again. Troy read the label of the jam jar and Jane looked to the coffee pot over and over again saying nothing. Chris opened his cell phone and continuously looked at the time. He thought five more hours now, what am I going to do? Pace the grounds of the estate as yesterday.

Jane got up and instead of going to the coffee maker she turned on the television morning news show. It was talk of the virus either that or talk of the hurricane and where it now was. Nothing really of interest just something to pass the time and making an excuse for not talking to each other. It held their attention for about 30 minutes then they all parted ways. This family who had always felt like a harmonious group had seemed to each drift off going their own ways and feeling their own path. Where was unity, it was at this time gone.

When it was time to leave, they went in three separate cars. Jonathan of course alone in his. Bond went with Troy. Chris and Jane traveled together with no words spoken. In the parking lot each walked separately to Attorney Randell's office. Jonathan checked in with the receptionist. Chris eyed him while he did this. Only Jane sat down. There was enough seating for all but the men preferred to stand. More eager for the hunt. The door was opened by the receptionist and she led them to his office door and softly knocked. She opened it as he straightened a paper file on his desk top.

He did not stand to greet them or even smile to them. He waited until he heard them all seated and settled, "Let's see there are five of you here today as there should be. This might be a little unsettling for some of you but remember we are all adults here getting over a tragedy of the passing of Vincent." At this point he hadn't made any direct eye-contact with any of them. He did scour through the room looking to each one of them for her physical reaction to being there. He already deduced that Jonathan looked like a lion tamer waiting for his crown. Chris looked like he was waiting for a medal. Jane looked like she was waiting for a check. Troy just looked eager. Bond was the only one who looked sad.

"Vincent has had a will made out, since the passing of his wife many years ago. He has made many and few changes to it, all legal. The question is who if any of you or just one of you will be his successor- the family business." He paused leaned back made a circling view of the room again. "Would anyone here like some water?" No voice was raised. "Okay we'll get on with this. Jane, his eldest son's Christopher's wife. You Jane will inherit all of his books, his entire collection." Her heart dropped hearing this, thinking these is all? "Oh, and YOU will be inheriting all of his departed wife's jewelry." She untensed herself, which showed to all in the room.

Jonathan you are inheriting his priced gun and weapon collection and coin collection." Jonathan thought, okay maybe the end I will be the one taking over and is just this for now." He showed no emotional response. "It seems that there is a new person here, a Troy?" "Troy, acknowledged himself." "It seems that he didn't know you, but he made a provision in his will if there comes to be a person to help settle things as in a case that the boys, that Chris and Bond are working on and this happens before his passing that person, being you, Troy will inherit, $60,000 and a job"

Chris's stomach had more than tightened, it was now a contest between him and his brother. He had always been the first that his father talked to him and gave power to him. With what just happened to Bond, he felt that it was his just simply be himself following the rules of succession, it would go to him "Chris, he felt very highly of you and always spoke with you first. He is leaving his noted car collection to you and all of your various clothing sporting equipment and your personal belongings. You will be number one in the field,"

"Bond, it has come to my attention that you were fathered by Vincent, but Vincent's wife was not your mother. So, some might classify you as illegitimate." Bond closed his eyes feeling himself tremble to his feet, this had been a locked secret and he thought that his father treated him as a son. Only once did, he feel a disconnect. And now hearing this, tears welled in his eyes. "Vincent had to let this be known so that nothing would or will be challenged now or in the future. He did all of the necessary steps legally adapting you, Bond you are his son and you Bond are the one that is taking over for Vincent, the power is yours the ownership of the business it is yours, 100%. The estate yours the bank holdings are yours and one Hummer is yours.

Bond felt like he was a flower growing up to the sky cracking the pavement above it. He was speechless. The attorney stomped the papers on the table top and closed the file. "Congratulations, Bond, and may good luck follow you." He got up from the desk and went out of the room leaving the door open. Only Troy went to congratulate him. He was still, sitting there in a frozen state, feeling happy joyous and a bit scared, though he would never let on to it. All of them left the room, with the exception of him still sitting deadlocked in the chair. The lawyer looked back in the office, "It's okay you can take a few minutes, I am going to need your signature on a few papers before you leave."

He thought of when Chris was away and Vincent was training him in the office. One event led to another and he just kind of thought no. Father always had the intention that I would take over, he knew that and apparently never changed his mind or decision about it…Now am I going to lead this family when it has spilt itself apart? Just remain myself and things will come together. He left signed the needed paperwork, and peacefully drove home. Pulling to the front gate and waiting for it open, he smiled, "My home." Getting out from the garage his puppy James ran to him. "Did you have a good day, James? As it turned out, I did."

Inside he was surprised on not smelling anything cooking in the kitchen, he saw no one. But wasn't surprised at this. He went to his room changed out of the suit, put on comfortable clothes on to relax for the evening. He fixed James his food and put the bowl outside for him, he stayed in the house and turned on the music stereo. A classical song started, he changed the music track, the music of the group Bon Jovi filled the airwaves of the house. He relaxed his body and mind. And came out from the kitchen with a ham sandwich, some potato chips and a bottle of Pellegrino. He sat to the right-side corner of the couch relaxing and feeling rewarded. He made up his mind he wasn't going to let anything bother him. He had always strived for the best, never feeling quite satisfied wanting more and to make things better and father knew that, He did slip off and maybe needed more time but he now had so much more to do and felt rewarded with this fact.

By coincidence he finished the sandwich and the music stopped at the same time. He reached over and took another sip of water, then took everything to the kitchen. He opened the door to a barking James who scratched at his leg to be picked up. He held him walking to the office, and placed him on the floor. "I'm going to have to get you a rug in here." James was already in the process of falling asleep laid on the floor by the door.

Bond opened the computer he opened the files, one in particular, the financial file. The one where Jonathan said that they were basically wiped out. He scrolled down to these figures then keyed in the other needed password to access the correct figures. He softly laughed to himself while typing this in." How could I ever forget it?" He typed in the word Hallelujah. The correct figures to all holdings and what the holdings were showed. He went through the records and balanced new figures to tally the new month holdings value. He sighed then smiled. "James, we came out 30K plus. Probably from not having our needed employees here. But we need them James, especially right now." He scratched the side of his nose then reached for a glass of water that wasn't there, he grunted.

He turned off the computer, then took his cell phone from his pocket and starting texting, in about 15 minutes he was through, He breathed in to what turned out to be two yawns. "It's time for bed." He got up looked at the sleeping pup, "You're not sleeping in here tonight. Come on." He held the door open the puppy moaned. He then found he had to pick him up and carry him to his bedroom. Coming out from the bathroom dressed and ready for bed. He thought "Am I now supposed to take over Vincent's bedroom?" He thought he liked the idea of being able to lock his door and no windows in his present room, where he did feel safe, With the present family turmoil, he thought it best to stay in his present room.

He turned off the lamp, and looked to the darkness of the room which he savored. "There is still a feeling of emptiness, I can't let it haunt me." He turned from side to side then laid flat on his back. "Tomorrow will be better." He again closed his eyes and moved around on the bed top. "With the feeling that the family wants to throw daggers at me." "Jane was the one that came to me with all of her troubles. Jane, I can't ignore her but I can't let our feelings reemerge. She doesn't feel this way to me anymore, she can't." "Neither can I." He closed his eyes and this time he did fall asleep.

He following morning he left his room looking neat and professional, wearing black slacks and a light blue cotton button down shirt. James was at his side. He went to the sliding patio door and let James outside. He looked to his left and to the right of the outside area of the property and liked what he saw. In the kitchen he sat at the table looked through a stack of signed papers, then moved his arm for coffee to be poured in his cup. Troy came in and saw this. Before he could say anything a cup of his favorite tea was placed on the table. He sat moved the cup looking to Bind poured himself some then looked back up to Bond. "How did you do this? We aren't supposed to have employees at this current crisis."

"No, employees on payroll. These papers that you see on the table they are all signed documents from the staff that they will work, but not on payroll, a personal payment from me and they had to sign a non-disclosure agreement that health wise whatever happens to them, is their known responsibility." "Is this legal?" "If it isn't. I'll make it so." "You are the boss." "Speaking of that, do you know what happened to the others?" "Others?" "The family." "Your brother?" "I do consider him family, yes."" He and Jane are here somewhere, at least they drove here last night." "Jonathan?" "He came here then he left, I don't know, if he ever came back."

Esmeralda asked him what he wanted for breakfast. "Just, a biscotti I am not that hungry." Troy said that he'd take some eggs. She smiled then cooked them for him. They talked of really nothing of importance just enjoying the company. She placed a plate of Bacon and eggs in front of Troy, Bond fallowed the smell of the bacon from his plate. She laughed then put a plate in front of him. They both instantly amerced themselves in eating breakfast.

Chris came in the kitchen, looking raggedy and unslept. Troy looked at him sideways then swallowed all that he could then got up and left the house. Esmeralda instantly cleared off his plate and cup from the table. "When did you get her back, how? We're broke." "Do you want to talk in here or the office?" "I want coffee." "Okay here then." "Are you hungry?" "She'll cook you something." "No, just coffee is fine," She gave him some. Bond told her to leave. She left going to clean another part of the house. "Looks like we are alone now. What do you need to know, Chris?"

"All about yesterday." Bond said nothing in return he just waited for Chris, to elaborate on this. He took a sip of coffee then reached for any way to compose himself, something that he had never had a problem with until now. "Everything that we heard at the lawyer's office was a shock." Bond lifted his head showing he knew. "Jane as you can imagine was upset and let me know it." Bond wondered on when to interject in the conversation but was interested in how long that Chris would take it or end it. "After a night of sleep or almost sleep. I put everything that we, the two of us have gone through and been through in life. The only sensible thing is for us, the two of us to do is work together."

Bond knew that Chris wanted to say more but he was now looking for a response from him. Bond got up and took hold of the coffee pot and filled Chris's cup. Chris was surprised by his action. Bond put the pot back and sat back down. "Chris." Chris looked to him. "Did you sleep on the floor last night?" He laughed, "How did you know?" "We are brothers." Bond went on to tell him of the company funds and how he got the employees back. At the end of the talk Chris felt much better. Now the problem was how they were going to react to Jonathan. Chris left the table to look for him.

He checked his bedroom, there was no sign of him there and the bed was made. He then figured that this didn't mean anything though she might have already made his bed or he could have slept somewhere else on the estate. He looked by the beach and felt glad seeing the outside patrol. The only place left is the front of the house or the garage. He went to the garage without even noticing the front outside yard. Jonathan's car was not there. He looked upset and sad at the same time.

"He must feel like someone took the floor out beneath him. The best thing that I can do right now is nothing. And no sign of Jane. This time he did not worry and thought or he hoped that she was doing something to calm herself. He went to the office and told Bond that Jonathan's car was gone. Bond looked to him listening to his reply. Then put his lips in and out. "Let's not worry too much on this. He is probably in Las Vegas singing My Way." Chris at first worried hearing Vegas, then caught on to the joke. "You haven't lost it, Bond." "You want to go through these things with me?" "Not really but I have to." He moved a chair behind the desk next to him near the computer to view it.

Jane was upstairs locked in the bedroom listening to an Elvis C. D. cranked up loud moving dancing and singing. She breathed out hunched over then went to the end of the bed and collapsed her body. "Why did everything get to be so hard? It seemed that we had it put together. When did we lose it?" She went to the bathroom and splashed water over her face, then looked at her reflection in the mirror and cried out. "When did I lose it? I don't even know who I am anymore." If I had some liquor in here, I'd drink it, the whole bottle."

She turned on the shower and got in trying to forget anything and everything. "At least with Chris we had sex, great sex, but we don't even have that anymore." Now out of the shower she dressed for the day in casual clothes that she wouldn't ware if she went out but they were good enough to wear staying home in.

In the kitchen she saw Esmerelda. She told her; sorry she just threw the coffee out but she could quickly make some more for her. "Just for me?" She shakes her head no then left taking an empty coffee cup with her. Esmerelda yelled to her as she walked away, "It is empty." She stopped in the empty living room and poured the first bottle that she picked up from the counter not even seeing what it was only knowing it was liquor. She twisted off the cap and poured some quickly in her cup, then recapped it and lowered it back to the counter. She went outside. Not even seeing that

James was there. She moved the chair and sat down and took a sip making a sour face after drinking it. "I never would have thought an Italian family like this it to have Tequila in their liquor cart. It'll do the job though." The puppy barked at the side of her leg. She looked to him, then back to her cup. "I am not going to give you any of this, believe me. It's mine." She sat there not even feeling the hot heat of the day shinning on her skin. Holding an empty cup, she twirled it then closed her eyes and the next thing that she knew she was back in the living room filling her cup again. Only this time she did not go back outside, she went back upstairs and locked the door.

CHAPTER **10**

T roy was driving around the island with no destination to go to, just passing time. He debated on stopping to get some fast food then thought later, maybe later it was still too early. On this drive he noticed all of the side road small businesses, the ones that before he had just passed by. At the left side end of a small shopping complex he noticed Jonathan's fiat or at least he thought it was his. He drove into the lot driving by it but did not park next to it. He went around the side and parked there then walked to this fiat and looked more closely to it, it was Jonathan's. The convertible top is up. "I didn't remember it being up before."

He looked to the shopping complex seeing what businesses were there. A closed bar, a wash and dry, an empty shop space and a gun store, "No Jonathan, don't be there." He walked to the side of it. It had no windows, other than the partial glass block door to enter it. He waited at the side of it, then looked inside. He saw Jonathan's back, he had guns rifles and a dagger placed on the counter and was talking to a man behind the counter. He slowly tried opening the door a partial amount to hear the conversation. The door jingled making a sound that it was being opened. He ran into the wash and dry knowing that he had gotten their attention. Afraid of being seen he waited there. There were people in there but they paid to attention to him.

He covered his nose smelling laundry detergent being opened then in looking out the window he did see Jonathan. He stopped to the side of his car and was counting a wad of money then put it in his pocket got in his car and left the lot. Once out of view, Troy went to his car and called Bond and explained everything that he just saw. Chris looked to him sensing something wrong. He got up from behind the desk and told Chris that they were going to be doing some field work. Inside the Hummer he told Chris what Troy told him on the phone.

Chris said that the first thing that they should do is get the weapons back. "Wouldn't it be kind of suspicious if we go there and take back everything that Jonathan just sold to them?" Chris agreed. There is another plan. Something to do with the fire department." Chris looked to him then nodded his head down, "Makes sense." Bond made a call from the car phone. Now to the side of that shopping complex was smoke and people running out of the shops and a siren blowing with a fire truck there.

Bond parked in the parking area across the street from the burning complex. "It seems that there is a fire there." "People are leaving these businesses." "I wonder if there will be an investigation?" "Did you bring a change of clothes?" "Always, in the back." "There is an Arby's right here that we can change in." "I am a bit hungry any way." "Come on let's go." They went the side entrance and went directly to the bathrooms. There they changed. Men wearing uniforms with dark hair and beards came out put still Chris and Bond, hadn't appeared back from the rest rooms yet. Was there a back window that they escaped from? These men went to the counter and got two roast beef sandwiches; the security camera filmed this. Still no emergence from the bathroom from them.

The firemen from the truck sprayed down the flames as the crowd moved back from the scene the smoke being unbreathable. The firemen entered the various stores looking for any survivors and clearing away debris. Two firemen came out from the gun store and took charred boxes to their side SUV. An emblem was on the side of it, Fire Crew Inspection. After placing the boxes in this van, it drove away. Firemen still remained there as it drove away. There was still no appearance of Bond and his brother from the side bathroom.

The fire van entered the freeway then took the vary next exit parked behind a grove of trees. These two men got out and peeled off mustaches and wigs. The taller darker one then pulled the emblem off of the side of the SUV, they each got back in the truck. Then Chris and Bind looked to each other and nodded their heads in unison. Chris opened the food bag and took out his sandwich and took a bite after swallowing he told Bond that next time, he would like to try their new fish sandwich. And next time he wanted to drive. Bond looked over to him and said "Don't push it, brother."

"Well at least we will not show up on the cameras, if they looked at it at the police station or air it on the TV news." "Yes, it is always good to be prepared and with a plan. Now we have to get these belongings of Father's back to the estate and put them away somewhere safe. And find out where Jonathan is." "How much do you want to bet that he is at the airport?" "How are we going to inspect the entire airport? Call Troy." Chris did. They went back to the estate to check the office computer and had Troy stand by inside the airport."

Now back home in the office Chris checked all outgoing flights. "Here it is, or here he is." "Where to?"

"Florida." "Florida, whatever for?" "Well retired old people like it." "He is only going there to get to somewhere else. Is it a direct flight?" "No, it stops off in Atlanta first There is a two-and-a-half-hour layover."" "A traveling hub to anywhere., very smart of him. What flight?" He, gave him the information; He called Troy and gave him this information. "Come on let's go." "Give me the keys, this time I'll drive." Bond tossed him the keys and sarcastically replied back, "Fine."

They ran into the airport departing gates and saw Troy. They went to side velvet roped off section separating the two sides. Troy spoke to them. "He has not checked in yet and he is not in the waiting gate for that flight." Bond became very nervous. "Standing out here we are sitting ducks that he shall surely see. How did you get in there?" "I bought a ticket for the flight." Chris asked him if there was a nearby bar, Bond looked to Chris and said "You have to be kidding you want a drink now." "No follow me, they turned around and backtracked to the first side bar that they saw. Looking inside the bar, there he was, sitting at the bar drinking a shot of Scotch looking at the soccer game on the bar TV and looking over to the side monitor checking this flight time.

They stood behind him and they could each see his spine tighten up. They each took hold of him from each side and pushed him, off of the chair having a firm grip on him. "Your flight has been delayed." Now out of the bar, Chris waved to Troy. Troy left the boarding area and gave his ticket back to the counter. Jonathan reeked of liquor; Bond sat in the back seat to the side of him, holding a bag for him to throw up into. He did many times.

Once home they put him in his room and locked away his car keys. "One problem solved, yet it still remains." "This is a fun job isn't it." Downstairs they met back up with Chris. "Well, gentlemen at least, we weren't bored today." "That is one way to look at it. I'm going to see if I can find Jane and see how she is doing." Bond, nodded to him as he walked up the stairs. "James, I had better go check on him, is he still outside?" He was, and he found that one of the guards had feed him, He thanked the guard. James pawed for him to hold him. Bond picked him up and held him tightly to his chest. "Don't worry boy, I would never leave you." He put his face up from the licks he received. "Let's go in the kitchen, I need something, you'll probably get something to." He received more licks.

Inside the refrigerator he found Enchilada casserole that Esmeralda made. He took it out and cut himself a piece of it then microwaved it. He opened a can of Coke put it on the table with the casserole and dug in, occasionally giving James a bite of the meat. He hoped that everything was okay for him and Jane,

Chris tried turning the knob of his bedroom door, it wouldn't turn, it was locked. He knocked and called Jane's name. No answer, he tried again only saying her name softer, still there was no answer. He stood back from the locked door thinking that he had two options. To either walk away or kick the door down. He sighed, there is no point on making the matter worse. He left the hallway and went back downstairs to Bond in the kitchen.

Bond looked to him and waited for him to say something. Chris stood there silent. He looked down to his plate, "Dinner is in the refrigerator." Chris nodded then took some and heated it and sat down with it and a bottle of beer. "Where is Troy?" He yelled his name. He came in and saw them eating and the exhausted looks from Chris. "It does look like a beer night." He reheated grabbed a beer and joined them. Bond took his empty plate to the sink and sat back down. "It felt good to get back to doing what we do." Chris agreed to his words." We do make a good team." James barked. Chris looked down to him, sorry buddy but this is too good.

Troy asked Bond what he did with the gun supply he got back from the store. Bond tensed up his relaxed state. "Chris and I put them away someplace else. They were father's, they can't be sold, they stay here like him." He got up from the table and left the room, James followed him. "Hey, I meant nothing by the question" "I didn't mean to upset him." Chris calmed him down and told him to relax, Bond was still having a hard time accepting Vincent's passing. Hopefully time will be the healer. Troy paused listening to him and ate the dinner, "This is sure good, I am glad that you got her back."

Bond went outside to the upper beach area holding James. He knew that James wanted to run, but there was still the fear of the tide taking him away if he got too close to the water. He wiggled in his arms so much that he went back to the patio area and put him down. He did run, Bond looked at him then up to the Moon. The sky was clear it was a bright new moon. "I almost feel at times that the Moon is trying to say something. Being that it is full and bright, maybe I or we did the right thing. Right now, I feel that I am my father's eyes." He held his arms over each other in front of his chest, trying to shield the forlorn look from his face. "It's you and me James." He looked to the moving puppy and smiled.

Chris went upstairs to his bedroom again, being the now late hour, he thought maybe she might have forgotten her madness and forgave him for whatever he did upset her. He found the door still locked, begrudgingly he went downstairs. He looked to the living room couch and shook his head. "The only other choice is father's room." He went there opened the door looked at the inside of the room then sheepishly went in, closing the door behind him. "Dad, it is not like I am taking it away from you I just kind of feel that I need your permission to be here." He sat down and brushed the bedspread and pillow. "We'll all miss you forever."

He then readied for the night and got in that bed saying a prayer of thankfulness before sleep. Bond came in the house, feeling rather surprised in seeing no one. "Well, at least no fighting. I wonder if he made up with Jane." Him and James walked down the hall to his bedroom, he stopped swearing that he could hear snoring from his father's room. He stood thee inches away from the doorknob, and put his hands to his face trembling. He silently opened the door and could hear the snoring louder. He closed the door keeping James and the noise of his barking out of the room. At the side of the bed he now saw that it was his brother, he smiled and left the room wondering why he didn't jump up from his presence. He must have known that it was me.

Now in bed sitting with his back to the pillow raised against the headboard, he wondered of the uncertainty of the world and how it would affect them. "It already has, Chris and I have gotten back together. It just seems that the family is still apart. Or, is it me? And what do we do tomorrow? After what happened at the gun store, we shouldn't do anything, especially now that we have the full crew back, and shouldn't. I can stay quiet and Chris and Troy can. Jane, I don't know where she is at in any of this. And Jonathan keeping him away from liquor and me too." Only the good Lord has the answer. I better pray." He thanked the Lord for everything mostly thanking him for his help in his own recovery now to give them patience with Jonathan.

He closed his eyes to sleep and was awoken minutes later to the sound of thunder. He rose up from the bed put on his robe and went to the widow of the living room, now seeing a darkened cloudy sky. "We just had a hurricane and now this. Is it a warning?" He climbed the stairs saying to himself that he had better go check in Jonathan. Standing three feet inside the room from the door he could already smell vomit, and he was laying on the bed, no motion or sound came from him. He walked closer then could hear him breathing. He left, now back in the hallway, he thought that he heard movement from his brother's room. He quickly went down the stairs to avoid anything with Jane if indeed Chris was not there.

At the bottom of the stairs, he said to himself, "That is the smartest move that I have made today." Inside his bedroom he saw the unmoved James curled in a ball asleep. "Yeah, I am going to do that too, just not in a tight little ball like you are. The morning came almost instantly Before he knew it, he was running Jams outside on the beach, He hadn't seen Jane now for two days and wondered about her, then thought no news is good news. He gave James his water and food bowl outside then went to the kitchen.

He went to the kitchen grabbed a full cup of coffee then went back outside to the patio table. The overhead skies were partially cloudy and clear. He wondered what the day would bring. Surely there was news on the fire, but right then he didn't want to hear of it. He was more than sure that someone from the family would tell him. Right now, he doing nothing was the best thing. The overwhelming feeling that something was missing still tore threw him, making him feel like he was holding up a falling tree that could never let fall.

Chris came out to him with sleep still in his eyes. He sat down to the side of him. He squinted from the sun's rays then moved the chair out its glare. From just looking at him Bond could more or less know how he felt. Chris moved his hands forth on the table. "No pot of coffee here this morning?" Bond swayed his body in the chair. "No, I brought mine in from the kitchen, Chris this may be none of my business but your we." Chris interrupted him at that point raising his hands in the air and showed a look of someone with a hangover on his face. "Stay here, I'll go get you some coffee." He halfway tilted his head up him in response.

On his return to the patio with the coffee, he saw Jane looking at him from in middle of going down the stairs. She just stood there holding tightly to the handrail saying nothing and looking like she was looking at nothing. He placed one cup on the floor while opening the slider then did the same outside to close it. He wondered why the usual helpful Chris didn't help him. "Here, this one is yours." Chris gave him a half smile, then took a sip seeming to have trouble in doing it.

"I feel that I have been silent of this for too long now. Chris what is the problem between you and Jane. You are both acting, I'll put it as gently as I can, off, both of you are just off." "I just fell asleep with head up against the headboard. And her, I think that it is just that time of month." Bond raised one eyebrow; Chris knew what this meant. "I saw you asleep in dads' bed last night, you don't need to say anything more, if you don't want to."" I don't."

"What are the plans for today?" "Nothing." "Nothing?" "After yesterday, it is best that we keep a low profile." "I have to have something to do." "Something to do or a reason to stay away from her?" Chris just drank his coffee in silence t Bond's question. "You want something to do, okay, look after Jonathan." Chris said nothing in response. Bond got up and went back inside the house, James followed him inside. On the way to the office he thought, his ought to be interesting two drunks looking after each other for the day.

He spent the foremost part of the day going through needed paperwork and studying up on things of the office. Every now and then, he heard someone at the outside of the door and the handle being touched but no one ever emerged, he figured that it was Jane. He kept reminding himself that she was a web that he didn't want to get caught in. He never did see a reemergence of Jonathan. Chris must be busy watching him or they are both passed out.

Later that afternoon Esmerelda knocked and told him that it was time for lunch. He didn't feel like leaving the now safety of the office. He asked her if she could just bring him a soda and yogurt. She did only what seemed like a minute later, He ate it then looked at James. I guess that I am going to have to leave here, you probably need to go outside. He went in the front yard instead of the backyard, feeling that he would meet no one there.

He saw Jonathan go in the garage and wondered where Chris was as he told him of the job of watching Jonathan for the day. Jonathan wore black all black which made Bond wonder. He opened the door and saw Jonathan looking frantically for something. He waited standing there observing him then asked "Jonathan what are you doing?" He jumped in fright. "I, I have to get to the funeral." He walked to him and sat his hand over his arm. "Relax, the funeral has already happened and you were there. You were great. Jonathan looked confused and slowed his actions, at that point Bond wondered if he was getting played. "Keys, keys where are my keys?" "Oh, your keys are in the house on the bureau on the entry way." "Oh, oh," He then walked quite good to the house. Bond then knew he was getting played.

Whether it was a coincidence that Chris was inside at the front door, he didn't know. But the two of them were able to grab ahold of Jonathan and in his state, and took him to the kitchen, "Sit down, let's get you something to eat." "No, no I am not hungry," Chris told Esmeralda to get a bag, she gave it to him just in time for him to again throw up in. "How much did this guy drink that he has been throwing up for two days now?" "Maybe he still has some in his room? Do you think?" "Esmeralda can you go clean his room, please." She nodded for head and went to go do it." What do we do with him the meantime?" "Chris this morning I told you that it was your job for the day to watch him, you go outside with him and sit, with a bag, a box of soda crackers and some water." He reluctantly did this.

He went back to the office, with nothing in particular to do. "With this lockdown-it is hard to anything. Yes, we did something yesterday but nothing of caliber to what I should be doing." He swiveled in the chair behind the desk. There isn't even a rock star to watch over at a concert right now." He tapped the desk, that meeting that I was going to, At the time I felt that I needed it and now I can see, was this really a way to help people or just get rich. Everyone is looking for something right now. They even took credit cards.

The meetings were at that public beach park. No having to rent a building and prove documentation of an official business, no records, but taking the credit cards, another business perhaps doing this that they are working under? He leaned back in the chair sighed out, now this sounds like I'm working for the IRS. There has to be something more, something that I can do, other than just wait this pandemic out. I wonder how things are going in Vegas, I couldn't wait to get out of there. But I never saw the real true Las Vegas, again after the pandemic is over.

I am reaching for something that I cannot even see. He sighed out loud and got up leaving the office he thought of the only thing he could think of, and this was to check on the family. He looked out the window and saw Chris with Jonathan how he still looked dazed. Chris saw Bond looking out from the window and showed a hopeful face that he was going to go out there to them. Bond turned away Chris dropped his hopeful face,

He saw Esmerelda walking down the stairs with a bucket and cleaning materials. She stopped at the bottom of the stairs and looked to Bond. "Terrible, she then lifted an empty Tequila bottle in the air in front of her. "She returned to the kitchen. Bond stood there thinking, Jonathan will never get better if he has a supply in his room. He would have to have her check his room more often, and what is he going to do with him now?"

He just then thought "Where is James?" He returned to the office and didn't see him, and he didn't see him outside with Chris, he wasn't in the living room. He went to the kitchen; sure, enough James was there looking for handouts from Esmeralda. He picked him up and took him to the front yard of the house. He put him down then told him to run. He stayed there in place and sat down. He went back in the house leaving the puppy out there alone then came back with a ball. He throws the ball the puppy just looked it him do this. He then started running with the puppy as he threw the ball, James eventually caught on. It was exhausting for Bond though.

CHAPTER 11

In the quiet peacefulness of the air, he heard a distant gunshot that pierced the airwaves, thinking why, it wasn't here but close enough to hear, a warning perhaps or just some body that lost it. He went in the house with James, not wanting to find out the reason standing in the open like a pigeon. Chris and Jonathan were already in the house. Chris handed Bond his bullet-proof vest to wear under his shirt. He took and started putting it on, Chris told him that he already wearing his.

"I'll drive in case that you that forgot, you lost your license." This making reference to his time in the hospital, his driver's license had been suspended until a licensed M.D, signs it off, so you can get it back. Now wearing it and taking his guns from the front bureau he looked to Chris nodding his head that everything was ready to go. They left the house running to the garage and quickly driving out the front gate. Standing back watching this Jonathan thought but didn't say out loud, everything is getting back to normal here.

Bond talked with Chris as they looked for anything out of the ordinary and traveled to where to the sound came from, "The high-end neighborhood where we live, we don't know our neighbors, is it like that everywhere?" "You should know the rich want their privacy and only let a select few enter, like us." Bond pointed to the black iron hedge lined black wrought iron fence to the left. A gold Cadillac was halfway out the driver door was partially opened and the body of a bleeding woman laid out of it to the side. The only thing that kept her from falling all the way out to the ground was the seatbelt.

He parked across the street, they both got out with guns cocked looking everywhere around them and ran to the scene. "Is she alive?" Bond had his hand to her carotid artery; I am feeling a small pulse. Why is there no sound of an ambulance?" "Because one hasn't been called." "We can't move her; you know the laws." "Get the burner phone out from the glove box and call on that." He did. In just minutes later they could here an ambulance. "I know the questions, what, where and why?" "Do I go in there?" "Go lock the car and park it better, we'll both go in there." They ran in against the other side of the car. The sound of barking dogs instantly filled the air, the fear of the animals did not slow them down. The garage was still open. Chris wondered in this why would she leave and not close it. They each ran to it holding their guns up and ready to strike. There was a small yard to the right side of the garage that offered a small water garden, there was nowhere to even stand there. The door to the house was closed. They stopped and looked to the closed knob. Then Bond took a handkerchief from his pocket and opened it before he went in, he told Chris that the dog opened the door.

This woman purse or someone's purse was still on the kitchen counter. Why would she have left without it? Chris saw the alarm box on the side wall over the phone. He pressed on button and it went off, the sounds of the barking dogs stopped. In the process of doing a sweep of the kitchen/dining-room/living room combo, Bond asked him how he knew the right buttons to turn it off. "I just pressed, the off button." They came back from viewing all of the other rooms in the house which there were only three of, and nothing and nobody.

"We had better get out of here before the police find us here." Chris grabbed one thing from a machine to the side of the television center. They ran out the open garage and right back the way that they entered. Crossing the street, they saw the ambulance pulling forth. They ran after the other one. The crew now out from the ambulance. They yelled even louder. "You are never going to leave our house without the grocery list again! You buy what I want you to!!!!" They got in the SUV and left in the direction of the grocery store and not back to estate.

Chris drove in the lot and parked. "Why'd you stop it here. we don't really have a list?" "No list, but we do need mustard." He turned his head and sighed then got out, "Did you bring any money with you?" "I drove, I have my wallet." Five minutes later they came out with a jar of mustard then went back home.

Inside the estate in the living room Jonathan was there waiting for them. They told him what they saw. "Looks like we have a case." "Where is the "we", you sir, are an alcoholic, you can't do anything." "Come on I got drunk that one night and now you are not making me forget this. I have a sinus infection and I am taking pills for it; they do make me a bit drossy. But I have not had any liquor since that night." "Jonathan, there was an entire bottle of Tequila missing from the liquor cart."

Chris checked the cart," There is more than just the tequila missing there is a bottle of Bourbon missing too." Bond called in Esmeralda and asked her what she found when she told him of the empty bottle she found. "No, no it was not in Mr. Jonathan's room, it was in his (she point's to Chris) wife's room. I haven't seen here all day either, the door is locked."

They all sighed not knowing how to combat the problem. Bond took this thumb and fore finger and wiped them over his mouth then replied out, "Dump them, all of them and just do not throw them away, empty them down the sink first." She looked to him. "But there are a lot of bottles there, are you sure?" "We don't need them, she thinks that she does, that is the problem." Esmerelda obliged to his wishes, right at that moment.

"Now we have two problems to deal with." Chris apologized to Bond. "Hey, we have all been there in some way. It's okay just, I don't know. It seems like we need a doctor here. Let's go get something to drink and cool off." In the kitchen, Bond took his usual soda so did Jonathan. Chris had a beer, and said that he wasn't ready to give that up. All three of them at the table Bond asked what are we going to do? "It seems that the way this has happened- it is something to get involved in." Chris opened his mouth then stayed numb capturing their attention. "What is it, Chris?"

"It was staged. I mean look at everything that we saw, it points to someone else, but why. And nobody else being there or her purse taken.

Turning off the alarm just by pushing off a button? I have never seen that before. No actual dog, just the sound of one on the alarm that did not go to an alarm company or the police department." "Why would somebody, have done this?" "It seems that it has been pinned on us to find out." "And why, why do they want us?" "For one thing, we are not the most neighborly family. Remember the expression, let sleeping dogs lie, well fellows one just woke up."

Jonathan turned to both of them with his usual silent demeanor and composer," Maybe they are not targeting us, but they want someone or somebody in particular to see what is there." "After dinner. I'll start working on a plan." "Do you think that Jane will be joining us?" "Only she can answer that question."

Esmeralda made of mixed salad for dinner and her homemade jalapeno corn muffins. They all ate with no words just satisfying their hunger. After dinner, Jonathan returned to his bedroom, Bond went to the office with James and Chris went for a walk on the beach. He thought of Jane with every footprint he made in the sand. "If she could just meet me here, look at me and tell me what bothers her so that she has to drink. I haven't changed what is she running from? She's always known of my line of work, I thought that she even enjoyed the danger and romance." He stopped walking then looked away from the beach and to the house. He looked to it in question. "Is it age? Fear that I cannot do it anymore, or is it her fear that she doesn't want to do it anymore." He continued his walk telling the Lord, that he didn't know.

Bond turned on his computer and scrolled through the daily news. He did see news of the fire at the shopping complex, he instantly scrolled down past it. He should ha paid attention to it but a more pressing matter he was thinking of. "There, there it is, something like this does exist." He looked to James, who was drifting off to sleep. "Well, no approval from you but this is what we'll do tomorrow." He looked to him more, "Right now, sleep does sound good, let's turn in James." He went to the door and waited for James then went to his room. He reached to the doorknob to open the door; it was warm. Meaning someone was just there. He thought of the hidden James and he felt fear down his spine that she would be in there.

He thrust open the door swiftly pushing it all the way against the wall and instantly turned on the light. The room was void of any living matter. James went in and took his spot. Bond thought what if she is in the bathroom, James would have barked, but maybe not. He went there reached for the wall switch for the light and looked at an empty bathroom. No one here. He went back and closed and locked the bedroom door wondering why the knob was warm. Maybe Chris or Jonathan was looking for him, whatever reason they could have had to want to see him it wasn't important enough to wait for him or find him.

Inside the bathroom feeling the jets of the shower against his skin relaxing his tenseness he hoped that she was okay and her and his brother will work things out. Now back inside the house Chris looked at the empty liquor cart and wondered what her reaction to that would be. Do I go upstairs and try that or just go to father's room for the night, again? What would she do if she had her senses about her? She'd go upstairs to me. He went upstairs, he held his hand to the doorknob, still deliberating on going in. Okay, my hand is on it. I am on the process of turning it, he lit up with joy and success that he was going in. It didn't turn. Still lost in the love they feel for each other, he knocked and said her name then waited, and waited and waited. He slid his body down to the floor sitting there waiting for her to open it. She never came, sad and broken he went downstairs to his father's room to turn in for the night.

In the kitchen Chris and Jonathan were already sitting at the table having breakfast. Bond went in surprised in seeing the early risers. He asked Chris how the night went, "Same as last night." He finished taking a sip of coffee then asked of either one of them had even seen her yet. Both responded no. Chris did say that he thought that he heard someone waking around during the night. He didn't worry too much about it because of the guards. That and he didn't want to get his hopes up.

"We have a full day ahead of us but she is the top priority." He moved his head to leave all three went to the base of the stairs. Bond already had the master key in his pocket. They knocked on the door, Chris thought he heard moans. Bond nodded his head and unlocked the door pulling in in they went inside. She was passed out on the floor. Chris dropped his body to the floor in panic, saying her name over and over. Jonathan quickly knelt down beside him and felt for a pulse, He looked up to Bond, she has one, and it is fast. Bond stood back took out his cell phone and made a call. Chris looked up to him, "Did you call an ambulance?"

"With both you and father each been picked up here in the last weeks. No, I called our doctor, he is one his way, I don't want us being a news story." Jonathan got up and got her some water to drink if and when she regained herself. Chris sat there dormant in fear looking to her, feeling lost. "She feels cold and is pale." Chris looked to Bond, "What are we going to do? She is my life." "Just stay here with her until the doctor gets here." They stayed.

The white elderly male doctor that Bond instantly recognized stood at the open door. Bond said hello then led him to her. They moved Chris out of the way. He examined her and asked them some questions. The doctor stood up and spoke to them. "Gentlemen this is not just simply being drunk. Do you know if she is taking any medication? They looked blankly to him. Where would she keep medication?" and Bond walked to the bathroom. The doctor followed him and picked up a prescription bottle from the counter. "This explains it." He walked out from the bathroom with it. "I take it that it is a pain killer, it is codeine, which is an Opioid. A look of shock came over Jonathan's face. Chris looked puzzled, only Bond appeared to be listening to the doctor's words.

"An Opioid, works by altering your perception of pain." "Doctor" Bond stood silent calm and strong as he asked this question. "What is the treatment?" "Ideally she should go to the hospital, for intravenous fluids." "Can you do this?" "I can give her some activated charcoal at this moment. She will need the prescription Naloxone, otherwise known as Narcan." He put his things back together in his bag, and replied," I strongly recommend that you get her to a hospital." "Can you write her this prescription?" "It would be unethical for me to do this, without her getting professional; treatment, sorry gentlemen." He left.

Chris looked hopeful to Bond. "We have no choice." "Yes, we do. Troy gets the Hummer out and bring it to the front of the house. Chris, I'll help you bring her down the stairs." They got her in the backseat. Bond took over the driving. Chris reminded him that he was not supposed to drive. "I know, we just need to get her there and quickly and I know the route." "Where, where are we taking her? Even Troy knows the way to the hospital."

Bond parked in front of a nursing home, one that they have gone to before in situations similar to this. They got her checked in and put in a private room. She was hooked up to an I.V. Bond spoke with the attending doctor there. He left as the doctor walked away. Chris, I think that you should stay her with her, when she regains herself, she will have a lot of questions, be careful how you answer them. We'll be back later today, hopefully…she will be able to go home." Chris didn't verbally reply but looked thankful to him.

Now back at the vehicle Bond threw Troy the keys., he caught them and got in the driver's seat. He looked to Bond as he buckled his seatbelt. "Where to?" Bond didn't answer, Troy turned the key and backed out of the space. "We have to go somewhere." He repositioned himself in the seat looking uncomfortable. "This has put a crimp in the planned day. I really don't know." Troy turned out to the street and was now in traffic. He didn't know where, he had never been in that part of town before and was just following traffic laws and going in a straight direction. "Turn around and get back on the freeway, we are going to the cemetery."

"You are kidding right?" He looked to the Bond, he showed no emotion and didn't answer him. "To the cemetery it is." Out from the car he walked directly to Vincent's grave and placed his hand on top of the headstone. "Father you know, you know everything even right now. I need some help." He stopped his movement then slowly started bending his thumb back and forth. He bent his head down then lifted his hand and ran it through his hair on the top of his head. "Everybody is just falling apart and I can't." He looked at the silent gave for minutes more then turned away kissing his hand then putting it over the headstone, made a cross over his heart then returned to Troy who waited by the vehicle.

Both inside Troy asked him were to now? "Home, just home." Inside the house he went to liquor cabinet and checked it, Even taking his hand and wiping the empty shelf. "This stuff is supposed to make you feel good, how can it work the opposite at the same time?" Janes ran to his leg and just stayed there instead of pawing his calf as he usually did. "It makes you forget and it numbs you. But uncertainty remains." He clasped the back of his neck and leaned back. "I still do not know what to do." He looked down to James- James went to the kitchen. He followed him and snickered. Life is so simple for a dog.

Troy went to him at the kitchen table. He sat down and asked him if he had any new plans. "We are going to play dress-up." Troy sneered at this comment from him." I got to get something to eat first, I didn't eat breakfast." He opened the refrigerator and saw a cheese plate; he took it out and ate it, Troy joined him. Troy asked him about the doctor that visited the house. Bond told him that he has been "making house calls" for the family for years and he was trusted.

They met outside at the side of the SUV. Each wore dark green uniforms. Bond removed adhesive tape from the back of the label he put on the back of Troy's uniform. He stood back and viewed it, "It looks good, and mine?" "It looks good too." They drove to sight of the condo where the woman was shot yesterday. They were both surprised that the iron gate was open. They drove to and parked in the driveway. At that time a police investigation van pulled up and parked to the side of them. Bond looked totally composed and showed no sign of surprise. Troy picked up on this and stayed calm and said nothing.

The police investigator walked right to Bond, standing face to face. "I wasn't told that anyone else would be here. Bond explained since the onset of the virus that they were there as a precaution, to them doing the full investigation. Once they gave the all clear, he cold proceeds forward. The officer then told him that he had been informed of any of this, He left and went back to speak to another man from the police man from the van. Now back to Bond, he told him that they would return later that day. They were going to leave for lunch now, as they had gotten backed up. He then asked how would he know that everything was all clear for the investigation or if here was a possibility of the virus on the premises. Bond told them that they would leave a paper. The police van drove away. Troy waited until it was out of sight. "How did you say that to an officer of the law, I mean how would he not know?" Bond replied, "Timing." "Timing, how does timing figure in?" "It's lunch time and they are hungry and tired. They'll be back though. We have to hurry."

They went in the house opening the unlocked garage door. In the note was a note signed by her, Lenore that she was going to leave him she had enough she was a wreck. She apologized about cheating on him and just could not bear it any more. He took the note placed it in a paper bag and sealed it. The bed was made but looked like either a person slept on top of it or something happened on top of it. In the bathroom he found two medications in her name he also took those and sealed them touching them only with gloved hands.

He left the rooms and went to Troy, he noticed he also had a bag. It's been almost an hour; we have to get out and now!" They backed out hearing another vehicle approaching, nerves fluttered in both of them. Leaving out the gate they saw the police van pull in. It honked at them. Troy honked back, taking this as a sign that they were saying "hi" and not as a warning to stop. He pulled in front of an on-coming car, again he was honked at. Bond told him to pull into the next housing row. He did, then parked three blocks down. Bond jumped out of the SUV and peeled the banner off of the side of the it. Just put them in the back in the plastic garbage bag. Troy did that then got back in and drove to the estate.

"Shouldn't we have picked up Chris." "God, I forgot where he even was. Is the bag still in the back?" "Yes." "Get it and let's go in a different car." "They pulled put in the white Hummer." Driving out the gate Bond turned around to make sure that the plastic bag was in the back, it was." They made a stop at the back of business complex drove around to the back of it and threw away the plastic bag, then went to the nursing home.

Chris was sitting in the front reception area holding a Styrofoam cup of coffee, looking at it not drinking it. Bond placed his hand over Troy's chest," Lets ease up before we go in there, he looks very fragile right now" They calmly walked to him. He looked up smiled then looked back to the cup he was holding. "The doctor told me that it was a risk in letting her leave now." "Has she talked to you; does she know what happened?" "No, I mean right now, she'll look at me but she remains silent. No matter what I say and what I ask her." "Physically is everything at the right levels or however you say it?" "She is still dehydrated, but her blood pressure is fairly good and her heartbeat is good. Mentally though, they don't know." Bond backed up from them and walked out the front door. Troy looked at this concerned, not for him but for Chris. He looked to him with a sad face, "I am sorry about that."

"There's no need to, I know him, he is thinking." In five minutes, time, he walked back, in a stern look and voice said to Chris. "Go home, you need rest and food and sleep. I'll stay and watch her, she is family, now go." Chris said nothing he just left with Troy beside him. He asked an attendant walking the hallways if it was okay to go to her room. He checked then told him yes. He went there walked around to her bed, then looked to her and smiled. She smiled back. "It's good to see you, Jane." "Same here." "You're awake." "Yes, where am I? what happened?" At that moment he wished more than anything that Chris was there.

"You." He stopped his speech being lost for words. "You my dear lady, became dehydrated and you know that right now the hospitals are full. There was an opening in this nursing home and they are taking the overflow from the hospitals. "You mean I got this sick just from not drinking enough?" He thought is that ever wasn't an oxymoron on this situation. "I had better let Chris tell you. I just sent him home. He was here all day watching you and beside you, you are HIS WIFE. I am only here so he can rest." "You always were special Bond." He sat up from the chair. "You know I am really thirsty and I have to go to the bathroom, I'll be back don't worry."

He went to the bathroom, once out he thought of the timing if he or Chris had only been there for 30 more minutes. He went to the vending machines against the far wall away from the rest rooms. He put coins in the beverage machine and punched a button not even look to what he punched. Bending over retrieving it from behind a black plastic folding tab. He pulled it out opened the can and took a swallow then another swallow. He held the can away from him to read it. "I didn't even know that they still made Tab, well at least I am watching my sugar intake. He looked at the other vending machine. A candy does not make sense with a diet drink. I don't want chips, the only other choice is peanut butter crackers, chips it is." He punched the button, pressing potato chips but got pretzels. He shook his head and opened it ate a few then threw it away in the trash.

"Now what do I say or how do I act toward her, I feel that I am walking backwards. I mean I have already gone through this with here, in sorts, of yesterday." He walked back to the room with the can of Tab. She sat up in the bed with her back against pillows. "Is that for me?" He looked to the can he was holding. "No, ah do you want one? I can go get you one." "No, that's okay just come here and talk to me." His body showed apprehension to this, then he went to her and moved the side chair at the bed a little further away from her.

"Why so far away?" "I have been out all day and I might have picked something up; you never know." "I knew that you would be here." She smiled to him. He straightened his voice looked down to the floor then to her. "Chris was here, he just left as a matter of fact. He was so tired, you know he has been here all day watching you and talking with the doctors, and taking care of you, he was here." "I know, you already said that." "Why am I here?" "He didn't tell you that?" She huffed, "You just told me that he left." He scratched he back of his neck then looked around the room. "Nice room, flowers over there on the counter, I bet they are from him, Chris."

He got up and looked at them. "Hum, no card. But I **know** that they are from him. I mean they have to be." "Either that, or they were just there already." "I doubt that", he sat back down moving the chair another few inches away from her. "What are you so nervous about?" "Who, me?" "Come on Bond, I know you." "Yeah, you do but you know him better." "You mean, my husband? What is his name again?" "Chris, he is Chris, I mean…" "Relax, I know. I was just messing with you." He relaxed his torso in the chair, "I see that you have not lost it."

"What happened to you?" "When?" "Right now." "You already know, that. I lost it, the pressure I guess." "But, you…" "I know, I just fell. I was looking for something to make things better and I lost it. I don't know why but all of a sudden everything scared me. I ran and I ran- the wrong way to liquor and then I apparently overdosed on the medication. I remember drinking but somehow the number of pills, I do not remember. I even went to your room to talk to you about it, but I chickened out." "You, came to talk to me?" "Yes, that night. I had my hand on your doorknob, I remember I even turned it, but then I ran." "Why did you come to me and not him?" She looked down held her breath for a few seconds then replied back to him looking at his face. "Because, you always had the answers." She then breathed out and looked away from him.

He moved his body nervously in the chair. "I know that I just sent him home but I know that he should know that you are better." "Let's wait until I hear the word from the doctor, Bond I am not going to run out of here, why don't you go home too." "I will, but not right know." "Good, now I do not have to eat dinner here, alone." "I can't imagine what the menu will be." "Can't or don't?" They laughed.

They talked, then turned on the in-room TV. A repeat of Gilligan's aired, and brought a good relaxed feeling to each one. Before they knew it two dinners were placed on the pull-out table in front of her. He moved his chair over to have dinner with her. He told her to go first. She removed the plastic wrap of hers and he removed his right after her. "Yum, tuna casserole, and canned string beans and wiggly jello too. And it is the green one, I hate the orange." He laughed. "See this is good, you need the company," She stopped in taking a forkful of food to her mouth. "Thank you." "Don't thank me yet, you haven't eaten yet."

"I ate more of it then I thought that I would of." She wiped her mouth with the napkin, "Same here." Momentary silence filled the room, neither one of them knowing what to say. "Well, we ate." He moved the try away from her. "If you have to leave now, I understand. I mean dinner's over, they'll probably have me go to bed soon, I am already in bed, but I mean to sleep here. I really don't want to." He straightened up, doctor's orders, I'll stay just a little bit longer on one condition." "What is that?" "You find something else good on TV to watch." She picked up the remote and gave it to him. "You find it, this way I won't pick the wrong show." He laughed, "You are good."

Chris woke up in the darkened hour of the day, he instantly moved his arm to the side of the bed to feel for Jane. He felt only the flat bed sheets. He got out of bed, lost his footing and fell back down to it. He breathed in and just stayed there thinking. "She is there tonight? I want her here, but will I still have to worry about her going off?" He got up went to the bathroom then straightened himself and went downstairs. The light was on in the living room but no one was there. Well, this leaves the kitchen, office, bedrooms or outside to find anyone. "They're usually looking for me, not the other way around."

He went to the kitchen feeling hunger and heard the back-side door of the kitchen being closed. He followed the sound to see who made it. Troy was leaving, He partially ran to him then stopped, raised his voice. "Where are you going?" Troy yelled back, "I just need to get out of here for a while, I really don't know where I'm going." He walked back to the kitchen. Opening the refrigerator to look for something that he didn't know what it was until he found it. "Well, this now leaves only Jonathan and me and the dog, where is the dog?" He hadn't heard any barks or whines there.

There are no left-overs. Hum -eggs, cottage cheese or something from the freezer. She must be going shopping in the morning. He settled for a bowl of breakfast cereal though wished for a hearty meal. As soon as he poured the milk in the bowl of cereal, he heard the puppy whine. "I should have known that you would show up." Jonathan came in and asked him the news on Jane. He told her that she would be there until tomorrow.

He sat down to talk to Chris. "In regards to your last case." "Last case?" "The condo where you found the dead woman driver." "Oh, that one, kind of open and closed." "Not necessarily." Chris tilted his head wanting to hear more. "I was in bed last night watching an old episode of Colombo, the detective." "Yes, I kind of remember that show, I was a kid then." Jonathan made a slight facial expression that he didn't appreciate hearing that.

"It was her husband." "Her husband, why?" "The husband had *found a new life.*" "Maybe or in Colombo's case, the TV series case." "Yes, I know what you are referring to. The wife, had money, they had been married for many years, and he found a new lady and having his old wife die making it look like suicide did the trick for him." "So, you are telling me that he killed his wife, then staged her death, but why? I mean killing someone that you made a promise to be there for her? Why not just divorce?"

Jonathan opened his eyes wider, lifted his face moved it from side to side and replied, "Money. She had it and he needed it." "But they were married, wouldn't her money be their money?" "Not necessarily it depends on her legal arrangements, if any. There are marriages were maybe, a pre-nuptial was signed, what yours is yours and what is mine is mine." "That is terrible if it is true that he did that. But what benefit or what is the benefit in us solving it?" "Exposure." "What? We do not want to be exposed." "That we do good." "No, doing this may be good for the dead- her, but we do not need nor want this, I know I don't." "What are the factors involved?" "Jonathan, I am tired of guessing games. If you want to go into this further, proceed, but without me or the family, I don't want a television camera in my face."

"So, what are you going to do tomorrow?" "I am going to pick up my wife and bring her hear." "And then what?" "Here we go again, with the guessing games. Doing what as in what?" "Are you going to be by her side all day?" "Yes, she is my wife." "Well, if you get tired- you know what I'll be doing." He then got up took a bottle of water from the refrigerator and left Chris sitting there in the kitchen.

"Bond, is staying there all night? She is my wife. I suppose that maybe he thinks that I need the rest. Actually, I do, I feel so tired, but know that I won't be able to sleep..." He picked up the spoon, then looked at the cereal in front of him. "I wish had something better to eat then this." He got up dumped the cereal and left the room. He got his keys and drove to the convalescent center, along the way he stopped at the In and Out drive thru and got a burger, fries and soda.

Inside he went to her room, it was dark but he was still able to see her in the bed and Bond asleep in the corner chair. He tapped him firmly on the shoulder. Bond opened his eyes drowsy and confused. Chris motioned for him to leave. Bond did. Chris walked to the side of her looking at her and bent down to kiss her check. He ws surprised that she didn't wake up, she needed her rest. He pulled the chair from the corner closer to her, he looked at her with love then closed his eyes to sleep.

CHAPTER 12

Dressed in his navy-blue sweats Bond ran along the beach with James. Instead of going through the living room they entered from the side kitchen door. He noticed a piece of paper floating over the ground, he briefly ran to side where it was picked it up, then followed James to the door, they went inside. He placed this paper on the kitchen table without looking at it. Esmerelda asked him if he wanted coffee. He told her that he did but a glass of water first. Troy came in and raised his hand to her for her to bring him coffee, she instantly gave it to him.

Bond looked up from his empty glass and said good morning to Troy. Troy returned the hello. "I thought that you wouldn't be here." "Excuse me?" "The plan was for you to stay the night watching her then Chris would pick her up this morning." "He came and relived me there last night." "So, now we don't have to go there?" Bond finished a sip of coffee then told him, "Apparently not, which I do think that him doing this is for the better." Troy looked to the table and made no reply. Bond reached over to that piece of paper. He read it aloud, "The transparency of death? Where or what did you do last night?" "When I got back to my car in the parking lot it was on my windshield. "I repeat where did you go last night?"

Jonathan walked in the room briefly looked to them and sat down. This created a diversion for Troy not to answer the question which Bond was fully aware of. "Shouldn't you be picking her up or bringing her here,

I thought that you stayed there with her last night?" Bond breathed in and sighed feeling upset as he already answered to Troy of this and now, he has to answer this same question to Jonathan. Troy could since the built-up pressure that he displayed. "Jonathan, Chris decided to go there last night, and Bond came back." Bond looked over to him and gave a slight head nod thanking for him answering this question. Esmerelda placed tea in front of Jonathan.

Jonathan clanked his spoon against the cup whether he did this to break the quietness in the air or he did it for attention, Bond ws aware of the two possibilities and did not want to react to either one. After seconds of innerving noise, he stopped doing this and asked Bond if he had thought anymore of what he told him the night before." He swallowed hard got up with his coffee cup and went back outside to the patio through the living room with James following him.

He filled James water bowl then sat down and instantly got up. "If I sit, they'll come and talk to me. Father never had this kind of pressure or did, he?"

He stood atop the edge of the patio; James dropped his ball in front of his foot. "It appears that you want to play. I'll throw the ball for you, but you have to go get it and bring it back yourself. I am too tired to run, but it seems that is all that I have been doing is run." He picked up the ball and threw it out from him to go get. He felt a gentle touch over his forearm. "You're back." "Where have you been running? "" Nowhere…just the beach. Does Chris know that you are back?" "Who do you think brought me here?" "Yeah, (he shakes his head) it has just been a long night. I am glad to see you, I hope you are okay."

She stepped back from him, "Yes, the looney bin, released me." He moved his body nervously. "I didn't mean anything by what I just said." "Bond, be quiet-you are not being yourself right now. It was nice to see you. I am going upstairs now, bye." He scratched his head then felt the ball on his foot. He picked it up and threw out for the dog, then put his head down and scratched his forehead, "I don' even feel, (He stopped his motion and words) come on James, we're going to the office."

Inside the office with James who laid on his floor pillow. He turned the computer on, then jumped up from sitting at the desk chair. He turned on some music, it was Elvis. He stood in the middle of the room and just moved around then started mimicking Elvis. At the end of the song he even bowed, then saw the face of his puppy. "Thank you, thank you." The puppy barked. "Again, thank you." He moved back behind the desk and said to himself, I had better get to work now.

Their wine distribution was doing stellar. It seems that in this current pandemic, people are drinking more. He went through other of the business holdings, everything was doing well. There was no apparent need to do anything. "Why, do I feel emptiness just trapped in the air around me?" He leaned back and deeply sighed. "And there is nothing that I can do to keep my mind of it." He got up and walked back and forth in the room, he saw the puppies face observing every move that he made. "Come on James, I am going to go shower." James followed him to his bedroom where he closed and locked the door. James instantly laid on the floor on that floor pillow. After he showered and dressed for the day, he went to find Jonathan. He found him in the living room listening to Mozart on the stereo,

Just as he approached him his cell phone rang. He raised his arm to Jonathan then turned around and answered the call. "Yes, Dr. Stone, I know, thank you for the reminder, I'll be there." He went back to Jonathan. "It, ah, your plan, I want to do it." His eyes lit up hearing this. "I am going to need a favor." Jonathan stood up from the couch, "I'll drive you there" Bond put James outside in his cage then they left, Jonathan driving.

He waited in the car for him. Bond checked in, Dr, Stone herself went out to the waiting room and called him into her office. He followed her they both sat down. "It is good to see you here, you missed our last appointment. If you didn't come here today, I would have had to report if to the hospital. It seems that you, yourself checked yourself out of the hospital. But being the instance of why you did this, we have let it pass. So how was his funeral?" "You knew that?" "Not much escapes me Bond." "It was a funeral, a sad time. What else do you want me to say?" "The family, have they excepted you back in?" He paused, looked down then looked up to her. "Excepted me back and in now I am the head of it." "Impressive, are you able to cope with it and everything?"

"Time." "Time as in how much we have left or time being a factor to you answering this question?" Time as in, I do not feel that I have enough of it, time to figure out what I should do or time as in how do I act and feel to my brother's wife. There, is this enough for you?" "Which one do you want to start with?" He sat silent. "Let is start with what I feel is the most important one." "The last one that I said." She looked to him with showing the face of someone that just called bingo.

"Okay your brother's wife. How is she involved in this-your feelings?" "Oh boy, how do I explain it?" "This is what I am asking you." "I have been watching her for her safety, you know that. She just had quite an experience." "With you?" "No, not with me, with overdosing on both medicine and liquor." She made a look of now-I-got-it." "I guess that she couldn't handle the pressure and the liquor cart was right there, and then that night she just took too much of her own prescription medicine." "Did she, do this on purpose?" "She said that the liquor yes, but the pills she doesn't even remember." "Did she tell you before she did this?" He squirmed in the chair. "She said that the night before or the night that she did overdose, she tried to talk to me about it." "Why didn't she?" "She chickened out?" ""Bond, do you feel guilty about this?" "Yes!" "You are not her emotion you couldn't of have stopped her." "But if I'd have been there then." "What if she did this at three in the morning, would it have still been your fault and her husband was there, would it have still been your fault?" He shakes his head and said "No."

"Do you feel that you have more time now?" He stopped his breath, moved his eyes to the ceiling then breathed out looking like he just found the answer, "Yes, I do." "Now in figuring out what you need to do." "That one is never-ending, it is now my job." She lifted her face in response. "It is good for me to hear you have this philosophy on the problem, it shows the importance of thought and rationality. You are doing much better. So, two-weeks from now? Make an appointment before you leave." He stood up straightened himself and thanked her. He breathed in hope.

Back in the parking lot he found the car, Jonathan was listening and singing opera music. He tapped on the door. it opened it for him, but he didn't stop signing until the end of the song which was a minute later. Bond fastened his seatbelt and asked him if he had a signed recording contract yet. Jonathan turned it off then fastened his seatbelt and responded that he was working on it.

Jane went upstairs to her bedroom. The sliding glass window was open a gentle breeze blew toward her, she followed it then looked out to the ocean view. Hearing a noise, she turned around and saw her husband, Chris holding a tray. He sat it down on the table. She went to him and hugged him, he kissed her lightly on the check. "Sit down dear." She did. He brought fresh coffee and sandwiches cut in quarters. She poured herself a cup then filled his cup. "I can never tell you how very much that I love you and miss you when we are apart." "Why do you think that I brought you home?" "I never want this moment to end." "Ditto." "Didn't they already use that line in a movie?" "Yeah, but I can't remember which one so it'll just be ours." "Ghost." "Where?" "The movie." "It can never be as good as ours."" Our life, our movie, you are the star."" So, are you telling me that you'll give me a paycheck?" "Yes, and you make the amount as big as you want." "Do you have any backing for it?" "Yeah, you."

They helped themselves to the sandwiches. She asked him about Bond. He suddenly acted uncomfortable then asked her why she wanted to know. "Well, he is the one running everything now, do you think that he can?" "Wait a minute here, I have known him all of my life and now you are asking me if he is okay. I mean look at what just happened to you." She felt a chill go up her spine. And pushed her chair away from the table. She opened her mouth to speak then closed her mouth again feeling the chill but this time fought it. "I have always been here for you even when I was there, I was here for you. I mean, (she opened her mouth to no words) I am just asking because I am concerned, for him, for you for all of us." He got up from the table and left the room never looking back. She sat back licked her lips and squinted her eyes, "Back to square one, maybe I do know why I overdosed. This is going to be a long day. One that I don't want to be involved in."

CHAPTER 13

Jonathan and Bond entered the open iron gate of the condo. They parked and just stayed in the car looking at it. "Well, we came here and now I don't know what we're going to do." "We already looked through it, we need more than what we got." "Well Colombo, what did he do besides smoke a cigar?" "He went to commercial break." "We have to find out more about him and we can't do it here." "He was or is an account manager at Eastridge Investments." "I have never heard of it before, how old is it?" "It was just started two years ago." "Well at least you know that. Do you know anything more about him?" "He is originally from Miami." "We better get out of here before he shows up. We'll talk more about this later."

They went back to estate, parked and out of the garage, Bond's puppy James ran to him. He picked him up, wagging tail and all and got his face licked. Bond didn't say anything, but he wondered why he was out of his cage and whoever did this, where were they now? They went in through the back door by the kitchen instead of the front door as usual. In the kitchen Jonathan told Bond he was going to his room upstairs and that he'd see him later. He wondered where the others were. Instead of looking for them, he got James's food ready then took it outside for him to eat. He didn't stay there with as he usually did, he went back inside to the kitchen.

He more than felt like reaching for a beer but grabbed a soda instead. He knew his boundaries, and popped the tab and took a long swallow.

"Well Esmerelda must already be gone. He opened the oven door and smiled. "Oh, good, baked chicken with her spices over it and roasted potatoes, he took it out and set it om the counter. After plating himself some of it, he looked in the sauce pan and saw green peas, he helped himself to those as well. "Oh my gosh, I almost forgot." He got up and washed his hands thoroughly at the kitchen sink then sat back down to eat, saying a prayer before biting into the meal.

On his second piece of chicken now, he heard and saw Troy come in the kitchen. Troy washed his hands then fixed himself a plate and sat down at the table with Bond. "I found a paper that rolled off of your car. What it said worried me, The Transparency of Death, can you or will you explain this?" "Oh, that I went to a bar last night and it was there on the counter, I think that there was some explanation about it. It was a bit odd though." Bond made a face, thinking a guessing game again. ""What was odd?" "An older man was right there sitting at the counter by me and he was with a much younger woman, there was no doubt that they were a couple or she was trying for them to be a couple because they after a few drinks were talking about framing his wife, whatever that meant." Just like a guard dog picks up his ears Bond sprang to attention hearing this, then asked him what they looked like." "Oh, I can do better then tell you I can show you." He was baffled at hearing this. Troy took out his phone, opened it then scrolled to the picture. And showed it to Bond. "Can I have this?" "You can't have my phone but I can send you the picture, sure, why do you want it?" "Something that Jonathan and I are working on now, and this sounds like it is something that we are looking for and need." "A case, is there something for me to do in it?" "I don't know yet, but I'll let you know as soon as I do" Bond thought all he had to do now was get a picture of her husband, the president of Eastridge Investments there on the Island.

He could feel the spring in his body receiving this information. He was back to work the work that he loved. Later Jonathan came downstairs, just as they were finished eating. "I am going to my office now, thanks Troy." "What is he so happy about?" "A picture that I took and sent to him." "She must be quite good-looking." "No, it is a picture of a man." He breathed out and said "Maybe I do not want to know anything more on that, I'll just eat." "Actually, I took this picture by mistake, just in hitting the wrong button."

Upstairs in her room, Jane locked the door, then moves briskly around the room, going through everything that she had there. She went from crying in desperation to panic and fear in the next moment. "I have too, I have too, for my own sanity." She looked to the door and went to it at least three more times to make sure that it was locked, it always was. "The key? What if he has the key and opens it?" She swiftly moved around the room then grabbed a chair and braced up against the door knob, the panic showed over her trembling sweaty body.

Chris went to outside of the door and tried opening it, he couldn't. He knocked on it in normal fashion and called her name, no answer, he couldn't even hear her on the other side of it. With a firm hard fist, he started banging on the door. "Let me in Damn it, it is my room too!!!!!!!" Jonathan opened his door and saw this. The rage that showed on Chris's face alarmed him. He called the guards. Two of them had to pull Chris away from the door. Being the absence of Bond, they looked to Jonathan while trying to hold back the moving Chris flinging his body in an utter rage. "Take him downstairs and outside-give him his car keys. He can't be here right now." Both guards locked Chris's arms and moved him down the stairs and out the front door. The guards came back inside and locked the door. Now outside Chris screamed. Jane could hear his scream upstairs locked in her bedroom. She went in the bathroom and locked that door then moved her body against the door sitting on the floor eyes wide open as they could be a cold chilling feeling down her back and panicked fear embraced her skin. She sat there silent as she could., and whispered, "I hope and pray, he doesn't find me."

Surprisingly in all of this commotion Bond made no appearance. Was he aware of it and ignored it? Or did something else, possess complete control of him? Was he even there? One of the guards knocked on the office door. James looked at the door and barked. He was engrossed in his work, looked sideways to James, trying to ignore him and the sounds of the door knocking above the loud Elvis Costello music. He moved his head and made fists with his hands moving them tightly up and down, then went to the door. He asked who it was before he opened it, still fearing being alone with Jane at that moment. The guard announced himself.

"Yes, what is it?" "Your brother." He squinted hearing that, because he heard the voice of the guard and not the voice of Chris. He hesitated then opened the door. The guard explained what had happened. "Right now, he is outside then?" The guard responded, "Yes." He sighed that it was family drama again. He straightened up his body and went to the front entry of the house. Standing there he debated whether to go upstairs and check on her first or check on Chris first. He told James to stay and he went upstairs.

He knocked softly on the door. "Jane it is me I am alone." He then thought of the horror of what he just said. "I am just here to check on you, to make sure that you are okay." Sill there was no answer. "Chris is not here; he isn't even in the house." He waited, hearing nothing. "I need to know that you are okay" At this point he worried. "I tell you what call me on my cell number if you are okay, you don't even have to talk to me." He waited, this time tapping his foot on the floor. He saw no other option but to count to ten. "One, Two, three, four, five, six, seven." His phone rang once then went silent. He did the same in to her in response, called her number it rang once and he hung up.

He went downstairs, James leaned against his leg once he was there standing by his side. "And now for Chris? Does he have a gun? Is he drunk? For the first time in my life I am feeling fear." He motioned the guards over to him and sent one of them upstairs to the outside of Jane's room and went outside with the other guard. They circled the front perimeter of the property and saw nothing and heard nothing. "How does a grown man hide?" He went back to the front door then went back inside thinking he had to be in there somewhere. Bond found him in Vincent's bedroom.

He was sitting on the floor with a gun on one side of him and nothing to the other side of him. Bond looked to him; Chris looked back showing no anger toward him. He was relieved at seeing this. He stood there silent waiting to hear anything from his brother who remained silent. He thought of him being Bi-Polar and maybe this was a reaction from that, had he taken his medication? He lowered his voice as if talking with a hurt child. "Chris, everything is good, I am only here to be with you. You know, I am your brother, I know you in every way. I am here for you. You are good, you do good, I am thankful for you." Bond moved slowly to him. He notices the guard behind him and put his hand flat behind him motioning for the guard to stop his actions.

Bond lowered his body and sat down on the floor two feet from him. "You know I would never be who I am today, if it wasn't for you and how many times have you saved me? I am sorry I just haven't said it enough but I always feel it. Chris, you are the best." In this time that he was talking to him, he was moving his hand closer to the gun in each passing second. Bond now had his hand over the gun. Chris opened his eyes wide seeing this. Fear grabbed hold of Bond, for that brief moment he quickly caught himself. "It is okay Chris, you are safe, you are with me, I will always be here for you." Bond closed his hand over the loaded gun and retracted it to his body. The guard then slowly walked to him and took it away.

Chris got up from the floor, this was a tense moment, would he run for the guard who now had the gun or would he hit Bond? He moved to Bond then opened his arms and hugged him, quiet tears fell from both of them. "We are family Chris, I love you." Chris exhaled a deep breath that was trapped inside of him. Bond helped to lay down on the bed then gave him a glass of water to take sips from as he held the glass for him. Bond saw no option of leaving, he turned on some soothing music and stayed there until he fell asleep. Bond thought of back when they were in Vegas; practically the same thing had happened. He wondered had Chris been keeping his scheduled doctor's visits? Should the medication be changed? Has he been taking the medication? One thing that I know, I have to be here for him.

After he sensed Chris to be asleep, he quietly left the room and had a guard stay outside the door of his room. He went back upstairs to see if Jane had softened her mood and would talk with him. He found that he was hesitant to even knock on her door. He finally did to a soft knock then proceeded with a louder knock saying her name before each movement. There was no answer and no sound that came from the room. He thought this was very unlike her usual behavior, when she was upset by something. She would have the music from the stereo filling the airwaves of the room and surrounding area. He then rationalized that she was asleep, being the time and trauma of the day. He left and returned to his office and gave Dr. Stone a phone call. On her message machine he stated what happened with

Chris. And asked her what to do now in regards to this. After hanging up the said, "Life's a beach."

He opened back up the computer and then thought of James, where was he and was he alright? He didn't see him in the office. Fear shadowed his footsteps in looking for him. He found him in his bedroom on the rug to the side corner of the bed. He was curled up and a gentle snore came from him Bond smiled, "Thank God, that I have you."

He returned to his office hearing his phone ring, he ran to get to it in time, he answered it-breathing heavy from his quickened pace. The voice on the other end of the line asked him if he was okay. He explained and said yes. It was Dr. Stone returning his call. He explained everything of that night regarding Chris to her. She asked him if he thought that he needed to be admitted to the hospital at that time. Bond replied no, that even seeing a hospital right now, would set him off. She told him, that she had a full schedule the next day but his matter took precedence. She would work on doing some rearranging and call him but it wouldn't be until tomorrow. He thanked her and hung up.

He looked to the sleeping puppy. "We don't drink anymore, so how about some warm milk?" James woke up and went to the door. Bond laughed and followed him to the kitchen to make it. James had some on a bowl on the floor and he had a full cup of it. He took a relaxing sip of it then wiped his upper lip with his tongue and took another sip, He thought this was the time when someone with a problem would come to him and spill everything out to him to solve. He actually waited for tit, looking for them any one of them. The room remained his and his puppy's.

He took each hand up the side of this face and pushed them upwards then dropped them. "How am I going to leave to try and figure out that case when both her and Chris are like they are? How did father do it?" He rubbed the side of his thighs then looked up. "I have a strange nervous habit, don't I James?" He didn't even look to him he licked the bowl as hard as he could. Bond got up and took it away from him. "You were going to lick the enamel right off of it, weren't you?"

"I better go back and check on Chris." They left the kitchen. He stopped in his room to shower and change into pajamas and a bathrobe before going in Chris's room. He left James outside with his rug and chew toy. Chris seemed to be asleep. Bond sat down and tried to find comfort. His eyelids grew heavy then he heard Chris's voice. "Talk to me, just be here." "I am, I am. I am sorry but I really don't know what to say right now." "Tell me of something that we have done, remind me." Bond searched for something anything that did not pertain to his wife or anything that he thought might upset him. He reached back to when they celebrated Christmas in the fifth grade. Chris laughed at the story. Bond felt the pain in his mind, his older brother Chris who had always been a rock, his own person, his challenges, dangers, he faces it all and conquered all and now this was conquering him. Tomorrow would not come soon enough, he only hoped and prayed that the doctor would find an opening.

The next morning, Bond woke up at the first sign of daylight, mostly because of how his body hurt from sleeping upright in that chair all night. He noticed movement from Chris. He stayed there wondering if he was just moving in sleep or if he was indeed was waking up. It turned out that he was just moving in sleep. He opened the door to the outside hall as quietly as he could. Once outside he asked the guard to go inside Chris's room, he did. Bond went to his room and dressed then went outside to James. He always enjoyed seeing that waging tail. He took him for a brief walk then went back inside the house.

Esmerelda was not there yet, he thought of the early hour, of course she wouldn't be there. He opened the coffee maker to put coffee grounds inside it and was surprised to see that they were already there, the water was there also, all he had to do was press the switch. He turned on the morning news show only to see a commercial advertising their line of automobiles. He lowered the volume. Then looked to the coffee maker that wasn't even half full yet. For something to do to fight the dullness of the morning he took the half and half out of the refrigerator and places it on the table next to the sugar. The news show started back up; the talk was the position of the democratic to Republican lead for the Presidency. He turned it off. "That is not news, it is purely opinion."

Turing around again he saw the coffee drip, one by one slowly falling in to the pot. He took his cup to the side and poured it full, hearing three drops hit the burner and sizzle dry. Sitting back down with it trying to place it on the table some slid out, he wiped it dry with a napkin, then saw a handwritten note on the table. He read it, it was a note saying that she would be late, her car wasn't working and she would get a ride there from someone else. She even said that she was sorry. "Well it's a good thing that all I had to do was press the button." Feeling jittery from the lack of anyone there, he got up and went to the front door. He opened it and saw a taxi. He closed the door, not interested in being seen by a stranger then went outside to the patio. "That was Esmerelda being dropped off, she'll have breakfast made soon and might even bring it out to me.

He answered his cell phone, he was surprised at this early hour that Dr. Stone was returning his call. She now had an opening at 10:00 to see Chris and he had to be there. He assured her that he would have him there. He felt wabbly probably from low blood sugar and took a candy off of the coffee table in the living room and went back outside to the patio with James. Before he knew it, he was back in his brother's room checking on him. Chris was awake. He stayed in his room while he showered and readied for the day.

They went to the kitchen. Esmerelda ws there, frantically trying to do everything quickly as she could. Bond told her to slow down, they didn't have to be anywhere for a couple of hours. She smiled and went on with her routine. She made French Toast. It was god but they both only had one piece, not feeling very hungry. James barked. Bond looked to him; no this is not dog food. "You do feed him treats; I have seen you do it." Chris then broke of a small piece from his uneaten slice and gave it to him. He swallowed it faster than he could have shewed it.

Esmerelda handed both Bond and Chris a piece of paper that she just picked up off of the far end of the kitchen counter. Bond replied, "Another note." He read it and then told Chris that Jane wrote it, she has an early doctor's appointment this morning, some Dr. Sullivan. Chris said, "Well she is taking care of herself; I just don't know why she won't talk to me." Bond remained silent to these words from Chris.

The taxi stopped at the departing gate of the airport. She paid the driver as he helped her with her bags to the side drop off area. She ran inside then looked to the gates and the airlines. "Right or left?" She turned and ran to the right. She waited in line at the booth with the shortest wait. The closest departing flights in time were all full, the closest one that she could get a ticket one was to Seattle in two and half hours, she purchased a ticket for that flight. With the ticket she ran to the gate. She sat down and looked to the faces of strangers wondering around her everywhere and wondered what their stories were. Liking her end of the row seat in the waiting area, she places her bags on it then went to get a coffee from Starbuck's there.

She returned thankful to see that her bags were still there. She put the coffee on the floor while taking her bags off of the chair then sat down and picked up the coffee. In just taking the first sip of the non-fat latte, she savored it. Finished with the coffee she swore that she felt her whole body tapping nervously waiting for the departure, would they come after her, did she have enough time to escape? AN announcement just sounded through the portion of the airport. There was an open ticket to the next flight leaving from the gate across from her. She sprang up from her seat and went to the counter to exchange her ticket for that one. They told her that there would be a credit for that was a less expensive ticket. She didn't care she just wanted it as she could see the line already forming to board this flight, she took her new ticket then stood in back of the line to board. She felt her heart beat faster and stronger with each passing second, hoping and praying that she would make it aboard the flight and that it would take off before they found her or came after her. Being the last person to board she walked down the aisle of the plane reading the row numbers. Her seat was the last row in the back of the plane, middle seat yet, but at that point she didn't care. She remembered all to clearly how Bond had once before walked on the plane and got her off. She didn't even notice the two people sitting at each side of her.

She thanked the good Lord when she felt the movement of the plane making it down the runway building speed for take-off. She held her breath and slowly opened her eyes to feel that it was now in the sky. She literally made the sign of the cross over her chest. Then listened to the stewardess reciting information on emergency landings. "Okay everyone, enjoy a safe and happy flight with us to Las Vegas Nevada." When she heard that she tightened her body rigid in the chair thinking oh no. Then after a brief moment she thought maybe all the better, they came back not liking it, so why would they want to return. "This turned out good for me, I can't wait to get there." She closed her eyes. It was a smooth flight.

After breakfast they went out to the patio and left James there in his cage, "Bye buddy, we'll be back soon." Jonathan drove them to the doctor's business office, once in the parking lot he asked them how long they'd be. "Why don't you make it two hours." He left to go do shopping while they went to see the doctor. Bond stayed in the waiting room while Chris spoke to the Dr. Stone. He was escorted to her office by the receptionist.

Behind her desk she looked forceful and dominant. He paused standing at the side of her desk. She made a look to the chair with her eyes. He followed her direction and sat down. "So, you have missed your last appointments giving us no reason as to why. From what your brother has told me, it seems that you have had a bit of a breakdown. I will plan and simply ask you question One, have you been taking the Lithium that I prescribed you? She received no answer. Well that is answering the question right there. What is your reason as to why you haven't been taking this prescribed medicine? It is for your own health. What do you feel?" He started to mentally form a sentence then looked up to her demanding eyes then realized that he could only answer her with the truth, which at that moment he couldn't form in an answer to her question.

"You are just like your brother." He looked up to her and wanted to know why she thought this. "Go ahead, you can talk, that is what I am here for. Something has a great hold on you, tell me of your or this problem?" He swallowed then looked to her square in the eyes, "Me, I am, my problem." She commended him on his honesty and told him that they would work on this issue. "There are two Me's, and I do not like one of them, it confuses me. I don't mean to say." He tensed up. She motioned for him to relax and then said it aloud. "I don't mean to act the way that I do at times. I mean look at me, I had it all together, I sometimes heard voices in my head but I tried to ignore them, thinking that maybe I just needed to relax. How do I relax with the job that I have?" He left his mouth open breathing out and looking first to the ceiling then to her.

The remainder of this session she asked him questions needing to find a diagnosis and wanting to hear him vocally being honest with her for the first time. Yes, he was Bi polar but the bigger issue was an offset of Bipolarism and that being Trait Anger. A characteristic where one experiences frequent anger with varying intensity, mild to intense rage, emotion of envy, resentment and even hate and disgust making it difficult to disentangle.

She asked Bond into the office while Chris was still there. She told him of the utter importance for Chris to take the daily dose of this medicine. She would work with him weekly on this critical issue. She reminded Chris and looked to him telling him that he was very important, and if she wasn't there or him to talk to, he could look to Bind or a friend of the family, and if they weren't there at his time to relax. Listen to music start a Journal, go for a walk, exercise. These were and are options.

She walked them out and stopped at the desk to make sure that he booked an appointment for next week. And then sent the prescription to the local pharmacy. And she reminded them that she would call the pharmacy to make sure that they picked this prescription up. As they left, she looked to Bond and told him that he could do this. They went to the pharmacy in that same building and sat and waited for it after receiving it and paying for it they went to the parking lot where Jonathan had just pulled in.

Driving away, Jonathan asked them how everything went. They both responded at the same time, "Good." Jonathan's opera music played on the drive back to the estate. Once inside, Chris told them both that he was going to go rest. He walked up the stairs. They wondered of Jane was there if there was going to be fighting. Halfway up the stairs he turned around and went back down then went to his father's room and closed and locked the door. Bond thought. Some feelings take longer to heal.

He went outside the see James and let him out of his cage the usual reception of a wagging tail and licks were received as he petted him. "You know, I think Chris would benefit from you. We've got to work on this." Right now, he had a choice of going in the kitchen or going to the office. "Everything has just become so predictable and closed off, in a way I feel closed off because of all of this social distancing. And places and things that you just can't do anymore."

He went to the kitchen, Esmeralda instantly welcomed and asked him if he wanted lunch. He felt a bit hungry but if he ate now what would be in store for the rest of the afternoon. He told her no, then took an orange off of the counter went back to the table sat down and started peeling it. He moaned, on just the lack of not doing anything when there was currently so much to do. He turned on the television, as usual the news was on talking of the current virus outbreak condition in the world the country and the state.

It zoomed to a picture of the Honolulu airport, it wasn't even half-full of people walking to and from fights. Inbound flights from the Continental United States were banded until October. He watched the show paying close attention to the limited number of travelers. He opened his eyes wide sprang up from the chair and stopped the picture with the remote. "How do you get a close-up on this thing?" Troy entered the room and told him, "You can't on that." "It's Jane, look." He moved closer to the TV and agreed with him it looked like her." Bond ran to the office and took the written her written note to the office computer. "Dr. Sullivan here on this island, one works in theology and the other one works in geriatrics. Neither one applies to her." "She is escaping."

"Troy, we have to get to the airport." "She might have already left." "We have to find out." Bond already had his keys on hand running out the door to the garage, Troy got in the SUV while it was already moving. Frantically running in the airport, they found out that they couldn't go to the gates. In a panic, he purchased to tickets just to get them in the gates, never intending to board the flight. They ran down the halls looking for her, she was nowhere to be found. Bond went to a gate attendant and showed her the picture of Jane on his phone and asked her if she had seen her. He received "no" answer. An attendant took over the spot where she was standing and said to her thank you for the break. He turned around with a dazzling smile to this young lady and asked her showing her the picture. "She was to board this last flight." "Where to?" "Just look at the board, above your head." "Seattle, she took off for Seattle, why?" "Come Troy let's leave." "There is one more thing that I think that we should check out." Bond was already walking away leaving the gate. "And what would that be?" "Security camera footage."

"My God, why do you want to see if a harden criminal boarded a flight or not?" "No, I want to see if she did board, she might have chickened out and be back home as we speak." "You know, that sounds like her. Let's just go home." "You want to bring home a pizza?" "Yes, but we won't get it here, I want retirement money, we'll stop at Marco's on the way home, you can order it from your phone once we get back to the car." Troy agreed and looked happy about this.

They got home with the standard pepperoni and a classic vegetable. He handed both the pizzas to Troy and went outside to get James. Back in the kitchen, he could see Troy washing his hands after seeing this he did too. "Now to get everybody?" "What if Chris is sleeping?" "With the current plans for today he can go back to sleep any time that he wants to." He went to Vincent's bedroom to get him, there was no answer at the door and he wasn't even in there. He then thought, he is upstairs with his wife but just to be on the safe side and also not having to climb up the stairs he checked the office. Much to his surprise Chris was there sitting behind the desk using the computer.

He nodded to Chris. Chris looked up to him. "You two went to the airport." Bond was taken back by this comment, "Yes, we were." "You didn't find her." "No, we didn't, I am sorry. We did find out that she went to Seattle." "No, she didn't, she went to Vegas." "But she bought a ticket for Seattle." "Yes, she did but she exchanged it at the last minute for an open seat to Las Vegas Nevada." "How did you find this out?" "From what father taught me, and this is a move that I would have probably made." "She is smart." "But we are smarter." "What does that mean?" "We're just going to let her go."

"But aren't you afraid of what might happen to her?" He put his head down then immediately looked up to him. "This is something that she needs to figure out for herself. If you or I or anyone goes after her right now, she'll just end-up doing the same thing again and again." "Right now, you sound like dad."" "Well, there is the saying- good things come to those who wait. Right now, she is looking for us, in her conquest to be free of us." "I think that you are right. There is pizza in the kitchen." He got up from the desk and asked where they got it. "Marco's" "That is good I was afraid that you were going to tell me, Little Caesar's." "Like that would ever happen."

Troy had the table set, cans of sodas and the pizzas on the table. Chris went to the sink and washed his hands then sat down to have the pizza. He asked them if they could say a prayer before the meal, they closed their eyes and said his prayer that Chris recited. "This time more than ever I feel that we should be close and thank the good Lord every day. And tomorrow,

I want to go to church." "We haven't been to church since…" "Since the passing of father. It is time that we go back."

They ate and finished the pepperoni. Troy wrapped up the remaining half of the vegetable and put it the refrigerator. "Where has Jonathan been, why isn't he here now?" "He left saying that he had some shopping to do." Chris tilted his head and raised an eyebrow. "Do you believe that he went shopping?" "Just see if he comes back with any bags and what is in them." "Hey, he is working for us- all I want is for him to be careful."

They went to the office. Bond held James to take him outside because she was vacuuming the living room and the vacuum is the mortal enemy of dogs. Even now that he was outside in his cage, he still barked. Going inside and seeing Chris behind the desk, he didn't take to kindly to seeing, but knew that he shouldn't show his feelings. He sat by Troy and listened to what Chris was going to say. "Okay from what I have seen of your notes Bond, we have a pretty open and shut case." Bond felt like saying "We do?" but he kept silent. "She was driving out from her house and just keeled over at the steering wheel in be process of leaving." They both shook their heads to what he just said. "If this is the case, why was her car in drive and not reverse? She wasn't leaving she was going home." "Her purse was on the kitchen counter, why would she have gone out and left her purse?"

"Troy you saw her husband the head of Eastridge Investments at a bar with a young woman talking of how shall I say it, offing her." "Offing her?" Bond looked calmly to Troy and told him killing her. "And gentlemen what would the reason be?" "Money, and so that his bar maiden could be the new misses." "Chris, but isn't that too easy?" "You think that it would be." Bond had gotten more than tired of this yesterday they were playing guessing games and now his brother took over his position and is having him play this guessing game again. He stood up, then lashed out, "If you know the answer, tell us, do not have us guess." "Ewe, when I got home, I took my pill, apparently you haven't taken yours yet, calm down and I will tell you. And for me sitting here when it is your space, I am just here right now because I think that it is easier for the two of you to pay attention to me., Bond I am not taking your place."

He saw him relax after he said this. On checking his social media accounts. Troy looked to him asking, "Why would an investment firm

President have media accounts?" "Popularity, so people will invest in his firm." "Close one Bond, you see last year he went to California, San Francisco California- he stayed there for approximately a year, reason being he was learning more on how to handle the firm." "If he was there, who was here working, doing his job?" "He was." "You mean he was going back and forth, so everybody must have known this."" Except his wife." "Why would he keep his from her, I mean she was his wife?"

"This is what we have to find out." Bond looked to Chris behind the desk with his mouth open in question. He saw this and asked him what he needed to know. "Is his wife, that was taken to the hospital, okay?" "I haven't seen her name in the obituaries yet, so I presume so, since the advent of this virus, hospital information has become increasingly difficult to get, at least here on the Island." He got up and moved toward the door, "So are we all okay now?" He didn't hear a response so he presumed so, they all left the office even Bond.

Chris asked Bond if he could take James for a walk. He agreed and was surprised at seeing him put a leash on him. Chris noticed him watching, "It's never too early to teach them." He turned around stood to wall blankly and debated on whether to turn the stereo one. Then he saw Jonathan come in the house. Jonathan went to him, standing three feet from him then took off his face mask. "You've been drinking, I can smell it on you, either that or you dosed your clothes on a bottle of Scotch." He sat down on the couch, Bond followed and sat down a measurable distance from him. "This is because I have been doing some research on this case." "You told Troy that you were going shopping and now you come back smelling of a distil-, never-mind." "I was working, and I found something that you will all want to see." He stopped while he held down a burp. "Did you find out what their names are yet?" "Well, yes, he is the head of the business, his name Lee Richards and she is Stella Richards, they have been a long time married. His mistress, the one at the bar, there is something that you are going to want to see." He pulled a picture advertisement pamphlet out from his jacket. Bond read it aloud. "An internet dating service for all of your fantasies." He set it down on the couch, "Come on Jonathan, you know that I don't do this."

"Open it up and look at the pictures." "I already told you." "No, it has something to do with this case. Open it." Bond raised his head closed his eyes sighed then opened it. "It is her!" He paused his actions. "What is her picture doing here?" "She works for-well for the dating service." "So, this Lee Richards was with a… (He lowered his head nodding it) I mean why, well, I know why but?" "It seems that he has only been seeing this woman at the bar for two weeks now." "So, then she wasn't or couldn't be involved in this long time that he has been in S.F.?" "Someone has, and being that we have no information here, on this, it has to be there."

"There as In San Francisco?" They looked to the sliding door where this noise came from, Chris stood there. "How long have you been there?" "Since you started talking. Bond your dog does not like the leash. I gave up on him then saw Jonathan come in." Jonathan looked to Bond, "Well your brother is a spy." "We need to track down what he did who he saw and where he stayed in San Francisco." Bond raised his face and replied, "I'll go." "Now, I am overriding you on this one. Las Vegas is on the way to San Francisco, and you nor we are going to see her. I can't leave because of therapy and neither can you. Jonathan is going."

He gulped, "Me in San Francisco? He opened his eyes wide as he finished saying this. "You have experience in this you will know what to say and what to do and maybe even where to go." He leaned back, "I haven't been there since the eighties, that is probably when you were born." Bond stood up being thankful that Chris was not going to do this, being his medical obligation. He made reference to the possibility of him going to see Jane, he even wondered if he would do this, it was a flip of the coin, being what the outcome would be, even he didn't know.

"Come on Bond, would you like some help putting this all together. At that point he did. "I'll be right there Chris, I just need to do something first, the headed down the hall to the kitchen. A few minutes later he walked back to the open door of the office with two cups of coffee. "I know that I need this, and I thought maybe you might too." He set it down in front of Chris and saw that two chairs were placed behind the desk to the computer screen. He looked to Chris in thanks. Chris picked up on it. They then proceeded to make arrangements for Jonathan's trip to San Francisco.

After a little over an hour they left with the plans ready to go. Bond went to his bedroom. Chris went outside for a walk on the beach and took the puppy with him. Jonathan sat in the living room in silence mostly remembering past memories in silence. Troy came in the back door of the house with a large heavy box that he took to his room and opened it and plugged it in. He took the folded cardboard box outside to the side of the garbage cans. Then drove his car to the garage parked it there and came out back to the house holding a paper shopping bag. He placed a twelve pack of beer inside the now running mini-refrigerator. "Sorry, guys but I need this."

In his room Bond took off his shoes and socks then sat on the edge of the bed and rubbed his thighs firmly; he closed his eyes then rocked his body up and down. "I'll get through this; we'll get through this. I only hope that Jane is okay, both mentally and physically. Why did she go by herself? Because she left, that was her goal. Chris wasn't upset about it, why am I?" He turned on his stereo, hearing Josh Grobin's voice playing on the radio. A controlled loud voice and in perfect rhythm, the sound adorned the walls of his room. He had only heard of him, and now really noticed the control of his voice and that he was offering pure synchronized music. He could feel his heart beat slow, and body relax. He moved off of the corner of the bed and laid down with his head pillows against the headboard offering comfort and support to his back.

"I miss you dad. I know that you are watching everything that we do, I hope that we are doing it right, the way that you would." He closed his eyes to try and take a rest before whatever next became a challenge. He thought back too many years ago when he was married. The beautiful union of two people in love, her soft eyes, but then reality of life intertwined and there was his job and the miscarriage, the loss of his son. Then her violent change toward him and her leaving him, for good that time. He opened his eyes to look at the blankness of the empty room that only he was in. "I always told myself that it was for the better. I mean look what even happened to mom." He closed his eyes and held back crying. "Be strong, you have to be. You are the boss."

CHAPTER 14

Jane touched down in Las Vegas, walking off the plane with her purse and her bag she looked more than confused trying to find her way out of the airport and to the taxi area. She took the airport train to the departing area then took an escalator down to a lower floor. Now off of the escalator she adjusted her bag and purse and tried to be out of the way of people. Feeling overwhelmed she sat down on a plastic chair where people sat waiting to meet people arriving. After five minutes she got up and walked to the glass exit doors. An airport attendant asked her where she needed to go. She simply said a hotel. He pointed to the taxi area then told her that the vans that were cheaper and went directly to hotels. You just needed to get on the right van for the hotel that you want to go to, as each van went to different hotels.

She knew that there was a Caesars Palace and saw an MGM sign there in the airport and she saw the Veranda from the airplane window. She then thought just get in a line and get off when I feel that one is right. She ended up getting off at Trump tower. Walking in the first thing that she noticed was a lick of slot machines, noise and gambling. Checking in she was told that it was a non-gambling hotel on purpose. People could stay there relax and enjoy a small bit of peace in this otherwise busy noisy city.

After checking in she found the elevators and went right up to her room. Inside it was a nice room but nothing out if the ordinary. She unpacked her bag adjusted things in her purse then looked out the window and wondered what to do. "In a strange way I thought that this was the answer. All I feel right now is solitude. Of course, because I am sitting alone in a hotel room. "Go out walk around and see the city, wearing a mask. I think that I will take a shower and get all of that airplane off of me."

She went in the bathroom turned the shower on then waited for the water to warm, it was a nice short wait. Getting in and feeling the water hit her skin she wondered about her husband. Did he know that she was gone yet? Surely Bond must know that I am gone. Will they try and get ahold of and ask Lauren? It is a good thing that I texted her and told her that I was taking off. She acted like she didn't like it there anyway. I don't know- I suppose this is why I am here, at least I feel safe now. She reminded herself to remember this.

Out from the shower and dressed. She looked at the door then out the window, she walked to the door and made sure that it was double locked and pulled the chain across it then went to the window and closed the drapes. "Right now, I am safe, I am in locked in a room- miles away from them and I am safe." She reached for the Television remote and scrolled through the pay-per-view movies and saw a few that she was interested in. Then found the room service menu and ordered a soup, salad and bread dinner with a glass of wine. Then picked one of the favorites that she found and leaned back and relaxed to view this movie while waiting for room service. Once they knocked on her door and she saw that it was room service, she asked him to just place it outside. Watching him leave down the hall. After he was gone and the there was no one in sight she opened the door and slid it inside then immediately locked double locked and chained her door closed.

She moved it to the small table then heard the telephone. She wondered about the call but saw no other option then to answer it. She picked it up and said nothing. A pleasant voice come over the phone and asked her if she received her dinner and if everything was alright. She breathed a sigh of relief and said "yes" then hung up the phone and went back to eating dinner enjoying the wine and the movie.

The morning light beckoned her to wake up shining brightly through a small opening between the drapes. She fought the urge to go and try to close it more, and took the pillow from the other side of the bed off and covered her face. She was now in darkness but couldn't breathe, finally she got up went to the drapes and pulled the left side over the right side. She got back in bed adjusted her body finding the perfect spot closed her eyes and it came open again. She looked at the time on her cell phone, "It is seven in the morning, I don't even think that Vegas is up yet, or it shouldn't be."

"Right now, I am craving coffee, and I can't go downstairs to get it already made and sit outside on the patio waiting for Bond. Waiting for him and hiding from Chris. She jumped off the bed and went into the bathroom and locked that door. "What do I do now, take another shower, dress and sit in the room all day?" She turned on the shower and told herself no, she had to get out and see people, maybe not talk to them but just be out in public without fear. She fixed herself up then went down to the main floor and had breakfast in the restaurant, while reading a pamphlet on tourist activities in Vegas. She ordered bacon and eggs, over medium white toast and coffee and ate every bite, enjoying it immensely. Paid then leisurely left and walked a block to catch a tour bus to view the Vegas strip.

Aboard the bus which was more the size of large van, she debated on the left of right side, she took the left mostly because she had usually always lately been the passenger on the right, a small change. Seats were blocked off with tape so passengers would not be seated in too close of proximity to each other, she liked this idea of space. Once everyone was onboard, which was only half of the bus, a young long blonde-haired woman-stood in the middle of the aisle in front by the driver and said that everyone should now be wearing their face mask, if they had a problem with this they should leave now.

She sat against the window seat and hadn't even noticed until this woman finished her speech that a gentleman was sitting in the aisle seat of her row, which had three seats, the middle one being blocked off. She thought that he looked to her and smiled, but she truly didn't know being the mask facial covering. The bus moved and the tour started. Information on the various hotels was given as well as some of the history of Las Vegas. She had a hard time concentrating on what was being said because she wondered about this man. Was he strictly a tourist as she was or did the family already track her down and had her being watched, hence she would be put on a flight back to Hawaii? This escape had now become unnerving, she tired in desperation to remain as calm as she could.

For the one-and-a-half-hour tour, she was in a cold sweat and couldn't wait the end of it which now was. The bus emptied with her being the last one still there, she literally was called off of the bus. Stepping down the stairs of it she couldn't bring herself to look at anyone there on the sidewalk area, she only looked to the ground and made quick steps leaving the area. At around 40 feet from the bus stop she looked straight ahead, a couple of blocks down was a large shopping mall, she blended in with the foot traffic and went to it.

As with most malls a Macy's was there, then the high-scale Neiman Marcus, with some other various stores and center mall vendors which she quickly walked past as they just seemed to follow and never-stopped talking at you. At one end of the mall is a food court. She purchased a health shake then sat down to enjoy it and basically watch people go by. She noticed that at this trying time, of going through this horrid pandemic everyone was following the rules and wearing a facial mask. Of course, though to eat or drink you needed to take it off, people on their own were spacing themselves apart. She had her eyes closed sipping the shake then opened them back to look directly in front of her now sitting across from her table was the same mystery man from the bus.

She choked on the very next swallow, he looked to her and handed her a napkin from the table in front of her. She took it to her mouth and covered her lips then wiped her mouth and set it back down on top of the other napkin on the table.

"I really didn't mean to frighten you, I just recognized you from the bus tour. I am here on vacation; my name is Mark. It really is nice to meet you if we do actually meet and you don't run away." She smiled to him then nervously scratched the back of her neck then moved her hands off of the table. "Oh, I am. I am Jane, nice to meet you too. Same as you, I am a tourist." "Oh, really where from?" She definitely did not want to tell him Hawaii and neither California or Chicago. She thought of someplace any place then blurted out "Topeka Kansas." He smiled and asked her where in the city that she lived or worked. "Ah, I work for the city, and I live on the North east side of town by Carl Jr's."

"You are a pretty woman but I know that you are lying to me, you see I work for the mayor of Topeka Kansas, and there is no Carl Jr's in Topeka. In this part of the country, it is called Hardee's. "She flinched her body and was speechless. "I understand, you are here by yourself and probably just want to be safe. I would act this way too, if I were you." She lost her feeling of fear and panic, she felt embarrassed but he was cordial and polite to her, maybe he was what she needed at that time. She softened her composure and asked him, "Can we try this again?"

She took her left hand to her chest then said, "Hi, I am Jane, nice to meet you." He did the same saying his name is Mark, nice to meet you too." They instantly started talking to each other and enjoying each one's company then went on another tour together, this time to the Ethel M chocolate factory in nearby Henderson. They walked the gardens then went inside listened, each one left with a piece of chocolate. He caught her off-guard and put his piece of chocolate in her mouth, she ate it laughing then did the same to him in return.

Back in the bus, her heart already beat for him and she hoped that he felt the same way toward her. For the first time in this trip she forgot about Chris and his family. She relaxed in pure enjoyment. Now back at the strip -the end of that tour she reached for words to say to him so that time with him would not end. Standing on the street off of the bus near him she wondered if she should blurt something out or if he would take the initiative to do this. He turned from her and walked away. Her face, body and heart dropped, watching him leave. She thought she was still trapped in a web. In the next moment she turned to his voice calling to her from a distance away. "Will you meet me here tonight at eight o'clock." She yelled back, "I'll be here."

Instead of going back to her hotel room she returned to the fashion mall. Trying on looking for clothes and make up and even some new jewelry. Now back in her hotel room she paced the floor waiting for time to go by until that evening hour. She was showered and dressed for the evening an hour before she even had to leave. It seemed that her only option was stay there for another hour and watch television which she did, listening to the evening news. More news on the horrors of the pandemic, and all of the deaths throughout the world. She wanted to turn it off, but thought of how it was important to be aware of everything. A cure for this virus was being worked on by four different drug companies-maybe next year they will be ready.

After minutes of hearing this she turned it off thinking that she shouldn't turn herself into a sad feeling before a date. She perked up, "A date! At my age I am going on a date. I wonder if he knows my age, I wonder how old he is?" She breathed out got up then sat back down. "It didn't seem to be a problem in the time that we spent together. I just wonder why he isn't married? Maybe he hasn't found the right woman yet." She smiled and got up from the bed then looked out the window to the darkening sky of night time then turned her eye to the ceiling. "But I am married. This just seems like a different universe- and I so much want to be in it. This universe not the one that I left."

He picked her up outside of her hotel. He walked up to her kissed her check to her by the hand and walked to a black limousine. He opened the door for her. She got in adjusting her dress and he closed the door and went to the other side and got in. They traveled to an off-strip small restaurant, Batista's. They couldn't even drive in the small parking lot. It stopped before the parking lot entrance then he got out went around to her door opened it and gave his hand to her to hold while getting out of it.

It was Italian food but not the usual pizza and spaghetti these were specialized dishes and some of the usual Italian fare. He ordered sparkling wine. At the end of the meal she couldn't even remember what she ate. They went back to her hotel. More than anything she wanted to be with more that night. He kissed her on the check and aid good night she kissed him back then watched him get back in the limo and leave. The doors of the hotel were opened for her she went silently to her room.

She felt happy on the evening but felt let down because he was not there with her. She wondered if she did something to push him away. She took off her shoes and her dress then felt loneliness. Her mind the went to think of Chris. "Am I abandoning him right now? She moved feeling lost and again went to the shower. Before getting in she said. "I came all the way to Vegas to shower." Now inside the shower with the bathroom door again locked someone knocked on the door to her room. His hand went to the knob and tried turning it, he knocked again, he waited and no answer. He dropped the red rose to the floor and left.

The next morning, she saw the red rose on the floor of her door and thought that it was from the Hotel. She checked out and took a taxi to the airport. The driver asked her which airline. She had no idea which one and at that time she didn't even know her destination. "Uhm, just go to the airport, I'll look for my ticket. She opened her purse and made noise looking for something that didn't exist. Now driving on it was a choice of airlines on terminal A or terminal B. She told him B, then picked a gate at random for him to leave her at.

She got out, went inside and found the board that stated outgoing flights and their destination. She held her purse and her bags stood out of the way and read the soonest outgoing flights. "Let's see, the soonest one is to Hawaii. That would be redundant. San Francisco CA, Salt Lake City, or Kansas City. "None of them sound like paradise. I'll just go to the gate and see which one is available.

At the counter she put away her wallet then went to the correct gate for the short flight to San Francisco. After checking in at that counter where she found that she didn't have so she sat down on one of the chair banks and felt bewildered and lost, then she reminded herself that she was safe. The woman that sat next to her on this flight told her that she had seen her around Silicon Valley before, she remembered her face. "I am really sorry, yes I did work there and live there in the Valley but I am sorry I do not remember you." The woman talked to her the rest of the flight and it turned out that she was entertaining and not annoying which proved all the better.

Deboarded from the plane and walking through the airport even in just looking out the window she already felt at home. A happiness that even outshined the feeling she got when she first met Jake. And then she told herself not to be upset about him. But she knew that she couldn't, he would be a memory that would be hard to forget.

Now leaving the airport, where do I go? I can't go home to Las Altos anymore, though the way I feel right now, I would like to. It probably wouldn't be the same. I am in Tony Bennett's city, he left his heart here, I feel that I have left it nearby. The outlandish hotel prices here, I can only stay here for a day or maybe a little longer. I hope that I can find a less expensive place, say a motel. Here in this city, that is dangerous. Maybe by the wharf though, but then safety and the pandemic. She took out her cell phone and checked on line prices.

"There I can't beat this, the Inter-Continental Mark Hopkins, $135.00 a night! but there will be fees, but I can't pass this deal up. She got a cab and went there. As usual there were many people standing in line to check in. She huffed- I will spend the next two hours just waiting to check-in, but I already made the reservation on-line. She smiled then found a self-check in where all she had to do was swipe her Driver's License and credit card. It was declined. She thought, what did I do wrong, she tried it again and got the same result.

The very first thought in her head, was they found me. Her eyes circled the people standing by her, she didn't know what to do. Unprovoked fear was the only thing that she saw. Now getting out of view was the most important thing, but where? At just that moment Jonathan turned from the counter after checking in and saw her. He then noticed the panic on her face. The reservationist behind the counter asked him if there was something wrong. He looked surprised then explained to the reservationist that the woman that had just tried to check in on the self-check-in over there was his niece. He wondered what the problem was. The reservationist told him that he could not expose any information about this woman to him. Jonathan then put forth his credit card to this man and told him that he wanted to pay for her room. This man talked to another worker behind the counter and his wish was granted. Jonathan then whispered to this man and left the counter to the elevators in his usually gentleman pace.

An employee dressed in the business uniform causally walked up to her in her frazzled state and calmly told her that there had been a problem with that self-check in machine and she was all set. He handed her a key card, then apologized and asked her if there was anything else that he could help her with. She moved her head puzzled, then looked up to the ceiling saying thank you, after a brief minute she left where she was standing and went to the elevators to get to her room. Now in his room, Jonathan opened his lap top, typed in some information, "Ah, there is the reason. Her Driver's License expired today. That is how she was able to check in, in Vegas but not here. I wonder if she'll renew it? She is going to need our help in getting back to the Island."

He texted this information to Bond. He was working on a plan to try and find more information out on the Richards. He was going a bit crazy because he no longer had the freedom to just drive off whenever, like he had been used to doing. James got up made noise in just circling around his rug. This bothered him, he took his eyes off of the computer looking to this noise to check and see what he was doing. Hearing the sound of a text coming in, he looked to the dog. "You're off the hook of being in trouble, did you sense this?" He checked the text from Jonathan. "Nothing could have been planned this way. What is she doing in San Francisco, she was just in Vegas for one night? Did she lose all of her money, if that were the case she couldn't possibly be in Frisco? Suspense. I just feel that I going a bit batty. Whether it is the lockdown, the medical condition, the job, it is just everything building up." He got up and told James that they were going outside of a run. James was already ahead of him.

In the city, Jonathan took a taxi to China Town getting off at a random location. Playing the role of a typical tourist. He went inside various gift shop, wearing his face mask of course. He even purchased a book on the city. He walked more of the streets, seeing ducks roasting in restaurant windows. On the side walk moving out of the way of busy foot traffic. He walked back and forth in front of one particular building, thinking maybe the name on the outside of it did not match the actual business that was on the inside of it. He double checked this address on his cell phone then found no other option but to go inside. He thought this surely cannot be the headquarters of Eastridge Investments.

He buzzed for the door to open and he went in. He thought it odd that there was no sign or signs of a business, an investment firm would have an open area to check in and go to different desk with employees to help wait on a patron. There was just brown narrow wall on each side of the main hallway, that was it no signs no doors, the only options were to walk down to the end and see if there was something there. He gathered courage then walked to the end of the hallway. There it was at the end on the right-hand side, finally a door. It was a wood door standard sized with no writing on it or to the side wall of it. Another odd thing for a legitimate business as an

Investment firm. He relaxed thinking that it probably led to an elevator to go upstairs as this was a three-story building.

His only option was to press the button and go up. There wasn't a button to the third floor he pressed the only other option of the second floor. He got off and walked to a receptionist area. There were numerous desks and all male secretaries at this desk on their phones. A young middle age man white with black hair buzzed on each side of his face and heavy wavy hair on top of his head he had two pierced gold earrings on one ear and a white button-down loose shirt with black bloomed long pants that looked like they dated back to the original Miami Vice TV show. He walked forward to him from on back of the reception stand. "Ah, a new client, I see welcome." Jonathan wanted to stand back from him but kept his footing. "Uhm." He knew that this was not what to say when at a formal meeting, starting a sentence with "uhm" "I am looking for Eastridge Investments." "Oh, I see that you are here from Hawaii?" "Yes." He went back to standing behind the raised welcoming desk. "We are already full for tonight, but if you leave me your name and number, we'll call you if anything opens up." "Tonight? I thought that this was an investment firm." "Yes, an investment firm for sex." "Sex?" "Yes, and how do you like it?" "Ah, uhm, is this gay sex?" "Is there any other kind?" He smirked. "Uhm, do you have a card?" "We don't do business that way, we are referral only. Who referred you?" He had become totally off-guard, and said "Lee Richards." Not meaning to. This gentleman then put his hand over Jonathan's back and told him that they would certainly accommodate him being that he knew Lee." Jonathan more than unnerved turned away and walked at a very quickly back to the elevator pressed the button, the door instantly opened and he went in pressed the main floor button with his back turned away, facing only the back wall of the elevator.

He walked out of the building and up the street where the cab had let him off and hailed one counting the seconds until one came. Ten minutes later inside the taxi, he told the driver just to go back to the Mark Hopkins Hotel. He didn't view the city or notice anything, he just wanted out of there. It wasn't that this was bad, it was just not what he was expecting by any means. He said to himself, it was not like I could open an account there." Getting out of the cab and walking inside to the elevators, he smelled a whiff of the famed sourdough bread and looked to see where this wonderous smell came from. Some tourists that were walking inside the hotel held a bag with it inside, he could see the top of a log loaf sticking out from a paper bag that they held.

I feel like following them and taking it. I just need to calm myself down, he stopped turned out of the way of people walking toward him, then spotted the hotel bar to his side. He went there and ordered a Tom Collins then sat down at a distanced table. The bar maid brought it to him sooner than he expected he motioned for her to wait while he got his wallet out. He paid for it and gave her a tip at the same time. He then looked out to the open lobby and saw Jane walking hurriedly by, she was one her way to the elevators. He took a long sip of his drink and said to himself, it is a good thing that I side-stepped here. I need to tell Bond but I need this first, he looked to the icy glass in his hand.

Waiting for the elevator to open a number of people went by her side and also waited for it. She was becoming nervous. Who were these people, right then and there she wanted total distance from everyone, not only because of the virus but because fear still enveloped her? She was pushed to the back of the elevator by the crowd. She looked down trying to relieve her present fear. The door kept opening and people getting off, she sensed that now there was only one other person in it riding with her. Panic held her as she hoped above anything that this person would get off before she reached the floor that she was at. It didn't happen. The door opened, she looked to the lit button, number 9, all of a sudden, a hand of what she could see was a man held the door open for her. She had to find strength to move forward off of the car.

Now out of it and standing to the left side of this person, that didn't move -she didn't know what to do and remained trapped there in her footing. The hand of this person reached over her shoulders, "Of all people to find here, I tried knocking on your door last night and even left you a flower. I thought that I had lost my dream." She recognized his voice and relaxed her heart then looked to his face. "Mark, how did you ever find me?" "Were you running away from me?" "No, it was just a series of events. I don't want to talk out here. Are you on this floor?" "Why else would I have gotten off on this floor?" He took his key card out and showed her. "Follow me", she did. He stopped at a room two doors from hers." "Now, there is a question here." She looked to him for what he was going to say next. "My room or your room?"

"Well, you already have your card out." He opened the door she followed him in. She looked bashful and asked him if she could use his bathroom. He smiled to her opened the door and walked away to the window looking outside. "Are you okay now? Is that why shall I say, so uppity?" "Yes, that and us meeting again, I mean things like this only happen in Danielle Steele novels." He laughed, "I have never read one. I take it that you have." "A few." She paused not knowing what to further say to him now, still being amazed by everything.

He took off his shoes and told her not to be alarmed, but his feet were killing him, in walking he hit the curb and could still feel his toes throbbing. She wasn't concerned by this and said fine. He sat down at a chair at the small table. She sat on the side of the bed." "How old are you?" She was a bit annoyed that he asked her this question but then thought of the closeness that she felt for him. "Over forty." "What about you?" "The same." "Are you involved with anyone, married?" "Long time divorced. What about you?" Being the fact that she could not give him a true answer to this question she stayed silent. He got up from the chair and went back to the window.

She wanted more than anything to hear words from him, something, anything the room stayed still and silent for her. "How much time do you have, I have a long story to tell you, and as strange as it is going to sound every word of it will be the truth." He stayed standing there looking out the window then lowered his head looking like he was debating a verdict. "You know I feel deep love for you and I want you in my life. I know that this might sound strange to you, but I am simply stating the way that I feel. This is why I am willing to hear you out and do not say story, tell me the truth and I will listen."

She felt relief but also felt a weight being dropped on her at the same time. Now she wondered where to start. "Start at the beginning, I am listening and at any time if you feel like it, you can walk out that door and leave, and I promise, I won't follow you." In the soft words that he just said to her offered relief but added pressure at the same time. "You might want to order a bottle of wine for me to tell the whole story, the whole truthful story." He got up; she became scared in seeing this. He went to the phone and punched some keys. "Yes, it is room 944, I want to order a bottle of your best chardonnay and Cabernet and two glasses in a bucket of ice, (he paused), 15 minutes, thank you."

He sat back down, "I am ready when you are." "Okay it all started in Chicago." She went on to tell him the entire story before and after the wine was brought up to the room. When she finished the day had become night. "Wow, you have really been through a lot, I am surprised that you are still standing and in one piece… I have an important question to ask you now, are you ready?" She wondered if she should pick up her shoes and grab her purse to leave him. "Will you marry me?" She opened her mouth to hear the greatest question in the world. She stood up and hugged him then kissing him, "Yes, yes., but there is one small problem, I am already married." "No, you are not, you have been separated from him for more than seven years thinking that he was dead and you were kidnapped. Then had to wait for him to be brought back, 17 years later, I'd say that was abandonment, heartache and grief, grounds for ending a marriage." She closed and opened her eyes. "I never looked at it that way before, but my daughter is still in Hawaii going to college." "We can talk to her about that." "I don't believe it. I am mean, I have thought that I felt it before but it was never like this, you Mark are love. The love that I want to and need to feel, thank you so much. The missing piece." She hugged him and kissed him, when they released from the kiss, he said thank you to her.

"I do not want to go to my room now." "I don't want you to either and it is already night." "How are we going to do this?" "This, right now? oh I think that you remember." "I was talking about the whole picture, everything and the move the wedding, but this will do for now." They dropped their bodies to the bed for a night of pure romance.

CHAPTER **15**

Jonathan finished his drink left the bar and went back to his room. After making himself more comfortable, he called Bond. "Yes, Jonathan?" "You sound out of breath, is everything alright?" "Yes, I was, or am running James on the beach." "James?" "The puppy" "Oh. Yes him." "I have some news to report to you on Eastridge Investments and how it relates to Lee Richardson." "Can you hold on a minute, until I get to the patio to hear you better?" Jonathan didn't like this, but he waited in seeing no choice. He ran to the top of the stairs and then put James in the cage, sat down at a patio chair to talk to Jonathan.

"This a two-parter." "Two things?" "Yes, involving, Mr. Richards and Jane." "Jane? Where exactly are you?" "In the city by the bay, San Francisco. I did find Eastridge Investments, the address that you gave me of this business." "Jonathan, your voice dropped, is there a problem? Were you able to open an account there?" "Believe me, I do not want to open an account there. It is a business with ties to Eastridge Investments in name only, and this Lee, he is perhaps fooling around but not with another woman, or lady." "Then who?" "Try a male for male dating service." "He is gay?" "It looks like it. I have to do some more investigation but in a very careful way." Bond breathed on all the air that he could then resumed his speech. "The second part to the, or the two-parter, what is this?"

"Your brother's wife, Jane." "Yes, she is in Vegas, how do you know about her?" "She is here." "Where you are? Does she know that you are there, have you met her there?" "No, she hasn't seen me here and I intend on keeping it this way. She is up to something; I can tell by her actions of when I have seen her." "That woman, I mean the whole thing of her always wanting to run away yet she wants us to be here for her all of the time." "Does she?" "Jonathan, in what you just asked me, a lot can be read into this question. I think that I will just let this pass for now. Do you need any other help? Do you want Troy there?" "No, oh no, I have to keep this as low-profile as I can. Just don't let Chris know anything. We have to keep this as low profile as we can, and stay away from the Richard's residence." He hung up, so did Bond.

Telling me not to do anything? James barked, Bond got up and let him out of the cage. Bond worked with him on the sit command, James already had this one down, it was the down command, he only obeyed 10% of the time. Chris came out to the patio. "I saw you on your phone. Is everything alright? Have you heard any news from Jonathan?" He said no, this way he wouldn't lose it trying to explain everything. "It was just a reminder of a medical appointment. I was on the phone for a while because I kept being put on hold." "Oh, one of those annoying calls. Are you alright though?" "Yes, and my driving restrictions will end tomorrow, just a reminder for me to keep today's appointment." "Being that Jonathan is gone, Troy will drive you then?" "Yes." "Maybe I'll come along because I need to get a refill on my prescription." Bond agreed nodding his head and thought how am I going to tell Troy of the latest news now?

They went back inside the house with James to get some coffee and breakfast. Esmerelda was already in the process of cooking it. "I could just follow the wonderous smell in here." He looked to the stove and saw bacon cooking. They sat down to bacon and eggs and coffee; he saw the morning prayer then started eating. Chris asked Bond what they were going to do on the Richard's case that day. "Ah…we are just going to leave this alone for a while. I have to and need to develop a plan." "I thought that you liked what I found out." "Uhm, yes, uhm, I did, I just…uhm, I need more time." "It is a good thing that you are going to see a doctor today, you presently do not look so well." "Yeah, I am feeling a bit of a sore throat, I hope that it is nothing." "Me, too, this is a great breakfast, Esmerelda, thank you." She smiled and refilled their coffee cups.

Troy came in the kitchen from the back hallway he looked to Bond, then motioned his head to Chris. "Good morning." Esmerelda offed him breakfast, he declined and took a health shake from the refrigerator opened it then sat down. "So, Bond when do I need to drive you?" "Not for a couple of hours. Chris told me that he wants to go with us." He again looked questionably over to Bond. Chris picked up on this. "What is there a problem with me going with you? Do you two have something planned?"

Both of them responded, "No" at the same time which made it all the more suspicious. He looked to each one raising his eyebrows. He got up from the table took his half-finished plate to the sink and left walking toward the entrance of the house. They waited listening to his every move. Bond turned his head to Troy and whispered, "No, I don't trust him, he could be anywhere, later." Troy nodded, then took another drink of the shake. Bond hadn't noticed until that moment, but James had wiggled his way to the table and was now at his feet. He looked down to him and his wagging tail. "The smell of bacon, hum?" Against his better judgement, he broke off a piece from the strip and gave it to him. "I didn't even see you chew it. That's it no more." He whined Bond looked down to him then gave him another piece, "Okay, that is it, no more." James still whined. "I don't have any more" he lowered his plate down to him and James started licking the plate. "Bond, you are going to be sorry that you did that, he is going to expect it, or something from you all of the time now." "Yeah, he will, and he'll get it."

Chris was outside at the side of the house, hitting the punching bag that he had earlier set up. Not purely for exercise, but at that time to try and release frustration. He said, that he didn't to the family, but he greatly missed Jane, feeling broken-hearted. He felt that he had more than tried. There was not a way that he could turn back time and change anything or be there for her, it was for her safety. He had always protected her. He missed her so much he could feel his heart sink as he fought the loneliness that was trying to consume him.

In hitting the bag, he went from just lightly tapping it to increasingly harder punches, at one point he thought that the bag was going to fly off. He stopped to watch this happen and got hit by it instead, he grasped his arm that it hit, but then did not nurture it, he walked away, leaving the pain, that pain any way. Bond stood right at the corner of the house and watched this from a hidden distance. "Boy, this is going to be harder than I imagined. The pillar tower of the strength he possesses will be challenged to the very limit." He went back in the house to ready for the oncoming appointment.

Troy drove them to the clinic, Bond noted the difference of listening to the steady opera music that Jonathan always had on the radio to the modern music that Troy played, basically the top 40. He sat at the passenger and opened that door then frowned when he saw Bond already there. Bond sat in the passenger seat; Chris walked to the SUV and opened that door, then turned away from the SUV, Bond thought of the less composed Chris, and instantly got out then waved his hand for Chris to get in. "I know that this is always usually your seat, I apologize." No words were returned to him, but he understood at that time any way

In the parking lot, Troy asked them how long they'd be. "I have the usual appointments time of basically an hour to 90 minutes, I don't know how long that Chris needs." Chris walked back to the van only to the driver side of the van not the side that Bond stood. "Make it 90 minutes, I'll be around here, somewhere." Watching them leave, he saw that they each went in different directions, Troy wondered what had brought this on. Did he hear them talking or had something happened between the two of them in the meantime? Needless to say, he traveled to the beach area to watch the surfers for the wait.

Bond was instantly called into Dr. Stones office. She told him that her last appointment finished a bit early for some reason that she couldn't pinpoint. He felt a little jittery at that appointment. She sensed this and asked him why. He responded that he didn't know. She knew how to work around this problem. "Bond, this is how you told me that you wanted to be addressed." He nodded, still not looking directly to her eye-view. "Unless you tell me the problem, I will not sign the slip for you to retain your driving privileges, ergo your License."

He looked down then directly up to her eye view. "The problem is not with me, in fact I think that I am handling this new problem, good. The problem is Chris." "Chris, yes your brother. I haven't spoken with him this week yet, tell me of this problem and how it affects you." He told her that

Chris's wife left him."" That is a deep problem? But why Bond are you making this your problem and not his?" "It is not **my problem it is his.**"

"Okay we will talk in a higher pitch. How can you keep yourself in control?" "I have no problem with this, I have spoken to the two others everyone is working on cue. It is just that I cannot deal with this problem, it is a problem that the two of them are going to have to work out. And one of them is going to be hurt. I know that the one that will be hurt is my brother. Tell me how can a person not hurt when their own family member is being hurt." "So, are you just going to let this play out then and not get involved?"

"I can't get involved; this is something between the two of them. I just am going to be supportive of my brother, he is blood." "And how will this affect your actions?" "It won't, I already have what I need planned out and really whatever happens to and with them will not affect business." "Bond from what you have told me of your father and his rational mind and he was that he did things, it sounds to me that you are taking his place whether you now know it or not. I don't know if you are doing the meditation exercises that I gave you to do or if in fact you have found a way to release your angers and your fears. You are now doing something and I can tell." "It's a puppy, James."

She writes down in her notebook. "A dog, a puppy is causing you to be rational? What kind of dog is this?" "A German Shepherd, they are from what I have been told a challenge to raise, but he is smart, and a bit stubborn at times." "A little like you, then?" She hands him a piece of paper. "You Bond, have earned it, her is the paper to recover your driver's license and I still want to see you on a monthly basis, here you go" She handed him the paper and he leaves her office.

Back outside he spots Troy driving in the parking lot but sees no sign of Chris and he wonders. Did he take off? Just as Troy stops to the side of him, and parks for him to get in, he spots Chris. He's standing at the far side of the building talking and what looks like flirting with a young short slim Oriental lady. Bond reaches over the steering wheel and honks the car horn.

He looks up to the car then talks more to her and takes his time leaving, touching her arm and shoulder before he departs from being close to her. He walks to the SUV at a regular pace then stops at the side of Troy's open window, pauses there for a moment, then goes around the side and gets in the back door. Bond was a slight bit upset from what he saw, but knew that he shouldn't say anything about it, especially being that Jane had just run off. Like Dr. Stone told him, it is not 'his' life. He did say, "Did you get your pills?" He said 'yes' as he fastened his seatbelt. Now driving back to home, Chris asked Troy if he enjoyed his beach watching, he replied, yes. Rock music from the car radio then played making the excuse for talk, unnecessary.

At the estate, they each go their separate ways. Bond watches seeing Chris take James out from his cage and run him in the beach. He quietly leaves going back to the office. Then takes the paper from the doctor out and goes on line to enter needed information on retrieving his driving abilities, then sends a copy of it. He looked to the it intently waiting to hear and see that it went through. He says to himself. I will not be or have balance until I hear back from Jonathan. Now I am more concerned about hearing what she is doing then this case. He hears a knock on the door and says come in. To his relief it is Troy. He pays attention to him waiting to hear something from him, they still had not talked to each other.

Troy tells him that he is just going to out and if he needed him to just call. Bond doesn't verbally reply, only shaking his head to him as he walks out the door. Wanting more than anything right now, he just wanted to talk to someone, even his dog who always listened wasn't there. Now was the time that he missed Jane and their talks. He wondered what his brother really did feel right now. Bond then opened a Binder and turned the computer screen to work. He found numerous documents sent from the accountant that needed his signature, his signature. He completed this then went on to another item to attend to. At numerous times looking to the empty dog rug on the floor. Hours passed involved in work. He moved his body from side to side on the chair, then turned the computer off, and got up stretching his body and left the office. Feeling and needing company, he walked the house looking for anyone. He saw no sign of James or Chris outside so he went in the kitchen thinking that would be the next place that they'd be. Only Esmerelda was there. He smiled to her then took a can of soda out and left. He went out the front door. He saw Chris talking on his cellphone, he looked deeply involved at whatever he was talking about or to. James then ran to him. He spotted a dirty look from Chris so he took James back inside with him and closed the door loudly.

CHAPTER 16

"So many words, so many thoughts." He took his car keys put James on a leash and told him that they were going to go for a ride. He took the precaution of taking a towel to put under him in the SUV. James put his head out of the back-side window, he looked happy panting with his tongue sticking out the window. He saw this was cute then closed it up leaving an inch open fearing her might fallout. He took the longer road at the fork to drive by the once coffee shop that had become boarded up when she left.

Seeing it from the road, he felt delight, seeing that it wasn't boarded up anymore and it looked like it's being fixed up to move in. He wanted to stop and find out, but drove by instead thinking later. He traveled to the cemetery parked and walked with James on his leash to his father's grave stone. He was surprised that James was calm and laid down as he placed his hand on the headstone. He breathed out and looked to the ground at the gravesite. "Dad, you already know that I am going to cry and I am going to tell you what you already know. So, I will just get to the point. Should I try and bring her back here to him or just let her go?"

He swore that he heard his words saying "Let her go" He thought of how this was had become a Twilight Zone episode. He turned and saw the same Priest that delivered this father's eulogy standing there by him." Father, how did you know?" "You, my son, is not the only one who is here."

He then looked up to the sky, placed his hand on his shoulder then walked away. "Let her go, I don't want to, but life goes on. Let her go." He placed his hand back on top of the headstone, told his father that he loved him and thanked him. Grabbed hold tighter on the leash and returned to the SUV with James, leaving the cemetery feeling stronger.

He took James outside to the backyard, only this time did not cage him. He let him free feeling confident leaving this puppy to his own free will. He was more entranced with running around the swimming pool then going to the sandy beach. James fell in the pool but unlike acting of the paranoid father to him that Bind was, he stood back and watched. Instead of acting in fear James swam to the edge and climbs the stairs out. Now out of the pool, he shakes himself off then ran around the edges of the pool again. "James, you are a leader."

Jonathan had taken pictures of Mr. Richards and his male love. Pictures from going in to and out of the building address and of going to and from his partner's home address. He notices his partner looking in his direction, he causally left from the side of the building and walked away in a normal fashion making it appear that he ws just taking a walk. Jonathan knew that the most important thing for him to do now was get out of that entire area. He went back to the Hotel.

In the elevator with other people all wearing their mask, he counting the stops and listened to the people get I and out. He paused to sneeze, even as he did this wearing his mask, the people in the elevator gave him a snide look then moved away from him. He got off at the next elevator door opening and took out his key card and walked down the hall to find his room. He heard other voices from behind him. He calmed himself and said they aren't following me; they are just going to their rooms. Their voices became laughter. He then looked to the numbers over the doors and saw yes, he was at the right room number, but the wrong floor. Only then when he turned around to leave the hallway and go back to the elevators, did he see Jane and her arms around another man. He paused in seeing this then turned to the side of the next hallway to listen to them and see what he could before they went inside the room.

He heard her voice first, and yes, it was Jane's voice. "I still cannot believe it, all of this. We meet by what could only seem like mistake and then fall in love." She kissed him. A long deep kiss, from what he could see. "And now, we are getting married. We'll make one small side trip back to Vegas, tie the know and then head back to Topeka." They kissed again. "Kansas, I never thought that I even ever go to such a place." "Such a place? I live and work there." "Whose room are we going to go in?" "How about, we go into our own rooms, until dinner and then I'll meet you, well right out here." "Where are we going to have it." "There is a nice restaurant right here in the hotel. Say 7:00?" "Sounds good." She laughed then went to her door and opened it, he went inside his door at the same time.

Jonathan moved forward, surprised hearing a maid ask him if there was a problem. "No, just, I got off it turns out I am on the wrong floor." She nodded then went back to her cart for work. He went to the stairs and climbed two flights of stairs to the correct floor for his room. He went inside and sat down, breathed in then stood up and looked out of the hotel room window. "I can't tell Bond or anybody about this until I am a bit more, abreast of everything. I will be having dinner at this restaurant tonight. I just need to do something about it first. I had better go talk to the maître d.

Later that evening Jonathan went to the restaurant and looked to the maître d, who sat him at a table himself. Jonathan sat composed and quiet, he ordered a drink from the cocktail waitress and looked at the time on his watch. "In about 5 minutes now." He took a soothing swallow of the Tom Collins drink then picked up the full-size menu that covered his entire face so that she would not see him walking by to their table. Both Jane and her mystery man were seated at the booth right behind Jonathan, it was spilt by raised greenery. This offered him camouflage and the ability to hear anything that they said.

When the waitress came to take his order, he placed his hand to his throat trying to signify that it ws sore. He pointed to what he wanted on the menu, she left with his order. He worried that they were going to speak softly or whisper in their romantic conversation but that wasn't the case, they spoke in normal volume. He heard her say to her date that she was worried on proving her identity because her driver's license has just expired. He told her not to worry as most DMV offices were closed right now and were offering a grace period. He learned that they were planning on going to Vegas for a quick wedding then were going to fly off to Kansas, and live their forever lives. At that point, he felt sick and flagged down his waitress to make his order to go and he would take it to his room to eat. She did it came 10 minutes later. He paid then left for his room.

This time getting off at the right floor, he found his room then went inside. He used the bathroom and came out still holding the towel to wipe his hands. He looked to his wrapped-up meal then reached for his phone throwing the towel back to the bathroom. "I don't want to make this call. In fact, I would rather go back to the business, no I wouldn't. "What time is it there?" He looked to his wrist watch hesitated then started punching buttons of his cell phone, while waiting for the connection, he said to himself that he could already feel his loss and pain that he didn't want him to see experience.

Bond answered it on the fourth ring. "Jonathan." After saying this at a louder voice, he looked around to see if he could see Chris, he didn't but already knew that this did not mean anything. "Can you hold the line for a minuet? I have to move." Jonathan more than ever wanted to just hang up but he knew that he couldn't. Bond went to his bedroom instead of the office and locked that door then inside to the bathroom and closed this door. "I am sorry for the wait; it is just that I am being carful right now." He spoke in a shallow voice. "Are you alone now?" "As much as I can be. Why? You sound is if you are going to tell me that somebody died." Hearing this from him, Jonathan's eyes teared up. "I saw Jane and her new beau, today and tonight." "She really has one, I mean she is not just saying this?" "Yes, as strange a s it may seem, it is right out of a romance novel. She meets him in Vegas, then somehow, they again meet her and now. ""Now, what? Don't tell me that she is coming back here with him."

"No, she is or they are going to go back to Vegas to marry and then they both are going to Kansas, where he lives and works at an Investment Firm, to spend their wedded life. And she's even told him about Lauren and how he is going to move her out of Hawaii and bring her there." Bond braces himself leaning against the bathroom sink. "It just doesn't sound right. It is a soap opera, pure and simple. And Kansas, as in Dorthey and Oz. Sounds to me like she is already flying, on something." "It is unbelievable. Do you think that she will leave this new man, Jake and fly back to Chris?" "This wouldn't be ethical but it does sound like what she would do. Can you find out everything that you can about this man Mark and send it to me. I want to look into him and his identity as well. I…I. uhm." "I feel the same way, I'll start work on this right now."

Jonathan sat down at the small table opened his laptop and the bag of food. One by one each got attention. He spent the next five hours getting information on this supposed mystery man whose identity in every way that he explored proved to be true and check out. There was now no mystery about him. He took his final bite of cod from the container, then said aloud, "I don't know what this is going to do to him, somehow I feel that I should warn him, but it is not my life. How could she have done this?" He breathed in a burp and then said, "I am leaving tomorrow."

Back at the door to her room, she laughed giggled and smiled to him moving her body up against the door, then handed him her key card. "Can you open it for me?" "Open what?' "The door." "You already have the card on your hand, why do you need me to do this, you can." She turned to the direction of the door not liking the feeling of what she heard. She opened the door herself. He stood back from her. "You look like you have had too much, you had better take care of yourself. I am going to my room now, don't bother me, I am going to sleep and I do not like interruptions. Be ready to leave at 6:00 a.m., sharp and have everything ready because we are not coming back. She looked to him puzzled, "Can I kiss you good night?" "We have kissed. You can't forget that fast, can you?"

She closed the door leaning her back against it and swallowed hard. "Did he just act differently then all of the times before?" She moved away from the door and went in the bathroom. Sitting on the toilet she thought of the wonderous romance and how he'd treated her in the past. "The past…3 days, and I am now ready to spend the rest of my like with this man. I don't honestly don't know if one thing that he has told me is true." She got up flushed the toilet then washed her hands and face, then brushed her teeth and changed out of her clothes for bed. She got under the bedsheets then turned off the lamp. Laying in the darkness of the room, she looked to the ceiling and said aloud, "Who am I living for?" She laid there still as a corpse and felt like one at that time."

In the early morning hour, he walked to her room and knocked on the door, he waited and waited and waited. He took his fist to her door and pounded it loudly. Another door from the hall opened their door to see the reason for this loud noise. He turned with a scowl on his face to them, the door instantly closed. "Come on Jane, do I have to break your door down or what?" He took out his cell phone and called the front desk explaining his problem. They responded that they could not do anything for him and for him to call her room number. He did there was still no answer. He looked back to his door to see if she was standing there, and he didn't hear her, no one was there. He went downstairs to the lobby and checked the restaurant and coffee Batista, she wasn't there.

In the busy check in at the airport she ran to the ticket booth of the airline with soonest flights to Hawaii. Panting and out of breath it was now her turn in line. She asked for a ticket for the flight to Hawaii that would be boarding in 30 minutes. The worker there told her that sorry that flight was all sold out. "But, can you take me as a stand-by, there is always someone that doesn't show up. He shakes his head, I already have 5 standbys and everyone for this flight has checked in, she dropped her body. "The next flight after that?" The flight after that one was a three-hour delay. There was another open flight on that day. She left the counter looking as forlorn and jilted as possible. Her only option that she could see at that time was to leave the busy airport.

Now in the front of the airport by the entrance doors, she thought of checking another airline to Hawaii, she turned away from the entrance doors and looked back to the inside of the airport. She felt a hand on her shoulder. Thinking it was her savoir Chris, she turned around to him with a huge smile on her face. He instantly smiled seeing her and her reaction to him. "You couldn't even have waited for me to leave and be here? It is good to see that you can't wait for our new life together. Our flight doesn't leave for an hour and a half, but we had better check in now." She showed a happy smile but felt disheartened. I had better prepare myself for a new life in Kansas. There is the Tin Man, the scarecrow and who else? I'll find out when I get there. Remember he told me that he loves me. They both smiled walking to the gate.

In her busy actions that morning she failed to see another on-looker, Jonathan taking pictures of her at the airport. He notices a security guard walking toward him. He fumbled with his bags and camera then said aloud,

"I had better go get some coffee before my flight leaves. He went to the direction of a Starbuck's stand, the guard walked right past him. He then headed to a different terminal to catch his flight back to Hawaii which would be leaving in an hour, he had already checked in on line. It was just an issue of trying to relax for the flight. He could only think of Chris, he was probably expecting her back now.

While sitting at the correct gate for his flight he sat their drinking tea and thinking of any other way that this could have a good outcome. He thought, maybe she'll find a broom there and fly home, now I am being silly. After a short wait he was already seated on the flight, and first class no less, a window seat on the left side of the plane. An older black woman sat next to him. She didn't talk to him and went instantly to sleep after takeoff. He did too.

Troy waited in the hospital parking lot and saw a taxi pick up Mrs. Richards, he followed at as it left the lot. It took her back to the townhouse that she shared with her husband. Getting out the back door of the taxi, she stumbled. The driver got out and ran to her to help. He held her arm while she got up from the curb then got her bag out gave it to her. He saw her thank him. The driver drove off. She again fumbled with her keys and dropped them, Troy fought with his instinct to run and help her. She seemed off balance was his from the medicine that she was given at the hospital or was she normally this way. He didn't know, but he stayed there and waited, watching her get inside. He waited a few minutes after she closed the door before driving away.

To free his racing mind, he decided to take a drive. He left James at the estate. He drove at a normal pace. He took the long way. He drove by the closed coffee house to check and see the progress being made on it. He wondered and hoped that it would open back up. But he doubted that she returned there. Seeing no visible sign that it had re-opened, he stopped there parked, got out and walked to the front door. From the side of the building he saw a woman carrying a large blank canvas. He went to her and asked if he could help her. "I don't have any idea of who you are or why you are even here, but this is falling out of my hands right now, yes you can help." He took it from her asked her where she wanted it. Just bring it on over the threshold and stand it up against the wall on your right-hand side.

He stood back from her, she looked to around 50, white skin dark hair and no visible make-up but her face was happy and pleasant to the eye. She looked to him for him to introduce himself. He stood there smiling to her and silent. "This is an awkward, moment. Do you want me to tell you my name first? Hi, I'm Claire." He caught himself, "I am Bond." "First or last and where is James?" "James, my dog is back home and Bond is my first name. I know I have been razzed about this before." "So, are you looking for something? Or somewhere, I mean why did you stop here?" "I used to come here when it was a coffee shop and I was friends with the female owner. I thought that she might have opened back up." "No, no coffee shop here, and I never even met her, sorry." "Are you putting in a business?" "Well, maybe I will make things that people may want to buy. I am putting in my own art studio." "Oh, is that what you do then?" "I was a social worker in California, but with all of the state cut-backs I lost my job, and my husband. I then thought, just make life happen and do what I always dreamed to do. So, I moved here retired early as I was lucky enough to pull it off and here I am. What about you?"

He smiled and hesitated. She noticed. "Let's see the name Bond, a man that doesn't talk of his personal business but wants to know all of mine. You are either a spy or a lawyer. Am I right?" "You are kind of on the right track, and that is all that I will say for now." "Ah, a man of intrigue and suspense, I like it. Now for part two of this equation, are you married, do you have a family?" He took a long breath out. "Hey, I don't mean anything by that question. Maybe I'll just go back to work now." "Ah, no, no, please don't leave. I mean, yes I was married and a long time divorced now and I do have a family that lives here on the Island and we live together, just me my brother his wife and her daughter and an uncle and a friend." You must have a big place, so it sounds like you are the Walton's then. There is one thing that you didn't answer." He tilts his head up to her, "What is that?" "Where does James fit in all of this, does he live somewhere else?"

He laughed; no, he lives with me. We have an estate." "An estate, hum. You are a puzzle. Our talk has been very interesting, but I am sorry I have to get back to work now. How about if you come here tomorrow with coffee and we can talk more?" He liked what he heard and he told her yes, then went back to his SUV and circled around and went back to the estate.

CHAPTER 17

Troy saw Jonathan waiting at the side arrival area at the Honolulu airport he was able to merge into entering and exiting traffic. Seeing that he didn't see him there he honked his horn. Jonathan looked to this sounds then waved and smiled to Chris in the car and walked over to him. He got in and thanked Troy for picking him up there. "So, how was the trip and the flight?" He moved his body in the car seat to find comfort then told him, that the flight was good, he slept through most of it and the rest he'd rather wait to tell them. Troy nodded his head to him then merged into highway traffic to get home.

"Bond, himself will want to talk to you about everything." "Yes, I have a lot of information for him. How is Chris?" I barely see him. I just wish that we didn't have to keep secrets from him." Jonathan sighed breathed in and said nothing. He saw him reach to the car radio; He was very surprised to hear that he and changed the station to the opera music that he enjoyed listening to. "Troy I am glad that you are here with us." He smiled back to him

Now at the front portico of the estate he got out then Troy moved the car to garage. Bond drove in and parked in the garage aside Troy. Walking to the front of the house he saw Chris watching them but didn't go to them, which he thought odd. Jonathan went to his room to recover from the flight. Bond went outside to the patio to check on James. He wasn't in his cage this alarmed Bond. He visualized the perimeter of the property from that point then heard Chris's voice, "He is with me. Here you can have him back. I saw Jonathan come back, is he alone?" Bond knew what he as making reference to, that Jane did not come back with him. "Yes, Chris our Jonathan is back. And thank you for watching James." "Oh, yeah, well, you are welcome. I am going to go lay down right now, See you later." Bond shakes his head to him in response, then but James in his cage.

He went to the kitchen and got a glass of ice water and drank it. He wanted to stall but knew that he had to meet with the truth, he went to the office and waited for Jonathan. A half hour later Jonathan knocked then went in the office. He went to the door opened it and motioned him in. He closed it behind him. "Jonathan, please have a seat. It is good to see you." "What do you want to hear first?"

"Whatever is easier for you." "Well there is no thinking on the answer to this one. Mr. Richards has a lover, by the name of Stanley, when in the city when he is not at the business, he is with him at his residence. The name of the Investment firm is a cover for the business there, which is very busy. A gay dating services. In looking at their Insurance policy: the one that he has here with his female wife, Stella. She is the one that with money from her family she was able to start him in his line of work. He has been going back and forth from the Island to there in the city for years and his romance has gotten deeper. His boyfriend has been putting pressure on him for him to commit to him and end his marriage to his wife. This gives ample reason to what we have found. I have it all written down on my lap top and now that I'm here on the Island I will send this to you, all the facts and pictures, everything."

He made a grateful expression and softly said, "Thank you for this. It sounds like we will be able to wrap this up pretty soon now. Would you like some water or something to drink?" "Not now, later. It already hurts." "I know, that this is hard, just take it slow and tell me what you can, on what you found out." "At first, she did go to Las Vegas, and there she met him, Jake. He knew how to pull her heart strings. She must have realized this, and that explains her sudden departure to San Francisco." He stopped to hear if Bond wanted to say something but he just laid captive to his words. "Surprise, she checks in a hotel and he of all people show up there, and stays only two doors away from her room. He asks her to marry him and fly off to another state to live their eternal loving lives together through eternity" He again pauses for him to say something anything, he only remains quiet.

"Early, early this morning before she was to meet with him to go to airport and go off to his wonderland. She has an attack of fear, paranoia, or thinks of the truth on how Chris loves her and all that he has done for her. She runs to the airport earlier then him to make an escape and fly back here to Hawaii." "Why didn't she?" "Well she checked the ticket counter at that airline and all the flights that they had here, were full. Instead of checking another airline she leaves the airport and, on her way, out, guess who is there to capture her and hold her in his arms and take her away." Bond looks utterly perplexed, "Jake, there at exactly that time? Are you sure that this isn't a set-up?"

"I have been through everything and more at least three times over and I cannot find it. They seemed to be a happy couple in love." "There is one word that you just said that throws me off." "What?" "Seemed, what changed?" "Him." "How?" "The way that he treated her, he became forceful and dominant over her unlike the gentle sweet giant that he portrayed himself to be before." Bond leaned back in the chair opened his mouth wiped his tongue across his lips then closed his lips together bit down and closed his eyes. "He has to know that she is linked to money. Ah, I am not saying that she isn't a catch, it just does not happen this fast, I don't care what universe that you live in, this just doesn't happen, things like this anyway." "The main thing now is Chris, how do you tell him, where is he?" "He told me that he wasn't feeling well and was going to go take a nap." "That sounds good, I am tired and now that I am home, I am going to go rest, see you later." Bond stood up from his chair as he left the room. "Jonathan can you send those pictures to my phone? He shook his head and left. "I would want to know, I have to tell him, maybe we'll take walk." He went back to check on James, just being near the cage he heard him cry, "I know what that means. Just a second I'll let you out and you can go do your duty." He stood there at the patio and watched to run to spot where they were training him to go.

He saw his brother walking toward him. He was holding something and had a big smile on his face. "Hi, I was going through my closet and I found this in the back. Remember boom boxes?" "Yes, that takes me back to our teens." "It even had a disco CD in it. I listened to that a while. It was fun to hear. Before coming out here to talk with you, I changed the C.D." "Yes, old memories, sometimes we have to make new ones."

"Chris, let's go take a walk on the beach and talk." Chris followed him down to the sand. Once on the sand they stood side by side and walked to the right to be out of the glare of the sun. "I am just going to set this down." He placed the boom box on a hardened piece of sand. "Chris, I don't really know how to start this conversation with you. It's something that Jonathan just found out on his journey." Chris briefly stopped his footing then looked to the oncoming tides. "Is it about her?" "If you mean, Jane, then yes." "I thought that this would be more than just telling about this latest case." "He found out more on that, but he ran into her on this last trip." "And?" Bond stopped and reached for words that he couldn't put in his mouth to speak to out to him.

"She did go to Las Vegas and when she was there, she met somebody." "An old friend?" Bond wiped his face and drew a deep breath in. "She met a man. It seemed that it happened on accident and then she met him again. She panicked and the very next day she flew to San Francisco, to what looks like escape from him. And as it turns out she met him there too." "Again? Who is he?" He walked numerous steps on the beach before speaking to him again. "I know that things haven't been, we've all noticed, both of you seem to be distancing yourselves from each other lately." "You are getting off track now, talk about what happened there and what Jonathan saw and not what I already know has happened here. You know that I don't like it when you do this and there is always an underlying theme when you do, it."

"She met someone, a romantic someone and they've made plans to get married. He told her since she has been separated from you for such a long stretch that technically she isn't married to you anymore." He quietly walked away from Bond and went back to where he left the boom box. Bond followed his steps in the sand and now stood face to face to him. "Don't you think that I know? I mean her things are missing from the closet. And pictures of the two of us together have been torn apart and thrown in the garbage. After a while you just sense when things are happening. I could feel it every day that she was further- distancing herself. I felt that she didn't want me to even try and get close to her, and I tried. I mean, we even slept in separate bedrooms... And why did she need to run away from me? She couldn't of just, talked to me?" He handed Chris his phone which displayed the pictures. "Give it back when you can."

Bond was now more than at a loss for words, he felt even felt his brother's pain and stood there for him. They both looked to the ocean looking for peace. Chris moved his body staying firm in stance, he looked Bond in the eyes then gave him back the phone. "I don't need to see these, just leave me." For a few seconds Bond stayed in stance, then walked away, headed back to the house. "I can be alone, I am solid, she was my weakness and I stood by her. Let her find out what life is like without me." He bent down to the boom box and picked it up. Then pressed the play button. He listened to the music, then commented, this song has the perfect lyrics for this to end." The song 'Someone That You Loved' by Lewis Capaldi played. He carried the box listening and feeling the lyrics of this song. He dropped his body to the sand swearing that he could feel every coarse grain touch his skin. "I don't need her. She has proven that she doesn't want me. I am strong."

He got up and walked to the house "I need to get out." He went inside with composure and quietness feeling unencumbered by her. "The best part is I get my room back, my room." He went upstairs to his room. From the under the bathroom sink the took a large plastic garbage bag. Opened it then started to throw anything that he found that was hers away. After an hour he left the room with a full bag. Bond watched him go down the stairs carrying it over his shoulder. He went out the back door of the house and threw it in the garbage can, slamming the lid down twice.

He went back inside the kitchen and washed his hands. He noticed her absence then saw Troy standing there looking to him. He didn't ask him what he was looking at or what he wanted. "Do you know what dinner is?" "Ah, I don't know but usually she leaves something in the oven or refrigerator, He looked in the oven then took the pot holders and pulled out a meatloaf. "Care to join me?" "Ah, sure let me just wash my hands first."

Bond came in looking at first fearful then eased himself seeing Chris's calm composure. "I don't know if I should wake Jonathan or not." Chris sat at the table, "Let him sleep, he'll come down here when he is ready." Bond put the milk carton on the table and that seemed to satisfy them. They warmed up the peas and mashed potatoes that were still covered on the counter, Conversation did not fill the air of the room. They were each involved in eating and enjoying each other's company. Just as Chris sliced his second helping of meatloaf, Jonathan went in the kitchen and looked to the table. They all welcomed him and reminded him to wash his hands. "I already did upstairs. He sat and enjoyed the dinner with them.

After dinner as usual they went their separate ways. Jonathan went to the living room to listen to music. Troy left in his car. Bond watched a movie on television. Chris walked back outside with James. He took out his cell phone and now wished that he had looked at the pictures. He checked to see who had called him earlier-the call was from her. He debated back and forth in his mind whether to play it or simply delete it. He played it, a silent pause for 10 seconds then a hang up. Either she changed her mind or he came to her. He, how could she have done this to me? Fly off on a whim and marry the first man that you meet? He bent down to James pet him, "Sorry but you are getting to big to hold."

"What was I to her, something for her to just pick up along the way, nothing more. I only need to become the old me, for the new me." He made a laugh then thought that sounded like a headline on a woman's magazine cover. "More than ever. I want a drink." He went back into the house found Bond watching the move and joined him to watch it.

After that movie was over, Chris said good night to Bond and retired to his bedroom for the night, Bond stayed to find and watch another movie. He noticed Jonathan half-asleep still sitting in the room listening to Beethoven. He took off his shoes before going up the stairs then almost sprang up then to his room. He opened the door wide visually encasing the room before going inside and closing the door." I suppose that the bed still smells like her. He stripped the bed of everything throw them to the other side of the floor then opened the sliding deck window and threw every sheet banket pillow outside then stood there and watched these materials drop to the ground outside.

"Tomorrow I will buy new bedding. I don't need her. God where is that boom box?" He went back to the open slider looked out to see everything on the ground outside, the water from the sprinklers were hitting everything, he watched as it all got wet and heavy. He wiped the sweat from his forehead then thought about Lauren. "She is still my daughter, does she know. Should I call her." He dialed her number on his phone, held it and his breath waiting for her to pick up, after six rings, it went to voice mail. He hung up. Either she is busy or doesn't want to speak to me. I don't know. Time will tell, if she even knows, yet." He went to the bathroom took a towel to his face, even this has her scent on it whether it is her or the cologne that she wears or both. He put the towel back on the holder and left his bedroom. Then back downstairs to his father's room and closed the door. "I'll sleep here for the night. Or this will just be my new room." He took off his clothes and went to bed.

Troy ran in the kitchen showing sweat from a morning run, he dropped the morning paper to the table it fell off. He heard the thud but paid it no mind, just drank his morning shake. Surprised at not seeing Esmerelda, she must have had the day off for some reason. He pulled the coffee filter open in the machine and saw that it already had the dry coffee grounds in it. He punched the start button then left going back to his room for a shower. Walking down the hallway he saw the door to his father's room partially opened, he opened it more and saw that the bed had been slept in. "Don't tell me that she came back?" He ran up the stairs knocked waited then opened Chris's room door. The bare mattress the first to notice then it looked like it was stripped of everything. "He had a hard night."

He went back down the stairs and meet James who had only made it halfway up, being his size." "Tine to turn around buddy, you made it almost all the way, good job." He had a much easier time going down he fell and from his body weight and rolled down the last few remaining stairs. "That's a quicker way to it." He went to the kitchen looked puzzled seeing no one there. His instinct told him Chris would be outside. He poured two cups, put sugar in one and cream in the other then carried them outside, stopped at the sliding glass door with his hands full, he looked down to James, "You want to get the door for me?" The door opened, he looked to him in amazement. "Relax, it is me." He looked up to Chris as he took a cup from him. They sat down at the table.

"Will you just relax; I can tell that you're tense. Relax, she found someone new, life goes on. For my, our lifestyle it is best, I no longer have a weight to carry." Bond moved in his chair not knowing how to calm his emotions. "I have another question?" He looked to him, concerned. "When we're out here. How come we never eat anything? I am hungry." "I'll go get us something." "No, I'll go in with you." They left the table Bond felt glad that the mood was softened for him.

"She is off today; I forget about this." He could hear Chris moving things around, he thought he is making something, I'll just be quiet and see what he makes. Spotting the newspaper on the floor, he picks it up and opens it to read. Chris put two plates down on the table. "What is the latest news?" Bind set the paper down and looked to the pate seeing that Chris had made them both, ham and cheese sandwiches. "That is different for breakfast." He took a bit then after swallowing, told him basically the same new. The virus and how it is getting worse. The democrat's complaining about everything. But really caught his eye was religious cults on the rise." Chris made a sound of recognition then bit down on the sandwich again. Bond then wondered about the religious meetings that he had gone to and whatever developed on that. He was on to something but then got side-tracked something his father would never have done. And the paper from Troy's windshield what was that? He became happy a case, a mystery to solve, his job. "Chris (he said his in a louder tone, he looked to him concerned) this is the best sandwich, thank you." Chris moved his head, "Ah, yeah, sure. You look like you found something for us to do." He didn't verbally answer only moved his head up and down twice.

They sent outside. Bond blinked then looked to it again then to Chris, "Do you see a bedspread moving around the lawn?" Chris looked to it and replied. "Ah, yeah," "You don't seem to be alarmed by this." He walked over and pulled the bedspread off of James. "Ah, I don't think that you want this anymore." "You're right, I don't."

Now in the office, Bond reached to the back of the bottom drawer and pulled a pamphlet out. "Here it is, I got this at a meeting that I attended at a park near the beach, over a month ago. Chris stood up and took it then read it. "I know that these are troubled times, but you went here? Was this when you were drinking or on that "pill" that you said you took?" "About that time, yes." "What happened?" He stayed silent and showed nervousness. "It's over, what happened?" "I only attended the first meeting, of this group, that at the end of the meeting, I felt like I needed to be a part of," "Sucker punch." He turned his head down and raised his eyes up to him. "Excuse me?"

"Sucker Punch, a punch made without warning giving the recipient is distracted leaving no time for self-defense." "Yeah, I guess something like that." "How much did they get from you?" "Why do you think that they got something from me?" "Because I know you. How much? "He tilted his head from side to side then put his index finger and thumb to the lower part of his ear and pulled down. Chris moved his body closer to him. "Two Hundred dollars." "At only the first meeting you gave then that much? How much would they expect at every meeting? And was there are reason for this contribution?"

He moved his up-tight body in the chair and breathed out looked down and said. "To support their cause, which helped people." "And they were the people and you like many others are the pigeons." "It didn't, it didn't seem that way at the time." "Exactly."" Are these meetings still going on?" "I really don't know, I only attended one." "Why just one? If you were having troubles?" "Troy followed me." "Thank God for him. Did these meeting have a name?" "The Group for Spiritual Enlightenment.", "At least you remembered that. Let me use the computer" he stayed there on the chair for a minute until he realized that he had to move out of that chair for his brother to use it. He did. Chris went right to work, punching the keys for needed information. "There it is The Church for Spiritual Enlightenment and the group that teaches us of the Transparency of Death are of the same company. Any idea of who owns these companies?" Bond shrugged his shoulders. "A Mr. Lee Richards. Eastridge Investments." "You're kidding?" "Nope."

"This means either this case has become easier or harder to solve. What are we going to do about her?" "Her?" "Mrs. Richardson, she just got out of the hospital." "She needs a helper." "You or me?' "Oh, Troy!" "Come on Bond, get your keys we have to take a drive and make a trip." Bond walked out following Chris. Bond opened the back slider to cage James, then took his then took the keys out of his pocket. They went to the garage and drove out of the estate. Bond drove out to main area off of estate. "Would you tell me where we are going?" "To a market or liquor store your choice." "But we aren't supposed to drink." "Oh, we aren't, we are just getting temptation." "What?" He pulled into a shopping complex that had a small market they both went in. Bond followed him right to the refrigerated beer section. "Do you know, his brand?" "No, he usually just drinks our beer, Stella." "I'll get that and a Bud, just to make sure, keep him happy. And let's pick up some steaks to." "At the price they are now?" "We have to have him working for is, for this case." "Get Porterhouse." They paid and left.

Now back home, Chris prepared the outdoor barbeque, the beer was in an ice metal container and chips were in bowls on the table. Bond ran throwing the ball to James on the beach. Chris just placed the steaks on the barbeque. Oh, the aroma that filled the air, Troy must have gotten a whiff of it, because he now stood there to the side off Chris. He set the table with plates and utensils. Bond and Troy sat down as Chris placed the steaks on the table then sat down to dig in.

Troy took a bite then another followed by a bottle of Bud. "This is great, what do you two want me to do?" Both of them were caught off-guard in finding out that he knew of their devious scheme. Chris explained. Troy answered back, "I have already been watching her." "How?" "Just being by her neighborhood, she lives behind those iron gates but there is a spot where I can park and remain out of her view of the condo's view and see all of the coming and going. Right now, a grocery mart, a pharmacy, a florist and one pizza delivery has gone there." "You did this on your own? I mean we haven't told you to." "You both have busy, do you think that I have only been driving around to go to the beach, pool halls or chasing the ladies?" "Pretty much, basically yes."

"There is a basic flaw, that you two didn't pick up on." They looked to him in question. "Mr. Richards, you found out he prefers the men, then why was he at the bar here with a female hooker?" Bond sat back, Chris answered right away, "Cover." "He scored one point, tata. Bond you have to be faster on the buzzer." "Does he own this bar or business that is going on there?" "This I don't know, Bond take it." "I will." Chris looked to him,

"If you already know about her, has she seen you?" "I don't think so, but basically hasn't everyone seen each other at some point?"

"I'll set this up, it would be too risky to set it up through the hospital or her doctor, her insurance company will have arranged this." "The sooner that we get to her the better." "I just have one question for you two?" Chris said, okay? "Who is going to pay us for all of this?" Bond stood up, "Someone always writes a check." He leaves for the office. "Doesn't she have any friends or family that visit her?" "Not that I have seen yet, but how would I know, who they are?"

CHAPTER 18

Jane had more than been welcomed by Jakes' friends and neighbors. She could not find anything wrong with living there. There were plenty of activities and greenery -parks and events. He had a large single-story home that sprawled out to 3,500 square feet. An encased swimming pool in the backyard as well as a paved walking trail of this 2-acre parcel that his house was on. The only thing that she didn't really care for was the master bedroom, it was all in brown. There were touches of beige and one red bed pillow but that was it. She didn't feel confident enough to do any redecorating.

He got home earlier than expected on that Friday afternoon. He walked to the sun room and put his hands firmly on her shoulders. His grip was a bit too tight for comfort but she said nothing of this only kissed his check as he moved his face to the side of hers. "You're early, I hope that everything has gone alright for you." "Why wouldn't it? I just finished early and came home to my house." "What did you do today?" "Oh, this morning after you left, I drove down to the plaza and got my hair done and then got a manicure and pedicure and came home." He loosened his tie and took it off. "You got your hair done; it doesn't look like it."

"We're going out tonight to the Drake Club." "That club is only for Men, what am I going to do?" "You can wait for me in the car, that way if any of them want to see you, you'll be there. And wear that new outfit that

I had put in your closet. Does it fit?" "I didn't know what it was in that garment bag. I haven't even looked at it." "You should have known that I put it there for you. Go try it on." "Can't I just stay home and at some time later if any of your friends want to see me-just have them come over here." "I could but I am not doing that, go change." She breathed in, closed the book she was reading got up and started to the bedroom. "What are you reading?" "To kill a Mocking Bird." He said nothing in response, she said to herself I feel more like a caged bird every day. The only exception is I would fly away."

Standing in the closet with only her bra and underwear on, she unzipped the bag, took it out and was first shocked by the color it wasn't the dull color that he had usually always bought for her. This dress was a radiant bright blue satin. In just holding it and looking at it on the hanger she loved it. "I see that you like it." "It's beautiful, thank you, I haven't tried it on yet though." He pulled her to his hardened body. "We have to do one thing first." She could only speak softly to him as he had such a firm grip on her. "What is that?" "Sex", he pulled her to the bed then laid her down and climbed on top of her while loosening her panties and bra. In thrust full motions he came down on her over and over until he came. After he came, he rolled off of the bed and went to the shower saying nothing to her. She felt bad from what he told her having to wait in the car for him, now after what he just did and he way it made her feel, she forgave him, got up and finished getting dressed.

Now leaving the bathroom she was instantly drawn to the vase of a dozen long stem red roses that where placed on top of the middle of the dresser. She picked up the card, that read to my Love, Jane from Jake. "He cares for me deeply." They had quick dinner at home of the previous night's leftovers of Chinese food.

On the drive there in his white BMW, she noticed the sky darkening and clouds overhead. At this point she wished that she'd of brought her coat then she quickly remembered, that he'd be sitting in a locked car in the parking lot. She wondered why she had to dress up. Oh yeah, it was if he wanted to show her off. In the parking lot in front of the club, there were scattered available spaces in the front and middle of the building. He parked at the far-right end space next to the garbage dumpster. There was no view of the building from there. There was just a view of a nearby softball field of the neighboring elementary school.

She didn't by any means like where he had chosen to park but said nothing to him about it. He reached over and gave her a kiss that didn't reach the side of her face then got out and closed the door never looking back. At that moment she felt unnerved and sat there silent. She looked to the car radio and didn't even have an option of playing it as he took the keys with him. It's a good thing that it is not hot because I couldn't even open the window and the only smell would be of the garbage dumpster. She saw bright lights go on to the front side of her where she had to lean forward to see. "Ah, a ball game at the school, wish I could watch it." She leaned to try to see it until she pulled her back out. "I want to see it and I need to do something. She unsnapped the seatbelt then opened her door to get out and view the game. The car alarm instantly came on, piercing the otherwise silent airwaves of the parking lot.

She debated whether to jump back in the car or walk closer to see the game. She walked closer to the game. The firm hand of her husband pulled her off-balance she fell to the ground. He stood over her and watched her with evil contempt in his eyes. "I told you what to do, did you not hear me?" She tried in desperation to get herself up and in the process ripped part of the dress fabric. "I only wanted to see the softball game." "And is that inside the car?" "No, sorry." He stood there and waited until she got herself back in the car with no help from him. After he saw her, back in the seat with her seatbelt on, he left.

"I have a new and different life that I ran to and escaped to be here, smile and wait." She stayed there sitting in the car barely being able to move, she could feel the lack of oxygen in the car. She fought with all of her might to just fall asleep knowing that this was not a dream that she could wake up from. In only being able to stare into darkness she fell asleep. Hours later he opened the door. She heard this noise from him but wanted to stay still in her safe cocoon of sleep. Now sitting behind the wheel and smelling of bourbon, he looked to her. She was afraid to make direct view to his eyes. He smiled to her and placed his hand over her thigh and slid her dress up then moved it over her crotch. She did not want to feel this but she knew that she had to respond. "When we get home." She felt the overwhelming fear of what his action might be to her. Above that fear was the fear that she had of him driving in his current drunk state. She prayed to God, that they'd make it home in on piece.

He turned the key twice before the motor kicked in, and made an abrupt reverse of the parking space. She was surprised that he didn't throw-up. She more than anything wanted to close her eyes and wish not being there, but panic and fear took over her instincts. She should watch everything, to at least be able to tell him that he was off-course or in the wrong lane or speeding. She opened her eyes fully to his actions of driving them home. He did speed noticeably and managed to get them home in one piece and without a ticket from a traffic cop.

Now parked in the garage the back automatic door still up, he walked to the back of the car to get out of the garage and once at the end of the car he side-stepped out and threw-up. He started back then moved back to the outside of the garage and threw-up again. He made it back to where she stood at the side back of the passenger side door, closer to the entrance of the house from the garage. She supported him into the house and to the bed.

With him laid out on his back on the bed, she disrobed him, he seemed asleep, she thought this to be all the better. He could just sleep it off. Just as she moved up off of his side of the bed where she placed him, he grabbed hold of her arm. She was shocked at how much force he had for the state that he was in. "I didn't tell you that I needed help." She replied calmly to him, "It looked like you did sorry." She had let her body fall to the weakness of the moment. In leaving him, he again pulled her closer to him. She sighed, thinking he'll just fall asleep in my arms. He pulled her down to his arms on top of the bed then hurled his fist to her face knocking her off of the bed and to the floor. She had never experienced so much pain in her life, and she remained quiet swallowing her tears and just praying that she would be able to roll herself up from the floor and leave. Two minutes after she did this, she left that room. Then she locked herself in another bedroom of the house and cried herself to sleep with the help of two aspirin. She said to herself, "There is no way out now. Thank God Lauren stayed in Hawaii to finish the year there."

The next morning, she woke up, looking to the ceiling hoping for an answer. She moved out of bed saying if only walls could talk. In the bathroom she saw her face in the mirror, it was swollen and black around her left eye and check. She splashed water on her face dried it and looked at her reflection again, seeing more than everything wrong with this picture. "I need to hide it. She worked very carefully putting make-up everywhere that she could even took some off that she had already put on thinking powder first then foundation. No matter which way she applied it, it was still noticeably there. After getting dressed, she wrapped a colorful lightweight scarf around her neck, hoping that would have someone look to the scarf and not her face.

There was no cook or maid as in Hawaii- she needed to get to the kitchen and quickly, to make the morning coffee and start cooking something for breakfast before he went to an empty kitchen. With every step that she took getting closer to this room she prayed that he would not be in there. She stopped and held her breath before opening the swinging door to the kitchen, she didn't see him or his reflection, but she knew from previous times that this didn't mean anything. Now inside, she pressed the start button of the coffee pot and opened the refrigerator for eggs and bacon. She had gotten the spiced bacon from the local market butcher, it smelled delicious, she thought he should like it. Just as she had cracked an egg into the frying pan the swinging door opened. She heard him say, Uhm, smells good. This was a relief to hear.

She looked sideways and saw him pour himself a cup of coffee. She scooped the eggs to the plate with the bacon then grabbed toast just as it popped up from the toaster and put it in front of him on the table. He started eating with no word to her. She refilled her cup took the one remaining slice of bacon from the frying pan and sat down at the table aside him. He moved his empty plate to the middle of the table then looked at her closed his eyes and looked directly at her face and eyes. "What on Earth did you do to yourself?" She looked to him in question. "Did you hit yourself with a frying pan or something, you can't let anybody see you like that." He got up and left the room and the house without telling her where he was going.

She sat alone in the kitchen wishing for someone to talk to that she could trust but she knew that she had to keep it a secret for now and forever. "Well, I suppose I'll just go and spend the day cleaning house. She left the room then instantly went back and started doing the dishes and cleaning the sink. Done vacuuming the living room and one hallway she recoiled the electric cord of the vacuum cleaner moved it back to the laundry room and asked herself, "What am I doing wrong?"

The doorbell rang. She couldn't imagine who it would be, but she knew that no one could see her now. She looked out the pep-hole of the front door and saw that it was Fed Ex. She opened the door just an inch and said to him. "Just leave it there on the ground by the door." He told her that he needed a signature. She searched for anything to say to him as an excuse for not opening the door to sign. She said that she had the virus, he left immediately. She closed the door leaned against it and looked-wide-eyed, to nothing in front of her. A moment later she looked out in not seeing him then she opened the door and picked up the package placed on the door mat. It was addressed to her husband. She walked to his closed office door and set it on the floor in front of the door.

"I can't even turn on the music any more, He told me that I can't sing, and dancing I look like a dork. The only thing left is to drink. But it is too early to." She walked to the bar grabbed a bottle of Vodka, poured herself a glass of it and said, "It is five o'clock somewhere." She looked to the ceiling then to her wedding ring and tried to twist it off. She couldn't even turn it in place. For the first time since she ran away, she questioned why she left Chris. Then picked the glass back up and finished what she poured in it and went back for some more. Looking at the now full glass, she looked to it and smiled. "Vodka, nice to meet you, my name is Jane, I hope that we'll be friends." Moving tipsy she said to herself, I had better go lay down, next thing that she knew she was on their bed.

CHAPTER **19**

Bond sat behind the desk at the computer, James chewed a bone on his rug. "There is no tie to this bar to him or Eastridge Investments. It appears that this place is just his escape. A place where people can see him. And as for her Insurance Company." He did a few illegal maneuvers on the computer and found the name of it and her policy number. Chris knocked then went in the office. He looked to him, "Do you want to take this or do I?" "What?" "The insurance company that'll call her and tell her of the in-home therapist that she will have." "I'll take it, you've been a little bit confused lately. Oh, and after I do this, I need a drive to go pick up some new bed sheets and towels." "Okay, as long as you don't throw what you don't like on James." "Deal." He moved out of the way for Chris to sit at the desk and do this. He took James outside for a bit before putting him back in the cage before they leave.

On the drive to the store, they listened to the music from the radio, they both knew that it meant they were each concentrating on the next move. Going inside the linen/towel store, they noticed women looking at them. It was hard to see their actual reaction to them being they were wearing the necessary face masks. Bond followed Chris down the aisles as he looked for just the right thing. He was surprised when he picked out a palm leaf pattern with red flowers on the bedspread with a matching sheet set. He picked out dark blue bath towel set and then took some in bright white towels also. Bond noticed this but said nothing at the time.

Stopped by his side as he put the bags in the backseat, Bond said to him, "I didn't know that you were a Dallas Cowboy fan." He looked to him, like what do you mean. "The colors, that is this teams' colors, dark blue and white." "You know that I am a Forty Niner's fan." Inside the car driving home, he asked what are we going to do next? "We can't do anything until we get Troy there and see what he can find out. I mean there are no ties to the bar, and he isn't at the business here. There has to be something at his place here that we just didn't see or his wife might let us onto. Hopefully we can find out something from her" "It just seems that there was something in S.F. that you missed." "I didn't go there, Jonathan did."" Well we had better work on the Enlightenment and Death, and see where that will take us. You're going to their meeting this Saturday, aren't you?" He said nothing in response as he knew that he now had to, he did not want to but it was work, he more than knew that he had to. "I'll just drive us home so that you can go and decorate your room." He smiled because he got the last word in, but he knew that Chris was already working on something to say back in retaliation.

Troy was in the backyard running James, they went outside to him. Troy ran to them and threw the ball in the other direction for James to run and pick up. "So how did it go?" "We just did some shopping, what about you?" "Tomorrow morning, she starts in home visits. I've already looked for exercises to give her. Oh, and I have a date tonight, Bond -James is all yours." He went back inside the house. Chris approached Bond, "Do you remember what he was originally like?" "Yeah, he wasn't so sure of himself and cocky, like now."

Chris washed and dried all of the towels and bedding that he earlier bought. Upstairs in his room he made the bed. He stood back and looked at the colorful bedspread and thought, maybe it is a little too much, it'll just take some getting used to. The towels looked nice, he first interchanged the colors then thought it looked better in just group of the same solid color together. In looking at the room it didn't seem empty but now he felt it. The absence of her. He walked to the sliding window opened it then looked out to the ocean, it was the darkest that he ever saw it, it even looked unwelcoming. He closed the window and drape, telling himself that he wasn't thinking right. "I am strong."

He grabbed his lap top and started to research if there was a group on the Island labeled, The Transparency of Death. He knew that Bond already said that he did, but sometimes things can be overlooked. He found it listed with executions, and how groups did not feel it ethical and how some states had not overturned the death penalty. There were no ties anywhere on the Island to there being such a group. He thought it a bit odd though, because Hawaii has never had a death penalty since it was established as a state in 1959. Maybe that ws just a random piece of paper that a tourist from another state put on his windshield. He felt it a relief, that they didn't have to figure anything more on that. He felt it was the times, this virus epidemic and the lockdowns everywhere had taken a toll on society. People were and now are acting up without provocation- it had truly become an unsafe time in both ways. He felt some relief that that he solved that and let that go. But now Jane burned in the back of his mind. "I only hope that you are okay. You just didn't give me a chance, but maybe you didn't want me. Bond was right, let her go."

He closed the lap top got up and placed back on top of the table. "I just have a feeling though." The only thing left to do now is sleep… hah, easier said than done with an empty bed. He got up from the bed and opened the nightstand cabinet on the side where she slept. She didn't take her books, well some of them. If you're on the run why take a book collection with especially as now as they have basically become a thing of the past with the Kindle. He reached down, a Hardcover-Devoted. That is rather redundant right now. I'll try reading it anyway.

He did and woke up the next morning with the lamp still on and the book open on the bed. He got up went to shower, saying aloud another day on lockdown. For our safety-hopefully this will end soon. With the lock down now, you can't go anywhere. Out from the shower, he debated on choosing the white or the blue towel until he felt coldness to his skin, he reached for the first one that he could grab, the white one.

Downstairs he met Troy in the kitchen. "Being that my brother is not here, he must be outside." Troy shrugged. "Esmerelda, it is good to see you back." She smiled and asked him what he wanted for breakfast. "You don't need to cook anything for me, I'll just have a yogurt." He opened the refrigerator, and looked at his selection. "Hum, blueberry, Strawberry or Lime." He pulled out strawberry then threw the lid in the garbage and grabbed a spoon. "He isn't back yet." He looked top Troy sitting at the table drinking his shake. For one of the only times in his life he spoke aloud what he felt. "I just don't feel like going out there and having another heart to heart with him this morning." She told him to eat. He liked this alternative. She poured him a cup of coffee as he heard James puttering his way to the kitchen.

He watched his brother walk to them and sit down. "What is the matter, you don't look good." "I don't feel good." "Is this because you are worried about everything that we have to do, or are you just physically not feeling good?" "I don't know, but something, somewhere is wrong." Troy, spoke up, "Something everywhere is always wrong, it is just now there is more." She poured him coffee. He took a sip before even putting the half and half in it. "Come on have some Froot Loops or something you have to bring yourself out of this especially today. He nodded his head. She put a bowl of this cereal with milk in front of him. "All of you are easy this morning." He looked to her and said thanks and started eating. "That's better." They all smiled to him.

"What color will the last one be?" Troy looked to him then Chris, "What is he talking about?" "It is a game that we used to play as kids. The last piece that remained in the bowl, we guessed on what the one remaining color, what it would be." "I'll take yellow." "That is what I was going to pick, I guess, okay I'll take red." He looked up to them and tilted the bowl to their view, "Sorry guys, it's purple." Oh's were heard at the table.

Troy left the table saying that he was getting ready for his visit to her. Chris looked to Bond, "There is a problem. Come on let's go outside." Now out at the patio area, Bond still looked to be in a remorseful state. "Do you want to talk here at the table or talk a walk on the beach." He didn't answer, he just sat down. "Come on, we have to work today." Chris waited in silence; it was so quiet he swore that he could hear the sound of a bird going by flapping its wings. Bond took his hands to his legs. "Stop right there, and tell me the problem?"" It is your wife." Chris sprung up in the seat. "Have you heard from her?" "No, it is just ever since I took care of her, when you were away, I just." Chris stood up, "Come on, it is over, let her go, as you told me. We have a case-this is the only thing to work on… You brother, seem weak, are you back on liquor again?" He looked up to him wide eyed and questioning. "Stop, you just answered my question right there. Where is it?" He heard him mumble, I, I…" That is not an answer."

He left and went to Bond's room, opened the closet, searched it then opened every drawer on the bureau and night stands, nothing was there, he didn't even find anything in the bathroom, he then checked the office, and nothing there. "My God, you don't mean to tell me?" He grabbed Bonds' car keys then went to the black SUV that he drove. He opened the passenger door and felt under the driver seat it and pulled out a half-finished bottle. "What the, my God, do you want to kill yourself or somebody else?" He took the bottle to the outside of the house driveway and poured it all out hitting the asphalt and set the bottle down then brought the garden hose with its water running and hosed off that area. Then picked up the bottle and walked to the side of the house and threw it in the garbage can.

He turned to the direction of the front door, there Bond stood showing tears in his eyes but no visible sign of crying. He walked closer then stopped ten feet away from him. "You may want to kill yourself but I do not want to see it. I can't deal with you doing this. I thought that you were over this? "He saw Bond trying to gather words to say. "No, I don't want to hear anything from you, especially right now. Just, just, (he took a long deep breath in) go to your room and pack; you are going away."

He called Dr. Stone; she sounded a bit disturbed then told him that he did the right thing in calling her. Four hours later a car came to pick up Bond. Chris followed it out the gate and to the airport. He was sent to a recovery clinic in Malibu California. He turned away in watching him being escorted down the entry to the airplane. "I only hope, that they can cure him and find his evils that are doing this to him. I mean he knows better. This one of the hardest things that I have ever done." He leaned his neck back and supported it with his right hand. Then found the courage and strength to walk away without turning back.

In his car driving back to the estate he thought, that was the reason of why Bond wasn't himself lately. He could not understand as to why he reverted. Maybe it was purely the pressure of being the 'boss'. From a jet set playboy spy, to the head of a mega spy ring, with numerous businesses to look after at the same time. Chris, then thought of how his father made it look all so easy. That and he had years of experience I doing it. He grew as the company grew. "I wonder what Jonathan is doing or how he is doing, I haven't seen him today. I just hope that he is home and not off on a gallant adventure to solve something, I need, we need order." He turned on the car radio and continued the journey home.

On entering the front door, he saw Jonathan sitting on the living room listening to opera music. He didn't say anything to him. He turned to go to kitchen for a soda. "Don't worry Chris I am thinking. Did you get him off?" Chris walked back to him and turned to his direction so that they could see each other. "How did you know?" "I watched and I listened. That is my job." He turned back to the direction of the kitchen, "Glad, to have you aboard." His footsteps faded. Jonathan smiled.

After he finished a can of soda, he changed into his sweats, loose tennis shoes and went outside to the lawn and practiced karate moves. He found that his gave him balance and a release from the life's stress. He had trained and is a blue belt. Jonathan watched him from the window then after a minute left because he did not want to create a distraction. Troy got home; Jonathan told him the news of Bond. He stayed still after hearing his words, then made no comment looking sad. He left him saying he was going to go and shower then they'd all talk later. After dinner they did meet in the living room for this conversation.

Jonathan sat in the middle of the couch Troy to the side right arm rest and Chris sat in a chair opposite the couch with his back to the window. James was outside tied to a long rope so he could move around but not far enough to reach the pool. Chris opened the meeting. "I hear that you have been told of Bond." Troy nodded his head. "I never expected something like this, I mean all that he went through and he seemed alright with the exception of today. How long has he been like this?" Chris sighed and breathed out. "Your guess is as good as mine. I just found out today." "So, you had him shipped out then?" "That sounds like I put him in the military. He is on the way to or is already in Malibu to the recovery center there, by the orders of his medical doctor. We are just going to have to do this without him, and I myself will miss that." They both nodded their heads to what he just told them.

"Troy tell us of Mrs. Richards where you able to find out anything?" "It was only my first day there, I can't be too quick. She is a nice lady; she doesn't know her neighbors and the neighbors don't know her. She has friends and meets weekly at a lady's card club. There is liquor in the house, but it looks like it is just there for decoration, crystal containers and matching glasses. Other than that, it'll just take time. She a nice woman." "Okay and for this club that meets by the beach." Jonathan interrupted, "I'll do this, it'll be harder to break me than you, Chris." He didn't know exactly what he meant by that, but he agreed. "Chris what is wrong? You look like you've lost something?" He did but he wasn't going to let on to it. He lost both his wife and his brother and now felt it but he couldn't let that get to him. "I am just thirsty. Well, that is it fellows, so see you tomorrow." He started upstairs then remembered his excuse and went to the kitchen and came back with a bottle of water.

Upstairs in his room in his pajamas laying against the headrest he opened a cardboard box from Amazon. "How to get over the loss of your ex." He picked it up and scrolled through it. "She is really gone. And she went to someone else." He dropped the book rolled his body back and forth seeking comfort. "And our daughter, won't even talk to me… Strength." He set that book on the floor and picked up Devoted. He read that until sleep overwhelmed him and he turned off the bed lamp and went to sleep.

Jane woke up a little before five o'clock on the evening. She tried to roll her body off of the floor and instantly felt dizziness and overwhelming nausea. She rolled to a piece of furniture and leaned her body against it to stand. She made it to the toilet just in time to throw up in the bowl. Her face was black and blue. She wondered if it was that way from him or from her drinking. If he was home, he would have found me, I don't know where he is but I had need to get ready for him. She felt her way to the kitchen made coffee and tried to find something to make for dinner. Even looking at food then made her queasy. She thought of the consequences she moved as fast as she could and poured a cup of coffee while it was still brewing. Hearing the sizzle, she put the pot back on the burner thinking it would eventually burn to silence.

She took steaks from the freezer and defrosted them in the microwave, then took a sack of potatoes from the bottom cabinet and peeled them to make escalloped potatoes. Now on her third cup of coffee she had the potatoes in the oven, the salad made, the steaks seasoned ready to cook and was now in the process of setting the dining room table. The house phone rang, she went to the stand and picked it up. "It was her husband. He told her that he had spent the day at the golf course then went over to a friend's house and they invited him to stay for dinner, he'd be home late. She told him to have a good time and hung up the phone. She fought an overwhelming feeling to just throw everything against the wall or the floor and break it.

She went back to the kitchen turned everything off and covered the steaks and salad and put them in the refrigerator and dumped the coffee down the sink. Now inside the dining room she saw the table set all ready for him. She felt an overwhelming feeling of loss. "If I break down and cry, I cry alone." She took a bottle of liquor off of the bar and went to the guest bedroom with it and locked the door.

The next morning, she wakened by pounding on the bedroom door and screaming from her husband. "You bitch, why is there no coffee and why aren't you in there for me?" The pain now ate at her. "What do I do before I am beaten again? Getting out of the bed she went to the bathroom trying to ignore his actions. She opened the bedroom door just as his fist slammed into her. She keeled over in pain; she saw him trying to reach for her with violent words coming from his mouth.

Loosening from the grasp he had over her ankle, she fell the got right up and ran the front door feeling him breath right behind her. She grasped the front door knob then felt her body being pulled back in pain. She slides to the floor clawing the finish off of the wooden stain being pulled back from the safety of getting out of there. She screamed, then moved to her side as her body was in motion. She heard him but not the words he yelled to her. She grabbed hold of the end table leg; the resistance slowed his actions. A heavy glass ash tray fell off to the floor she caught hold of it before it smashed into pieces then threw it at him, it hit the side of his head, He fell to the floor. She didn't know how it happened but it had to be from the grace of God that she gained he power to stand up and run out the door. She almost tripped on her bathrobe, she stopped for only a second and took it off. Running down the sidewalk she hoped for anyone to see her and more than anything she prayed for a police car to drive by.

She fell and saw herself falling, feeling every second that her body was dropping then crashing to the hard-concrete sidewalk on her knees, the pain roared through her body in agony and lost desperation of being defeated. She thought the only thing that could follow, was death by him. A hand reached down to her at her left side by the grass, she reached for her husbands' hand, she felt her body being lifted up she could feel the blood fall from her knees. Thinking there wasn't any way that she could do anything more to get away she looked to him, at his face. Hallelujah- it wasn't him; it was the neighbor's gardener. "I know that you are in pain but try to hurry, I have to get you out of here." She moved where he put her, in the front seat of the truck. "Keep low, and we'll leave, hold on"

He stopped in front of a Baptist church a few miles away. "I'll be right back." He was, and with two other people, they carefully got her out and took her to the back offices of the church and laid her body down on a couch. A woman tended to her and her wounds, bandaging them. She could hear the sound of an ambulance siren. "No, no please, no, he'll find me." "The woman from the church looked down to her, "Honey, who will find you?" "Jake, my husband." "Is he looking for you?" "Yes, yes, he is." "There is man running down the street in our direction, should I call him?" The siren became louder. The door opened... a man entered the room and saw her. "She's in here, bring the stretcher. Three men from the ambulance took her vitals then carried her to the ambulance and it drove away to the nearest hospital.

She was taken to the E.R. a short wait for them to do paperwork then a doctor went to her, he read her report- nurses hooked her up to an I.V. They drew blood. "Her blood alcohol is high, .03, did any one come here with her? She can't make any decisions for her treatment right now. Move her to the next ward, we'll have a psychiatrist look at her. She screamed, "No, no he'll get me, repeatedly, they didn't know if she was in actual danger or not. There was no I.D. on her. They asked her questions of her name D.O.B, her address, fear and panic were the only thing that she showed, answering no questions just pleading with them not to tell Jake her husband. "Do we need to call the police on this one?" A verbal yes, was heard shouted through the room.

They had to sedate her, from her violent rage that she let engulf her mind. The attending doctor spoke to the psychiatrist that was called to treat her. "She has answered no questions, it is quite clear that she is panicked of her husband. We need a statement signed by you, for this as so she won't be claimed by him. The police are on the way." The attending psychiatrist went to her and asked her questions. The only words that he was able to get out of her were, No, please no, Bond. "Is this her last name?"

They tried everything; the psychiatrist told then that at the current state that she was in he couldn't get anything out of her. After the doctor's examination she saw the bruises on her body and the black and blue face. It was in his estimation, domestic violence. They brought a Biometric Scanner to use for identification. A picture was taken with an iris camera that subsequently confirms her identity and pulls up medical records that has been linked to her biometric credentials. It compares her captured biometric templets against all stored templets. "Her identity, Dora Stevens, Chicago Illinois, she moved to California." "Her blood alcohol level is what concerns us the most, she needs to be put in a treatment center. What is she doing here?" Her paperwork was brought back to the offices.

"Get prepared. the victims of that truck crash are going to be here in 10 minutes. We need all available beds. What do we do with her?" "There is a flight leaving for California, L.A.X. in 4 and a half hours, lucky her, an opening in, Malibu. Our records show that she is from California. She'll be paying for it." "Okay get her ready to transport out of here." She was taken to the airport via hospital bus. The checked in with the needed medical info, and papers for the flight. From needed medication she was out for most of the flight, and non-violent and quiet for the remainder of the flight. From L.A.X. she was taken by Lincoln Town Car to this treatment center with a female nurse in attendance for the trip duration.

She was checked in then taken to her room and given times of meetings and appointments. When she did speak, she asked where her daughter was. They told her that she was okay and not to worry. Fear struck her without warning, "He can't find me. He can't find me." She was assured that he wouldn't. She was escorted to her private room and a nurse went over the following days plan with her. She was also remined to increase her daily water intake as alcohol dehydrates the body. The following morning, she had a one-on-one appointment scheduled for 11:00.

Bond left the L.A.X. airport via private Limousine, it headed north to Malibu. He sat by himself in the backseat of the limo, there were water bottles there for him for the drive. He ignored those and the scenery out the windows. He looked at the empty space around him, inside the limo and nothing more showing no reaction to anything. They checked him in then showed him his private room. It was on the second floor and had a private desk that looked to the ocean. Standing with the sliding door open he looked to the view. "I could see the ocean from home, why do I have to be here?" He clenched his fists together and pulled them to his chest then released them and sat at the edge of the bed rubbing his thighs over and over. "I don't want to be here. I was the head of the organization, why can't I make the decision? Who did? Just move me around where they want me. They don't appreciate me, never have and never will."

Jane spent that night close to the bathroom; her body was still going through the recovery stage. She got up from the toilet bowl, washed her hands then looked at her reflection in the mirror, "This isn't me, where did I go? Where am I?" She went and sat at a chair looking out of the window." "There is so much that I do not have the answers to. In drinking so much, I became deaf to the world…it was a way to cope with the ever-changing turmoil of life. Maybe I should save these words for the one-on-one meeting."

"Now showered and dressed and get ready for the group breakfast, and meet other people here. And what will my name be? Dora or Jane?" She turned on the shower got in and said aloud, "How about, D.J.? No, then they will ask me what radio station that I work for." She did take the time to work with make-up the nest that she could to hide her bruises. "More than anything I do not want to answer the questions of why I have these scars."

Downstairs at the eating areas. There was the option of sitting inside or outside at the open eating tables with the beautiful scenery. She opted to sit by herself inside at a corner trying her best to be out of the way hidden from the world wanting answers to her daunting past that she wanted to bury. She drank her cup of coffee, never taking her hand off of the cup turning it in every direction she could only stopping when she took a drink of it. The plate of food in front of her looked good but she could only bring herself to eat the toast or most of it,

Bond wearing his sunglasses went to the outside eating area, he noticed that female heads were already eyeing him. He scanned the available area, then honed in on a table of men with one empty chair. He went there and asked them if he could join them. He received smiles and yeses from all. The coffee was better than he thought it would be and in eating breakfast and talking with these men, he felt welcomed. And cherished the feeling of not having to run from the table to track someone down as with his job demands. And following orders.

She finished breakfast and instead of taking a leisurely walk through the beautiful outside grounds she went back to her room. She turned on the television and heard of the damage to the state from the countless wildfires sweeping through over a million acres. A scene of the Golden Gate Bridge where the surrounding sky was orange in color from the smoke fumes traveling. "I wonder if where I lived, I hope this area is okay." She got up from watching the TV turned it off then went to the bathroom mirror reapplied lipstick and brushed he hair and left the room, instead of going to the closer exit to her right she went to the left direction as exiting on that side would be closer to the office that she needed to go to. Bond walked to his room from the right-side entrance and said to himself the sound of the exiting footsteps sounded familiar. Then shook his head to what he just heard thinking of all of the people there from various places and nothing more than that. He went to his room on that hallway, stood back opened the door visually swept the room then went inside and closed the door.

Inside the office that she needed to be she was instantly welcomed then lead aside to the room by Dr, Burrows. She was comfortable in the fact that this doctor was a woman, thinking that it would be easier to talk to her about her problems then a man. Sitting in the room instead of being there a large desk between them, she sat on a comfortable chair with the Doctor sitting on one opposite her. Just the fact of the comfort of that setting made her feel more at ease.

"Let's see you have two names, Dora and Jane, which one would you prefer?" "I suppose that it depends on who is talking to me." "We will go into this, but right now, here, which one would you prefer?" "Jane." "Is there a reason why?" "Yes, but I would rather not tell you right now, at this moment." "Have you always drunk or did this just start? Is there a reason why it started?" "I…I ah, uhm." "Take your time I am not here to judge you, there is no right or wrong." "I only just started drinking, I mean before I drank once and a while, but not enough to get me drunk and that wasn't the reason on why I drank, then." "Okay, you are safe, here with me. Tell me why now you want to drink?"

"I started because it helped me forget about him and to become numb to him" "Was, he this gentleman those name that you have called out Bond?" "No, no, he is my savior." "So, you were calling out for him for help, help from who?" "My new husband not the one that I ran away from." "You have two husbands, then?" "Jake, the new husband told me that my husband didn't count." "There is some very important wording that I just heard from you." "What is that?" "My husband. Do you not like the new husband, was there a need for the new husband? I can see the external scars on your body and I feel the internal scars also."

"You, understand. I wish that I had been able to talk with you months ago." "Dear, help is always out there you just need to look for it. It feels that you are alone, but isn't that the way that he wanted you to feel? Alone and betrayed-you needed him." She opened her eyes then batted them to her, opened her mouth, she understood! She is hearing me. By the end of that meeting she began to feel self-worth. Now in smiling she could feel the reason why she smiled and it was now not just for show and trying to hide something. The doctor reminded her that she had many more appointments to keep and a workshop to look forward to be a part of.

"I am sorry, doctor but I forgot your name, could you please tell me?" She received a smile as she told her it was Dr. Burrows. "Why don't you go for walk and maybe make some friends to have lunch or just an iced tea with. There are people out there to meet and maybe you'll form a new friendship." Jane got up smiled to her and left the office feeling better and thankful. She went back to her room freshened up then walked outside to open area not now fearing who was going to see her. There was an immediate door to her right, she exited through that door.

Bond walked down the hall to see the doctor. He opened the door of the office, Dr. Burrows looked to him and asked him what he wanted. He told her of his appointment. "I don't have any appointments scheduled for now, is this your first appointment?" He said yes. "You want Dr. Hardy his office is across the hall and to your right, other side of hallway. He thanked her then went to the right office.

He knocked on the door and didn't get a response, then gently turn the door knob and held it he waited to turn it and walked in the office. No one was there. He didn't know whether to leave or not, in a way he looked forward to this meeting though felt fearful of it at the same time. He heard the door behind him open, he moved nervously further away from the door. He man that entered moved his hands forward then replied to him. "Hello, I am Dr, Hardy. I am sorry but I just needed to step out for a minute. Inside this next door is my office, he held the door open for Bond to walk through, he closed it behind him.

"Would you like to sit at my desk or the sofa and chair?" Bond sat in the chair, making the doctor feel a bit unnerved as he always sat in the chair, the doctor then sat at the side of the couch closet to the chair. "How would you like me to address you?" Bond looked to him questioning the question. "I mean by your first name, Bond or your last name or a nick name?" Bond more than anything wanted his identity hidden, in just hearing the word nick, he replied, "Nick." "Okay then Nick, where would you like to start?"

"My family sent me here, I do not want to even be here." "Your family sent you here, was this because of your drinking problem?" "There is no problem. They are the problem making my job harder, I need a release." "So, for a release you turn to alcohol?" "It doesn't judge me." "Do you feel that you family judges you?" "Yes." "Tell me of your family." "What do you mean tell me of your family? We all have a family." "How many people are in it; do you have a wife? Children? Brothers, sisters?"

"I have, or had a father, a brother, mother died a long time ago when I was a child. I am long time divorced, no children. And I am very close to my brother's wife. I had to watch over her, for months while he was away." "Why, did you have to watch over her, was she sick? Why was he away?" "I don't want to talk about this, any more." The doctor stayed quiet. The situation in the room became tense. Bond got up from the chair and nervously paced the room. "It seems to me, that you are looking for an out." He stopped his pacing and listened. "Until I sign a release, you are here. Indefinitely, nothing that you tell me will leave this room. If you aren't comfortable with me, another doctor can be found." "Okay, then. He walked to the chair, then paced back to the other side of the room and opened the door to leave. "It's your call, you are only making it longer of a stay for yourself." "I just do not feel comfortable talking to you, find me someone else, you know how to get in touch with me, everyone here knows." He walked out and the doctor waited for his return as this sometimes happens with patients, but he made no return.

He walked to the outside of the main building watching people, patients come and go. He wondered if he could just get inside one of the cars that brought a patient there. He watched the process. He felt a tingling feeling run through his body and shakes started, he felt that he wanted to and needed to reach out to something for help, but no one was there. His body trembled as he fell to the ground. Two men from that worked there came to him. One stood at each side of him, they helped him up then escorted him to the medical facility there. They put him in a room laid him on a bed, and a medical doctor showed up to care for him. "Mr. Bond you are experiencing withdrawal, the sooner you act to start this program he better for you. We are here to help you." "Okay, okay just get me someone different," "What did you not like about Dr. Hardy?" "He reminded me of my seventh-grade science teacher and I hated that class." Their moods were instantly relaxed. "Another doctor will be arranged to meet with you. Let us just watch you here for a little bit and then you'll be free to the grounds. There will be a meeting tonight, the information will be in your room."

"So, you have me on lockdown then?" "No, Mr. Bond, you are not on lockdown. After a meeting with a doctor, you will feel better about everything here." "You are telling me, that all I have to do is have a meeting with one of your doctors here and then I'm free?" "You will have made your first step." "I just want to go to my room now, please. Just let me go, let me out of here." After he opened the door of his room, he looked to the man that escorted him there. "Do you need to do a room check?" The man smiled to him then left. He went in the room kicked off his shoes, closed the drapes then laid on the bed. "What is everyone at home doing now?" He closed his eyes to the now evening hour of the day. "Chris is sitting behind the desk; it should be me."

CHAPTER 20

Troy worked with Mrs. Richards. Her face lit up as soon as she saw him. He asked her some basic questions, she was fine in answering the and talking with him. He had her do some range in motion exercises. That he picked up on the internet. That exercise seemed to tire her out, He told her to take a rest. She went to her bedroom and settled in for a brief nap, while he was there. He went to her husbands' desk. Choosing not to turn the computer on, instead he went through drawers and alas his checkbook was in the center desk top drawer. He thought this odd because wouldn't he have needed it for the trip. He put plastic gloves on, then held it open and took pictures from his cell phone of all the check receipts, and other papers that he found searching through the desk. He put the cell phone back inside his bag then thought that should be all for him to do that day, not knowing when she would wake up, He took a paperback novel out from his bag and opened randomly to a page and pretended to read.

She entered the living room where he sat on the couch with the book open, he looked up from it and to her with a smile. She walked to him and asked him if she could get him something to drink, water, coffee, soda. He thanked her and said no. "Well then, you can just work on the exercises that I gave you, until tomorrow then." She acted surprised, "Tomorrow?" "Is there a problem with this, I can see if I can change the dates if you wish." "No, no tomorrow is fine. I just have never received such good service before. My husband, says…never mind, about that," Tomorrow, I look forward to it." He smiled picked up his bag and left out the door.

Jonathan went to the next beach meeting. He was noticed, by a few older single women there and also because he is new to the group. They gave him a name pin to wear. He looked at it and det it in his pocket. He chose the name of Bob to be called. Listening to the meeting the main vibe that he got from it was a support group for the broken hearted with checkbooks. When it was his turn to talk and tell his story, something that everyone one savored, their time to shine in the spotlight. He simply said that he was single and retired. They asked him why he was single. He answered, plain and simple, "Because I choose to and that he was retired from being a garbage worker. There were no questions on this. Upon leaving, he noticed that they all lines up in a single line, to leave stopping a t a table first. He watched they signed their name and then either gave a check or cash.

When it was his turn, he asked them why he needed to pay. The reason was to support their cause. He felt like asking what was the cause, and how much money are you asking from what basically people do at Starbuck's, talk to people. He just told them that he was there without his wallet. He walked there and all he had with him was his house keys. The female attendant that sat behind this card table taking the money then got up from the table and went to the speaker standing to the side of a parked truck and whispered in his ear and then pointed to him. He went to Jonathan, a.k.a. Bob and told him that their meetings required financial support, he could bring payment for that meeting at the next meeting with payment for that meeting also. He then smiled wide thresher cat grin to him. He smiled back and turned and walked away quickening his pace with every step.

He waited in his car wearing his dark glasses. As the truck with the two people and the money drove away, he followed it. It went right to an ATM drive up machine at a bank and made the deposit. He jotted down the make and license number of the truck then went inside the bank. Inside the bank looking and acting as distinguished as he could he went to the branch manager sitting behind his desk. He then made it noticeable that he had forgotten to put this face mask on and then did it.

The Branch Manager stood up and told him of the ATM machines at the side wall or there were two tellers at windows that he could go to. He made an embarrassed look then stood closer to the side of him. "It is rather embarrassing this is why I have gone to the man in charge, the president of everything here. You see both my company and my business do bank here. I was just at the drive thru to make a large deposit from my business and I forgot the receipt. Could I get a duplicate from you, please, Sir?" The manager relaxed after hearing his, and then went behind the counter, and looked at the latest drive thru deposits. He returned and asked him what his vehicle that he used when he drove through to make this deposit. Jonathan told him, he waited for less than a minute and was given the receipt. He thanked the Branch Manager and left then went back to the estate.

That evening both Troy and Jonathan gave the information they got that day to Chris. "Wow, this will keep me busy for a while, you two just want to make sure that I don't get hooked on a soap opera." He expected a laugh from them but don't get one. Jonathan went upstairs to his room and Troy went to his room and got a beer then went outside with it. Chris put the information on the side of the office desk then walked away. I just do not feel like sitting there for hours on end, looking for something. I know that I will have to do this though. I miss Bond. Who am I kidding I miss Jane! I'll never hear from her again. James leaned against him and whined. "I feel that you know." "James, I know that you miss, him, I do too."

Locked inside his room at the treatment center he thought of how much he missed James, he wanted to reach out for something. He felt the emptiness of the room and now felt the emptiness of his life, something that never before bothered him. He clenched at the bedspread clenching it tighter and tighter then released it exhaling a heavy sigh, "She caused me to drink. The weight was put on me to get them back together. Then Nancy Drew, runs off to Vegas and marries a stranger, and he doesn't even know why she left."

He got up from the bed went to the bathroom then came back out put on his shoes, and left the building and walked to the outside grounds. He noticed the grass and the trees and the calming atmosphere. Maybe I should just give this a try and not resist. Who knows I may meet somebody, I need someone?" In the inside dining room, he met the same group of men that he had breakfast with, and there was an open chair waiting for him. He listened to their stories two of them actually knew each other from work and that is why they were there. The pressure that they experienced from work and the pressure that it put on their families. One of them was a retired NFL guard. The team that he had been on and signed to for 8 years released him without warning and no other team picked him up. He had been a free agent for three years now. He shared a duplex in L.A. with a friend, but now more than ever he was feeling the tightness. The other man there at the table was a farmer/cowboy from Wyoming. He said that when things do not go right it is just easy to reach for the bottle. They now turned to him for his story.

Rather than make-up a story that he might forget but this came with his job, living stories, he declined to say anything his excuse being, he just didn't feel comfortable speaking on this yet, maybe after a few more meetings with a doctor. This satisfied them and they went on to another topic of conversation. Looking from the table at a side view, he swore that he saw celebrities from the big screen there walking around. A man from this table noticed him and what or who he was looking at. "Oh, yeah, that is him, alright, and we didn't even have to pay $20.00 for a movie ticket to see him. We were told to not approach them as fans. If they talk to you fine, otherwise leave them be." Bond nodded his head and then turned his view back to the table.

The next morning after having coffee with the table of gentlemen he went to his appointment with the doctor. She answered her door to his knock. He retracted his face and body at seeing her, surprised that she is a woman. "Bond, welcome, come in." He sat at the middle of the couch she sat in the chair. "Relax, I am here to help you. This will most probably be painful for you to recall; we need to talk of your latest breakdown." "Latest?" "I have it here in my notes that this has happened before and treatment at a hospital was required." He moved apprehensively on the couch and made no reply to her.

"There is only one thing that you have to do, and that is plain and simple talk to me, whatever you say stays these four walls." He remained silent. He bent his arms over his legs and breathed out looking like he was going to rise up off of the couch, then leaned back. "Okay, let me get this over with, I think that I just could not handle the pressure, and I didn't have Father to talk to, not even Jane was there. I reached for what I could find and wouldn't judge me and that was booze, alcohol, vodka, whatever you want to call it. There are we finished?"

"No, we are not finished. You just made it much easier. For the both of us. Number one, you have admitted to doing this." "You have the proof that I did it, how could I deny it?' "Most alcoholics will not admit to the problem and hide the liquor." She stayed silent after finished with this last sentence waiting to hear a response from him." He couldn't mask over the question any longer. "So, you are asking me why the open bottle was in my car?" She again, remained silent. "I was hiding the fact the was drinking." "There we go, you are admitting to it, good. And the reason of why you were drinking was it the reasons that you already gave me or was there something else that pulled the trigger, for you to start drinking again?" "Isn't what I have told you enough? I mean I have never been able to do things good enough, Chris was always better. Or simply he got the recognition for the job that we did together, and I was supposed to be comforted by the fact that he was thanked, and know that it applied to me too?"

"Who thanked you, as you say him?" "As you say, him, pertaining to me? Father, that is who?" "But yet you tell me that you miss your father and his talks with you. Bond, he knew that you were there. And just in hearing you say that he thanked your brother and not you, this means that he knew that you didn't need it, but your brother did." He sat back and stayed silent thinking of what she just said to him. "He knew that I was strong. Yes... that has to be it. Chris needed to hear it and I didn't." "Was your brother ever at these talks that you had with him?" "No not the- one on one talk, father would talk to me first then Chris would come in, but he talked to me first." Bond's entire character and demeanor changed after hearing this said to him. He raised his body up and straightened up and showed a smile on his face.

"Well, Mr. Bond, I can tell that you feel better, much better than when you came in here. Is there anything that you want to ask me right now?" "Uhm, I not... right now." "Before you go, I do have one more thing that I want to say to you. You used liquor as your crutch. That is what you leaned on for support, you are stronger than it is, always remember this, you do not need a crutch, you do not need liquor. It is a crutch that will knock you down." He stood up from the couch standing firm and tall then thanked the doctor. She gave him a card for their next scheduled meeting and he smiled to her as he left out the door.

He went back to his room and changed into a sweat suit then went for a run around the property. For the first time that he has been there he relaxed and actually saw things the way that they are.at now' What did worry him is how Chris would react to him and could he himself be the boss? He stopped and bent over breathing in air. And then told himself not to worry for he is the boss. He stood up and regained his run, "I am the boss."

That night before the went to dinner, he changed into a suit, looking handsome and in vogue. Instead of automatically going to the gentlemen's table as he usually did, he went to the other side of the room and sat by himself at a table for six. A few minutes later a middle-aged couple joined him and explained to him on why they were there, basically to save their 19-year marriage. He was cordial but could have cared less about it. He heard a group of women talking behind him. The smell of the cologne that one of them was wearing caught his interest. There was something familiar to it, that caught hold of him.

A single woman sat at the table next to the couple that was already there. He said hello to her and she did in return. She was nice looking but there was something about her that just didn't catch his eye. His eyes circled the table there were now three empty seats. He thought of the possible temptation that could sit there. Another married couple took two of the remaining empty seats. He smiled to them but felt a bit disappointed, his chances were now greatly decreased. He took a drink from the ice water placed in front of him, thinking that, that evening was basically now a lost cause. Suddenly he smelled that cologne that entranced him and he could sense a person now sitting at the empty chair to his left side.

When he saw who she was, he almost dropped his glass of water from his hand. He couldn't believe that he was held captive to her. How did she ever get there and by herself yet? The couple that were first at this table, introduced, Jane to Bond. They smiled to each other and nodded hello, laughing. The others at the table asked them what was funny. "We have met before." "Old friends, so to speak", said Bond smiling. They went on having dinner with the others and listened to the talk of the table, which was nothing more than sports and what their children were doing and of course, the dreaded virus that held the world on edge. They were at the table to eat none wore their masks but the chairs were placed a good distance from each other.

Those at the table waited for dessert. Both Jane and Bond excused themselves saying they were full. Walking away from the table they heard a man there say that they probably want to catch up. Both were happy hearing this. She started to say something to him and he motioned her to be quiet. Now outside and away from other on lookers, he dropped his mask standing near her, so did she. He started the conversation. "What… I mean why are you her? Shouldn't you be of in the land of Oz with your new husband, or is he here too?"

She lowered her head and wiped the smile from her face. "No, he is not here and he is the main reason as to why I am here." Bond looked to her questionably. "I found out who the person that he is under the disguise." "You will need to do more explaining then that. No hurry, I am listening, and you know me." "I know you very well and I wish that you'd have been there for me. I needed someone, mostly you. "She dropped her head then reached her hands to support it. He saw this and was concerned.

He pointed to it. They both walked to a bench and sat down, allowing distance from the other. "It started out as a storybook romance., there in Las Vegas anyway. I mean nothing could have been more perfect. Then we got to his home. Bond, I saw more people when I was captive in Hawaii with your family… Is Chris there, is he alright, I mean." He bent down his head and shook it up and down. "Yes, he is there, quiet, he has been quiet, but you know him, it is just part of his nature." She moved her fingers over her legs retracting them and then bringing them back up then brought her right hand over her shoulder and rubbed it before placing them back down to her side and rest her hands on the bench top. "Get on with what happened, please."

"It was good at first, just getting used to his place and a new town. I spent 90% of the time trapped inside of his house. I went outside to go to the grocery mart and that was it. The mail was even put in a slot inside the house" "So, you were just with him?" "Yes. I could only do what he let me do, I even changed my life. I could clean cook take care of the house read and occasionally watch television, that was it. He wouldn't even let me play music anymore." "You, without moving around to your music, that was your release." "It was beyond being a Stepford wife. And then the beatings started, I couldn't defend myself and I even thought it was my fault. I masked them and him. And then I turned to the bottle, it seemed that it was my only release."

"Why didn't you tell me?" "How could I, I was in another world." "I am glad that you were able to escape from him." "That is just it I still feel that at any time I will turn around and he'll be there." "It would be awfully hard for him to get in here." "Maybe. He is strong in every way, power and money." "It sounds to me like you were his servant." "That is one word for it." They each became quiet. She looked up to the Moon, He saw her do this. "It's hidden." "I can see part of it, how is it hidden?" "If you look closely at it and it's diameter, you can see the part that is hiding to make it whole." He thought of what she just said to him and what she said applied to her current situation, but he said nothing to her in response.

She took her eyes from the sky and looked to him, at his face. Then moved her face to his, she kissed him on the lips. He stayed still, and didn't pull back, but did not move in response to her movement. "I love you, but not like that." "I am sorry." Quietness came to the moment from both. She held herself back from him, still sitting on the bench. "Are we good then?" He relaxed his body, "We're good-as friends, nothing more. Save this for Chris. And talk to your doctor." He stood up from the bench and said good night to her, as he walked away. She said raising her voice that he could hear here, "You're a great friend." He stopped in his footsteps. "Ditto, and I know that it is from the movie Ghost." She smiled and stayed there for a few more minutes looking to the moon before going back to her room

Would he ever take me back after what I have done if he knows it? Why did I do what I did? If I could turn back time. The missing piece, from the puzzle, it was the cowardly lion, that was the missing character from Oz, isn't it funny that I thought of this now? I need to go back. I only hope that I... I had better turn in and be ready to see the doctor in the morning.

CHAPTER 21

He following morning, she went to the dining room to get breakfast. Instead of sitting outside as she usually did, she went inside in looking for a table and saw Bond. She started in that direction then saw that he was at a table with men and no available seat there. It would have been to odd for her to go there any way. She backstepped her movement and proceeded outside to a small table set for two. The waiter filled her coffee cup. She looked up to the hazy skies and knew that it was from the smoky fires all through the state. Bond noticed when she went into the building but made no reaction to her. Sitting with the gentlemen at the table, he turned his head to the side and looked out the window for her, He saw her at the table set for two and resisted the sudden urge to go to her.

She finished her breakfast of scrambled eggs sliced tomato and toast. Slowly got up from the table and went back to her room to ready herself to see the doctor. She knocked at the door of the doctor's office and it was instantly opened for her. She sat across from her at the desk rather than sit at the couch, the doctor looked at Jane and could tell that there was something bothering her, but waited for her to comment about it. The room had been quiet for too long, the doctor broke the silence. "Our last session went good, I can tell that there is something wavering in the air, care to comment on this?"

"It is my former husband's brother." "And which husband would that be?" Jane looked at her puzzled. "You have two husbands, the first one and the second one that put you here." "She blinked moved her face and straightened her shoulders. "The first one, my only one." "Now, you are denying your marriage to the man that beat you? That would be too easy, it exists and he exists, you cannot run from it, it is there" "I want to go back." "You are going to have to tell me a little more-back to where?" "Not back to Oz." "Now, this is a two-parter, the land of Oz is fictious and your current marriage cannot be fictious. Who does this brother belong to? Which one? You told me that you were always alone." "The only one that counted and counts the one to Chris not Jake. And the brother is Bond, Chris's brother. The one that protected me and was my guard. We once before had an intimate relationship almost, I stopped it from happening and last night I saw him here, we talked and I kissed him."

"You kissed him, and this is what is causing all of this turmoil for you?" "It wasn't just a kiss; it was a kiss on the lips." "A romantic kiss then." She shakes her head in response. "With two husbands and you are still looking for someone else? What are you running from or who are you running to?" "That is just it, I don't know. I want Chris back but without any memory of what I just did." "Careful in what you say and what you do, there are no do overs in life. Think about what you did and why that you did it. This is off course of my treatment, but are you going through the change?" Jane pulled back at the doctor; how dare she ask such a personal question. She closed her eyes and breathed out. "Yes, yes I am for months now, I am okay at times then other times I just snap at everything." After she finished saying this last word, she left her mouth open, closed her eyes and breathed out. "Is this it, I am, I feel a different person at times."

The doctor looked at her, jotted down on her notepad. "There you go" Jane got up to leave. "Sit back down, it is not that easy. We are going to have to talk about how you are going to deal with everything. Menopause is not a release card; you still have to deal with the responsibilities of life. And mistakes, how to fix them and how to live with them." Jane sat back down listened to her and made no verbal response. "Chris would have the answer and be the answer." "Yet, you left him and now you want him back. What about Jake? Would you go back to him?" She tensed up in that very second, "Never!"

"You have the proof that you need to end the marriage to him. Your next step is to see a lawyer not me to do this. I cannot do this for you. You have to make this step, your first one. Do you need for me to write this down for you?" She gave no answer. The doctor handed her a piece of paper with this written on it. She took it and made a thankful look to the doctor. "Now you can leave, but the same time tomorrow and there is a group meeting tonight, the information on this should be in your room. Jane, you can be strong, do it." Jane left the office with a feeling of purpose.

She meets Bond in passing leaving the doctor's office. He looked at her in passing and showed no smile to her. She looked to him feeling strong-willed. "I need to talk to you and ask you something important, and don't worry I am not after you. Relax, you can breathe now."

He went to the door of the office and knocked; the doctor opened right up for him to go in. He sat at the middle of the couch, she sat at the chair beside it. "Did, you just talk to her?" "I have talked with a lot of people; you'll have to be more specific." "I saw Jane leaving from this direction." "Yes, I did see her, but that is all that I am going to say about it. You know why we are all here." "I saw her last night and I never expected to see her again let alone here." "And why is this?" "She escaped from us then flew away and of all things she married someone else and, never mind." "Obviously this is upsetting you, we need to talk about it. Why is she important to you?"

"She is married to my brother, Chris and suddenly she just up and left, ran away. It turns out that she married someone else and he beat her and she started drinking and then ended up here." "She told you all of this?" "Yes, I have always been her go to." "And why is that?" "Because I watched over her. When Chris was away." "So, you are your brother's keeper?" "No, I am not that. At that time, she needed someone to make sure that she was safe because the plan made by father was to reunite them after he finished his business." "Bond, how old are you?" "Why do you need to know this and wouldn't you already have this information about me?" "Okay, I will put this question more bluntly- you are a grown man why do you still answer to your father?"

Hearing and watching him say this she knew that she had uncovered something of great bother to him. "Relax, you are here with me. Tell me how you feel about this." "When father told me and just out of the blue, I mean it had been so long, why did he wait until then to tell me? I felt, angry, shocked, disorientated… and anxiety filled my soul. My utter being was shaken. I felt alone, isolated and manipulated, I mean this was all through my life. Why did they lie to me? It was like I was a commodity to make the family whole." He rose up from the couch and paced the room. "Nothing… the pieces no longer fit together. I was living in a mansion but I came to feel that I was walking on rubble. I could only hide any feelings that I had regarding this. It made me feel that I had to be grateful to them and not question anything. Do you know what it is like to grow up knowing who your parents are and then finding out different when you are 45 years old, that I was from an illegitimate relationship that he had, and his wife, my mother is not my birth mother."

"I am sure that this was a challenge to your self-esteem. But, let me rephrase this sentence. Didn't you grow up feeling that you were loved and appreciated?" He sat back down heavily weighing his body on the couch, and quietly replied yes to her. "Think for a moment on the timing of everything, do you think that you father had a reason of why he at that time needed to tell you?" He drew a heavy breath- "Soon after telling me this he died. Did he tell me to clear his conscience?" "I do not know what to think of something as important as this. All the time that you were growing up with the family that you had and still have, did you feel loved?" He sat in silence, opened his mouth and looked down with watery eyes. "Yes."

"Maybe in your father's mind, he put himself as you, and it wasn't until then did he feel that he could except you finding this out, Bond, I know that you have always been loved by your family and you are important to them." She paused and looked to him. What you have to do now, is be important to yourself." "I didn't think about it that way." "Now, these other things that you mentioned?" "I don't know if they are important now." She saw the current relaxed state he was in.

"Do you just want to pick this up tomorrow, then?" He looked straight forward and did not reply back to her. She slightly raised her voice. "How about if we just meet here tomorrow at the same time? Will this work for you?" He jilted his head toward her. Then closed his eyes and stood up. "Yes, that will work. Thank you, doctor," She nodded to him. He left the room letting the door close slowly behind him as he left her office.

Walking down the hallway to leave her office, he wanted to do something other than retreat to his room and be alone as he had done so very much in his life. He went to the outside patio area and took a can of coke from the steel ice bucket placed at the side wall of the building. He opened it looking up to the relaxed sun. Instead of being the bright powerful glaring sun, it seemed peaceful, limited cloud cover blocking its intense rays, but still emitting its power. He found peace in this. He took three sips then started walking the grassy area of the gardens. He told himself, it is a good thing that I came here. I wonder what she has to speak to me about? Is there a reason to worry? I feel that I should call home, but I can't, not from here. What is Chris doing now? Does he miss her? I only hope, so. First and foremost, I need to keep her away from me, in a sense.

He stopped closed his eyes then looked behind him seeing that no one was there, he started back to his room. At the side of the outside door to his room, she was there waiting for him to return. He saw her there and really did not want to approach her but went to his door regardless. He put the keys back in his pocket then stopped by her side. "I presume that you are waiting for me to have this "talk". It can't be here, or in my room. You can take that chair and we can go to where we were last night or somewhere else outside, there is a lot of free room here."

She looked up to his emotionless facial response to her and seemed to read his feelings. She got up and lifted the chair walking away from the hallway. He followed her then took ahold of the chair and carried it. The bench that they had sat at was clear. He placed the chair opposite the bench and told her to sit. She sat at the right side of the bench, he in turn sat on the chair across from her. "Okay, tell me this important news that you have. I am waiting." She looked to him peeved, then relaxed her composure.

She opened her mouth to start talking to him, then stopped and closed her eyes and mouth and took a deep breath in. "Talking with the doctor, she gave me insight of my problem, maybe I was too scared to realize what I have to do, but now I do know the first step. All that I am asking from you now is." She more than saw that he curled up his body sitting in the chair fearing what she was going to say to him. She stopped and took another deep breath of air. "All I want from you is information." He again tensed up fearing her question. "Can you refer me to a good lawyer, I want, or need to start divorce proceedings, to Jake."

She instantly saw air enter his body and noticed the silence in responding to her question. "There are a lot of things that I can say to what you just told me. I will say that I am glad to hear that you are thinking this way. My family has good lawyers, a group of good lawyers, but not specializing in this. I feel that you can find better help in this matter somewhere else. A woman's shelter possibly or even online. I can read you Jane; you want me to hold your hand while you do this. But there are some things and this is one of them that YOU have to do, by yourself."

She sat quietly on the bench and closed her eyes. He feared her response to him. "You are right, you just need to realize that since I was dragged away by the family, I lost my former life where I had, never mind, it is too late to go into this right now and I have to live the present moment. You are right there are places that I can look for help and I might even have to go back to Kansas. I am sure that I can find protection. I just more than anything, want to make sure that we are, you and me are still friends and family. I thank you for your time and everything." He sat back. hearing her words, he couldn't believe her stayed emotion as she said this. Whatever the doctor told her, worked. He the thought of her past actions and was still a bit skeptical that she would follow her words. It would be easy to now talk a walk with her but distance was something that she was now going to have to deal with, distance from him. He got up smiled to her folded the chair and placed it against the bench. "In a few days from now, let me know how you are doing. And there is something else that I want you to think about. I am here, and maybe I have problems, too." He walked away quietly not looking back. She sat there unmoved and teary eyed. Not quite sure that she wanted toto hear what happened as it did. She did not expect that response from him. She told herself, I have to mend my actions myself. I can be strong- I only hope that he will take me back as I am. Bond I always need you. I fear my response at times to everything. I had better go back to my room now and read the paper on the meeting tonight, I can put this puzzle back together, the puzzle of my life. I already thought of the missing piece."

Back in his room Bond circled the perimeter of the room pacing in planned steps. He was quiet though verbally moved his lips to unspoken words. "Can I figure out now, what I want in life? I always had to make excuses that I couldn't have things because of the family, but without the family I have no life. Now there is a two-parter, doctor. Why did my first marriage end? Because I went into it and stayed in it blindfolded. And then she lost the baby, or maybe she lost me. Now there is something to think about. It was just like I was supposed to turn the page on that part of my life, and not relive it or think about it again. A page that could not be reread at any time. Shit, no wonder I drank?" The only thing to do now, is go to that meeting, hopefully the guys will be there, right now I need support.

Later that night at the meeting, the large meeting room was cleared out with chairs placed in circles. There were two circles and each patient could choose which circle that they wanted to go to. This was determined by the people sitting at the different circles or just by the available spaces that there were in circles. He went in the room and was instantly called to by the men from the breakfast table. He stood back and smiled and waved to them but didn't go sit at their group circle. He scoured the room looking for her. She entered the door and stood back looking at the circles. He looked at the clock on the wall then to his wristwatch, making it look like he was checking it for accuracy, he does the famous spy look to his side and see her enter the room and looking for him.

A speaker goes to the standing mike in the middle of the room and tells everyone that it is now time for the meeting to begin and for everyone to take a seat. He walks to the circle at the far end of the room from where he stood. She sees this and goes to that circle and sits down. He in turn steps to the opposing circle that the men from the group were saving him a seat. He looks away from her view not wanting to see it or her at that moment. The meeting began with the man at the mike giving instruction as to what they would be taking about that night. First thing being the noted introductions of the members at the individual groups. He had sidestepped away from doing this at the breakfast meetings. He was now ready though with a perfectly concocted story not admitting to his identity but versed enough in it to remember everything. The meetings of the two groups began. He was surprised that the noise of the two groups conversing stayed quiet enough to hear each word spoken by patients there

----

That night at the estate things went on as they normally did. Dinner conversation, laughter then separating to her individual places. All through dinner Chris had the overwhelming feeling that something was wrong. A guard came in the house and told him that two of the guards were sick and would be leaving to go to their homes. The likely cause of their sickness seemed to be the virus. That guard said that he already had made arrangements for two new guards to take their place on the next day's shift.

The probability of this happening at this time was specious but then could be likely, at that time of the virus. The radar was now lit in his person. He felt unnerved and a bit shaky- the blood did not flow smoothly through his body. He went to the front bureau and took out a handgun, then checked to see if it was loaded, it was-every shell. He put on the safety and placed it at his back above his belt. Even now with it, he encases the room visually sweeping it for everything. He thought should he tell the other two- of the situation, or was he making more of it then it was?

An overwhelming fear ran through him, he fought the natural inclination that he had developed over the years to reach for a bottle. But knew that there wasn't any-now in the house anyway. He took his hand to his open mouth then closed his mouth and ran his hand over his face. He then overlooked his fear that he had there at that time and thought of Jane, was she okay? Was this maybe why he was feeling the way that he did? The dog, where was James? He wasn't barking. He breathed out and dropped his rigid shoulders. He went to the glass sliding door opened it while holding the gun with safety off. James did not come to him. He thought was he even out there? Why didn't he come to him? He thought maybe his is taking a dump, so he waited a couple of minutes and called him again. He didn't show up. He went back inside the house and locked the door and went to the office. Sometimes the dog laid there in his dog bed. He smiled walking to the office thinking that, that must be it. He first thought it odd the door was closed, so how would the dog ever have gotten in there. With gun in hand and his entire nervous system of his body on alert, he pushed open the door and held the gun straight-forward to the room while turning on the light. The room was empty, empty of James any way, everything else there was in its place.

He ran up the stairs to check his bedroom for James. He opened the door took a sweep of the room and bathroom holding the gun and found that he was not there. He looked out the sliding window still with gun in hand ready to fire, he saw the dog, he was laying sideways on the grass lawn of the backyard. He instantly turned around and ran down the stairway and out the door to the backyard to the dog. He didn't respond to his movement or smell, the dog laid still, unresponsive. He felt a pulse on him, he could feel something, but the lack of response greatly bothered him. Knowing full well that he was in danger and now a target he still dropped his gun to the ground and pulled out his cell phone and called the emergency vet to the house.

On his bent knees on the ground next to the dog, he cried. He dog was young and healthy, there was no way that anything like this could be happening to the poor innocent creature. He stood up then bent over and held the dog in his arms and brought him into the house. He laid him on the floor of the entry then ran back for his gun, counting the seconds that it took him to do this. When he went back inside the house, he saw that Troy was with the dog. Once he was at the dog's side Troy got out the way then answered the front door to the vet service that came in a van. "I buzzed them in the gate." Chris had to be pulled out of the side of the dog for them to examine it. They checked for the weak pulse then put it on a stretcher and to the van.

Chris stood at the open front door of the house in weakness and tears. Troy stood by his side supporting him. Someone came back the van and told both of them that they induced the dog to vomit. He said that the dog should be taken into the vet's and monitored for a period of maybe up to three days to recover if the dog can. It was defiantly poisoning. They were then handed a questionnaire to fill out. Troy helped Chris to the couch to sit down- he literally looked like a dead body at this point. The man from the van then told him of the urgency on the matter. Troy nodded his head then grabbed his car keys and followed the van back to the 24-hour vet service.

Chris sat at the couch feeling the weight of the world on his lap, keeping him trapped there, transparent to what he could do to fight or change. "I am not feeling well, I need somebody."" Me." He turned to look behind him at the base of the staircase, and saw Jonathan. "I am going to check the outside of the house, Chris rose up from the couch and in one second changed his entire composure, back to that of a trained spy ready for action. Jonathan was in awe of this and they each went outside. Jonathan to the front of the house grounds and Chris went to the back. He walked around the swimming pool and saw it all clear. Then stopped at the grass area where he found James. He closed his eyes and breathed out to the pain that it represented, then quickly caught himself to be on guard. He walked forward to the direction of the ocean, then swore that he heard footsteps, He thought that couldn't be, how do you hear footprints in the sand? Unless they were from the gardens above him and he had his back to the enemy. He jumped in a quick turn running closer to the emitting sound- he opened his eyes wide to the fear and racing panic of war, the whites of his eyes shining in the darkness of the night sky. A gun cocked, he felt that he was in the middle of a pinball game. He fired four times at the direction of the noise, unaware of the piercing loud sound rippling the airwaves. He ran to the direction that he heard a body fall. It was at the right side of the back area of the swimming pool next to the bushy area by the side trees.

He didn't recognize the body, and fought his natural inclination to reach down to it and feel for a pulse or check for identity, He just stood there looking down to the body showing no expression. Jonathan ran to him. He reached down and checked for a pulse. "He is dead. What happened? Do you know who he is?" Chris said nothing looking at him in his half-dead state. Neither said it but they both thought it, Bond, where are you?' He was the one that always seemed to fix things at times like this. Jonathan carefully turned the body then took his wallet out from his back pocket. He looked at the Driver's license. "This man is named; Jake and he is from Kansas. What is he doing here?"

Chris heard these words and played them over and over in his mind. "We need Bond- we have to get him, and now. I need someone, I need something, and I don't know what." He bent down and cried. Jonathan lifted his shirt and helped him up. They went back to the house and locked the sliding glass door. He sat him back down on the couch. "Where is Troy?" "My dog was poisoned and he is at the vet." "This strange man was here with a gun and James was poisoned and the guards both have left to illness? This was planned, and the motive? He was aiming at you, you were the target, why?" Chris was silent to the world at that point. "I feel that I should call your doctor, but, most importantly the body. The police will be combing this area, someone would have reported the sound of the bullets. And the guards aren't here."

"Ah!" he exclaimed;" it is just what do I do with him? Your gun where is it? Did we leave it out there?" Again, no reaction from Chris. Out of the blue there was a loud pounding at the front doors. Fear over overwhelmed Jonathan, Chris bolted up off of the couch and picked the magazines up off of the table and hurdled them through the air of the room. Jonathan looked to Chris who looked like he was starting a fit of anger-then to the front door, the pounding resumed. It had to be the police, but what could he do at that second. In order to be innocent- you had to act innocent. If they had nothing to be guilty off, why would they hide? And the fear of the gunshots, this is what triggered, his PTSD. He then moved quickly to the door and answered it without words. Now, standing there at the open doors, he dropped his mouth and could not believe what and who he saw. He stepped back for this man to enter the house, at a loss for words. The man that entered instantly went to Chris, who stood in the living room. "I am here, brother, it is okay, sit, sit down everything will be okay.

Jonathan closed and locked the front door then went to the living room and stood beside them. "You are in California; how did you know and how did you get out of that facility?" "I was there voluntarily not by doctors' orders. I signed myself out, they were not happy on me leaving but it was my choice. I just had an overwhelming fear that something was wrong- I got here as soon as I could. Where is James?" Jonathan sighed lowered his shoulders then told Bond of that night's events.

"So, Troy is with him now?" Jonathan shakes his head to him. "Good, we have a lot of things to do and quickly. You stay here a minute with him.' Jonathan shook his head and stayed by the side of Chris. Bond ran down the stairs with Chris's medicine, then ran to the kitchen and came back with a glass of water. "Here, swallow it." He stood over him and watched him swallow the pill. "Have you been taking them daily as you should?" He received no answer. "We are going to have to get him to a hospital. But not now, there, is an order." He stepped back from them and to the open entry, then called Troy. Troy was more than surprised in hearing from him. He got through this conversation as quickly as possible. He found out that keeping James there was the planned best course for his treatment. He asked Troy to get back to the estate. He was greatly needed there.

He motioned for Jonathan to cone to him to say something to him. Chris got up and went to at the same time. He knew that he had no time to deliberate on what to do with him at that moment. He then thought, power, the cards always seemed to play to a hand of power. He placed his hand on Chris's shoulder. I am glad that you are here, buddy, you are going to make this happen. The most important thing for us to do right now, is keep watch. And this is what you are going to do. You can best do this, upstairs at the deck of your bedroom. Keep watch over the ocean. Make sure that no one and nothing combs the shores. Later we are going to have to go out there, believe me I will let you know when. He watched Chris run the stairs inside the house.

Jonathan get a tarp out from the garage and bring it to the back patio. He instantly then made some calls. The tarp was now in the backyard and he was finished with the calls. Troy came in the house. Bond told him of the next planned move. Chris ran down the stairs and told them that there was a small boat on the outside shore of their property. Bond thought, Chris looked and sounded like he had it together, but still wasn't sure. Chris I am going to need you to stand by me. Troy came running in from the back side of the house. He said words to Troy and Jonathan listened to everything. They took the tarp to the dead body, Chris thought that it was odd, but Bond took pictures of the body especially the face of this now limp body. They rolled the body in the tarp and took it to the beach. The boat moved as close to the shore as it could. "Troy this is where you are going to have to swim, and I will too. Chris you watch and make sure that no one else sees anything. Got it?" Chris made an expression of understanding.

Bond took the front part of the tarp and Troy took the back, they moved it to the boat. Troy wore rubber gloves and did the driver of the boat. They moved the tarp containing the body on to the boat then unwrapped it. A silencer was put on his gun and a shot was fired directly to the dead man's body by clenching his hand to the gun and firing it at his own self, making it look like suicide. The area of the boat was wiped of any and all finger prints. He driver jumped out then Troy did and wiped the area dry where they jumped from. They all went back to land then walked to the house.

All now inside, Bond told them to all get showered, dried off and changed into their pajamas, being the late-night hour. They each did then met back in the living room waiting for further instruction from him. All assembled in that room, a loud sound of whirling helicopter blades vibrating in the otherwise quiet room. Troy ran to the back window looking out to the backyard and ocean. Bond instantly called him back away from view of the window. Then motions all of them to the walled hallway to the side of the office. He looks to him, for an answer. "It was a helicopter shining its spotlight down over the ocean. "I thought that it would be. The most important thing for us to do right now is stay out of view of anything, no going to the doors or windows, go to our beds and stay there, try your hardest for sleep. We don't know anything about this, or any occurrence, got it"

Jonathan questioned him, regarding Chris, and taking him to the hospital. "Yeah, right. I just do not feel that it is a good idea to leave right now. Chris, how are you feeling?" He received no answer. He thought that being he just took a pill maybe this would be enough. "No, I am not going to my room to sleep. Chris- I have done it before when we were in Vegas,

I'll do it again tonight. I am sleeping in the chair to the side of your bed. I don't want any comment from you, this is for everyone's safety, go it?" He didn't like the idea, but didn't fight it.

Sitting in an easy chair to the side of his bed, Bond thought, he should have earlier texted the doctor regarding his behavior, if he did it now, the timing wasn't right. The best thing to do is just wait for the morning. Being that he just got there to the island and estate, his excuse would be that he was just too tired to do this at that time. He more than anything wanted sleep to overwhelm his tired aching body, but it took its time to be able to drift off to it. Waking in the early morning hour, he looked to see Chris on the bed. He wasn't there. Fear incased his spine, to where he would find him. He got up and went to the closed bathroom door and heard the shower, just to make sure he opened it and looked in and indeed his brother was there taking a shower. Chris saw him peek in and replied aloud, "A little privacy, please." He instantly closed the door and replied back in a loud voice that he was just checking. "I know, and thanks for staying here last night." He started to say your welcome, but turned a left the room going downstairs to his bathroom and shower and dress for the day instead.

Esmerelda was in the kitchen with coffee made and warm fruit biscuits from the oven. They all were presently in the kitchen at the table with the exception of her being there. Bond told her to go and clean the rooms upstairs, she did. They now had privacy. Jonathan got up turned on the television remarking that they should hear if this story made the news. It did. At that very moment, a scene of the stranded motor boat floating on the ocean waters was scene then the camera focused on the dead body inside the boat. The commenter told the story then finished his last sentence with, "A suicide." The female news caster by this side then remarked how that this virus has made people go a bit crazy, they smiled then went to a commercial break. Bond got up from his chair and turned the TV off.

"Hopefully we were able to dodge this, but we don't know of how much further this police investigation will go." "We pretty much covered everything up", remarked Troy. "It just depends on who this person is and why we are target." "Could it be maybe as it was said on the TV, that this was just some deranged psychopath and nothing more than that?" remarked Jonathan. Bond got up then looked dazed at Chris. Jonathan, commented, raising his body then spoke up. "Gentlemen- there is something that we have all overlooked." Troy quipped, "And what is that?" "Where were the dogs?" Troy was instantly up from the table and halfway out the door replying that he was on his way to check on this. Bond too left saying, "I have the pictures I am going to go try to figure something out. I would appreciate not to be bothered, gentlemen." He left for the office.

Inside his office sitting behind the desk, more than anything he wanted to work on getting this over with, he quickly reminded himself to call the doctor, they needed cover. He texted her, and left a message. He found out that this man that targeted them for a killing was the same man that Jane ran away from. He somehow found out. He figured that since she ran away- she would be his target and he wanted to change her game plan. His main concern now, was-what would should do or react to finding this out? Since she was there, she could not be a suspect, but could they? being that he was there too near them? He checked the beep on his phone and read the responding text from Dr, Stone, "Bring him in, A.S.A.P." He put the phone back in his pocket and went to Chris, still in the kitchen, he motioned for them to leave for the doctor. He followed him out they drove there in the Hummer. Bond reminded him of what to say to the her, once there.

Bond stayed in the waiting room of her office. Chris sat silent, across from her at her desk. "Okay them, I will start this conversation. Chris, right now and pertaining to yesterday what is bothering you? Your brother told me that you went into a rage, care to explain this to me. And remember I am not here to judge you; I am here to help you." He moved in the chair expressing a feeling of discomfort then opened his mouth twice before verbally saying anything. "Okay, how would you feel if your spouse of many years out of the blue, flew off to parts unknown and then married someone else and then does not get in contact with you. And you find out that they have been beaten up in this new marriage and is now on the run. Would you want to save them, knowing that they left you and only now after something as horrific as what happened to them, only now do they want to come back to you… And you find out that you are now the target for that person to kill? How would you feel? Everyone just expects me to save her risking my own life when she without any notice leaves me. I do love her and felt that she is my life but after this? What comes next? My funeral?"

"You, have never been quite this vocal to me before and presently you sound more like your brother." He interrupts her. "Because I have always been tied to the bounds of both my job and my life. I had no choice on how to act or what to say. Right now, right now, here in this room is the only time that I have spoken about this and not broken any bonds. Of what? My loyalty, so that I can breathe?" "Chris, do you want your present life?" "At this point in my life, what else is there?" She sat quiet. "As for the case of P.T.S.D. have you been keeping up on your daily medication intake?" "Does, it even matter?" "Yes, yes it does, right now YOU are the most important being in this room and I am not just saying this. I want you to take a moment and stop, just stop thinking about the present rift of things and all of the things in your haunting past. Yes, I know of this. Think of the things and people that you feel for in your heart your good emotions, what you have strived for in your life." He breathed out trying desperately to shield himself from her words wanting to feel his own emotions then thought of her words in the silence given to him.

"Right now, I know that you want an escape- from everything that you have told me. I think that if I just send you home right now-you will try something, and probably, most probably, what it is will not be good for anyone. You need rest, to think about everything, without pressure, both the pressure that you feel and the added pressure that you out on yourself. She writes down an order for a hospital stay, then explains this to him, she tells him to stay there, then gets on her desk phone. He closes his eyes and seems to let his body rest while she does this. Fifteen minutes later, two men knock on her office door. She lets them in. They are orderlies from the hospital. They take hold of Chris's hands leading him out the door of her office and to the hospital via ambulance. He walks with them with no resistance. Bond watches observing all of this, he doesn't question anything and stands silent to the doctor. She explains everything to him and more than anything she tells him that Chris needs rest from everything right now, so no visiting. Before she leaves, she hands him papers with these orders written down. He folds these papers in his hand then goes to his Hummer and leaves to head back home.

He drives in silence looking like he was thinking of nothing, but everything and more beat at the walls of his brain. More than anything he felt he needed a release. He thought of going home to the wagging tail of James, but even he wasn't there right now. He thought, what about Jane? Does she know? How will she take the news? And where will she go when she is released? More than anything he wanted to fly there and bring her home protected. But maybe too this was the problem. She was Chris's wife, not his to protect and stand by, but it seemed just natural for him to be there for her.

He went off course on the planned ride home and went to the cemetery to visit his father's grave. Momentary fear paralyzed his spine as he found trouble in getting out the Hummer. He circled the perimeter of his view looking for the priest, seeing no one he thought is this safe? He engulfed his fear and walked out to the grave site. He looked to the writing on the headstone and wiped the dusty dirt off of it. "Dad, we all wish that you were with us right now, well you are, you always live in me. I don't think I have to tell you what is going on, you know. Please, father I ask you for strength at this all-important time. In a way I want to stay right here with you forever, but I know that we'll be together in Heaven, I just have a lot of living to do before I see you there." He placed both of his hands over the gravestone, fought his tears from falling then squeezed it until he saw red lines on his skin where he squeezed the hard stone. He released his hands then placed them over his heart. "I love you dad." He blinked then turned and walked away.

CHAPTER **23**

Back at the estate he saw that Troy was gone. He wondered how much longer that he should keep this going, as they haven't seemed to find out any more needed information. That entire case seemed rather insignificant now any way. Jonathan's car was gone, he had no idea where he was or what he was doing. His phone beeped that a text was coming in. He read it, it was from the vet, James was recovering and seemed to be good but to be safe they wanted to have him there for one more day. He texted back, yes, then scratched his chin looked down to his rug and breathed in. "Give me your strength."

A call came in right after he said this. "Yes, yes, the treatment center, I ah, I thought that I already went through everything with you, I am okay." He listened and instantly dropped his entire upbeat tone. "You told her?" He listened. "I still do not think that it was wise to do this in her fragile state" He tensed even more listening to the voice on the phone. The doorbell rang. "Ah, I have to get the door right now. Can you call me back or I'll call you back, I need to go?" He hung up before hearing the answer.

Answering the front door wide, he closed his eyes thinking of how stupid what he just did was, he had no protection at this time, but then how did whoever was there- get in? He opened his eyes to two police officers. Seeing them standing in front of him he gave a total look of overwhelming surprise. They saw this and told him to relax. "What, what is the matter?" "Sir, I am sure that you are aware of what happened here on the waters outside of your residence last night." He invited him inside, but they declined at spoke to him at the open front door.

"I had just gotten back from a trip to California and I was very tired, my brother well, he, I have the paper right here, he patted his body but the paper was not there. He told them it would just be a second and he would get the paper from the doctor. He returned from the office with it and handed it to the officer on his left side. The officer, unfolded the paper and read it. "His brother, Chris is in the clear, he was at the hospital last night." They left but stopped right before getting back in the police car to leave, "We'll be back in touch regarding this."

He read the folded paper that the officer gave back to him. It was an order by the attending psychiatrist, Dr. Stone, for hospitalization, and it had yesterday's date on it. Meaning that Chris was there last night. He then thought was this a mistake by her part or did she know that he needed an excuse. Regardless of what it was, he was thankful for it. He immediately thought of father and maybe somehow it was help from him. He went back to the office and thought of James and how he wished that he could pet him right now, there was just something about the calming effect that he had over him, the reassurance. "Tomorrow, buddy, tomorrow." He sat back and wiped his hand over the side of his head stroking his hair." Mrs. Richards, your husband is gay and running an illegal business and pocketing your money, should I just send her an email?" He opened the computer then grabbed ahold of his phone and called the clinic in California.

Once connected to the party that called him, he listened to their words Jane collapsed. This was resulting in them telling her that her current husband, had died. His body was found floating in the ocean waters off of the coast of Oahu, Hawaii, after a police investigation, it was called a suicide. The next course of action would be to contact a family member for her care, this is where her first husband Chris came into play. Bond thought Chris was now in the hospital for psychiatric treatment there was no way that he could tell them this. He calmly replied that Chris was still fighting off the virus and was now in the last stage. He then explained to them that he had power of attorney over him and that he- being his brother knew Jane very well.

He needed to send then confirmation of what he just told them. He hung up then called his attorney explained the whole problem and the attorney took care of the information needed and said that he would be back in touch with the next course of action. He got up stretched his body and went to the kitchen, stopping to look out the front door making sure that the front gate was closed. He saw Troy driving in and going to the back side of the house as he usually did, Now walking to the kitchen he wondered why he had come back so soon. Now there, he took a can of soda from the refrigerator then looked down the back hall for Troy. Troy waved to him, and said that he would be right there. He came out of his bedroom with a can of beer and looked exhausted. He sat then Bond did as well. Bond looked to him for an answer to a question he never asked. "I left early because she told me that her husband is flying home today. I stayed there a while longer- I then told her that she is doing very well, she no longer needed my help that she was doing very well, before I left though, I put on piece of paper by her purse." Bond looked to him and saw that he wasn't getting any further information from him, only saw that he was guzzling from the beer can. "And what information was this?" "He wiped his chin then looked to the table top, then halfway back up to view Bond's face, "The phone number of the Domestic Abuse Hotline." He sat quiet hearing this.

"How is your brother doing?" Bond relaxed his weak body slumping down in the chair and breathed out then looked to the ceiling. "I guess he is good news." Troy tilted his head and gave him the eye, "How so?" "Well after the police came here today and I showed them the doctor's orders- yesterday's date was written on it, meaning that he was in the hospital last night. He has an alibi. They did not ask about you or Jonathan. I volunteered no further information then what I already told them." "So, you just acted puzzled?" "I was. I mean the whole sequence of events, it was like they were planned out, the guards not being there, getting sick at the same time, everything." A deep forceful voice came from behind him. "It is called the spy game." Jonathan was there and said this.

"I found out some much need pertinent information related to the Richards case. The FBI in San Francisco is on this or his case. As soon as he sets foot off the plane he will be arrested. Gentlemen they figured it out before we did. It's a good thing that we have no involvement in this matter. And Troy, what are you doing here?" Troy explained. He reached for a glass from the overhead cabinet, then placed it on the counter and took a bottle of sapphire gin from a twisted closed brown paper bag. "Sorry, Bond, but I need this. I know what you are going to say, so you don't need to say it. When will Chris be back?"

"I do not know yet, I haven't heard anything." "I will be getting James back tomorrow, but I may have to leave to go after someone else and bring her here." He explained everything to him. "You cannot go, you are too fragile and she knows how to work you." Bond nodded his head in agreement to his words. "Right now, my attorney is working on everything, I can make no plans until I hear back from him." "As it should be."

Bond returned to the office as the men went their separate way in the house. Right as he waked in the door looking down to the empty dog bed, the desk phone rang. He answered it, it was the clinic in California calling him back regarding Jane. He was told that because of her current condition she was admitted to a local hospital, at this time someone needed to be there or someone needed to be responsible for both the cost of her care of her treatment. After hearing these words, he looked wide eyed to a desperate world of no answer. He in turn gave them a method of payment for her care and again reminded them of the contact with the attorney.

I wish that James was here right now. The phone buzzed; someone was at the gate. He got up from the chair and went to the door. He looked out of the peephole of the front door but felt he should not answer the door or make himself visible in any way. He felt thankful that there was one guard there on duty that brought this envelope that the guard had to sign for to him. He brought it to the kitchen table and opened it. Both Jonathan and Troy came there to watch him do this. They were curious on its contents He felt fearful, but there was nothing else that he could do but open it. He took out the two pieces of paper that were inside of the envelope. Troy instantly remarked that from the size of one piece of paper it looked like a check.

He read the letter then raised his eyebrows uplifted his body and smiled. He read it again. Both of the other two men were now extremely jumpy replying to him, "What, what is it?" Bond breathed out and looked at each one in the eye then back to the paper. "Gentlemen, it seems that our Mrs. Richards, already suspected the dealings of her husband and had a hired P.I. on this case. She knew of us, and that we were trying to solve this case as well. She was more than delighted at Troy's company for her safety. She thanks us."

He hands Jonathan the cheque made out to the family name. Jonathan read it then looked dumbfounded, Troy moved his head to view it and made the same expression. "She was rich! this amount is for $100,000." Bond replied back, "We don't have to worry about paying the bills this month."

They relaxed for the rest of the day and sent out for a chicken dinner. Bond was relieved that two of the guards were presently on duty. He could see and tell that the other two were relaxed. He could only give the persona that he was relaxed and composed, but he couldn't get his mind off of his brother and Jane. He hadn't heard back from his lawyer regarding what to do next, he could only wait. He knew that it was going to be a long night. There is a fine line between denial and hope.

He more than anything wanted to savor a fine glass of Pinot Noir and look out to the ocean, but he didn't want to have to start the program for alcoholism again knowing that right now especially he was fragile and that is the worst time to step-backwards. He went in the living room and turned on the stereo listening to soothing rapture of Verdi while drinking a glass of cranberry juice.

He slept to the morning hour of seven and showered and dressed for the day. He wore the black polo shirt that Jane earlier complimented him on and beige cotton shorts. Looking in the mirror he saw that it was time to get a haircut, but this something that could wait. He heard his cell phone buzz, He read a text sent to him by his lawyer, He needs to be at the airport to pick up Jane, and sign that he would be responsible for her, as Chris was still in the hospital. He replied back, Will do, then closed it. Then went to the kitchen grabbed a cup of coffee and went outside to the backyard. He was welcomed by the sound of a dog barking, he looked to the direction where it came from and saw Troy's smiling face then felt a warm hairy body against his leg. He looked down and saw James, he almost threw the coffee cup to the table, then picked him up, instantly feeling his weight. James licked the side of his face. He put him down then ran to the beach with him. Bond was laughing and James was happily barking on this run on the beach.

Later at the breakfast table, Bond told Jonathan of the earlier text and that in the afternoon; he would be picking her up at the airport. Jonathan replied back, "Do you want me to go with you?" After hearing these words, he instantly thought of the pro and con of it, then told him that he would do this himself. Walking to the office, he could feel James almost glued to his leg. "I missed you too, buddy."

The desk phone rang, James went to the ringing phone. He looked to the dog then went to the phone thinking, did this mean something. The call was from the hospital. Chris left- they couldn't find him and all of his things were gone. "No, I do not have him or know where he is…Yes, if I hear anything, I will let you know…." He hung up then called Chris's cell phone. The call went through, but no answer. He stood up and told James that they were going to look for him on the estate. James was already at the door. Jonathan and Troy looked for him as well. Jonathan quietly took to him at the front door, "Do you think that someone took him and he is in danger?" "I just don't have that feeling. There is one other person that I have to ask about this with." He went to the office, James followed him. He called Dr. Stone, and explained everything he was more than surprised at her calm demeanor. Hanging up from the call, she never gave him an answer either way, if she knew something but she didn't appear to be alarmed by anything. He checked the time on his wristwatch and saw that it was time to leave to pick her up at the airport.

Now at the airport after checking in with the needed parties he went to the gate where she would be deplaning from. Looking directly at the persons exiting the plane and walking into the airport, he didn't notice the other people standing their waiting to pick people up from the flight.

He smiled as he saw her leaving the hallway and to the airport waiting area. She was wearing a black tee shirt and beige slacks with the jacket folded around her waist. She looked nice, he noticed that she had put on a little weight, but this virus seemed to be doing this to everyone. He saw that she hurried her pace, almost to a run but was not going to him. She lowered her facial mask then jumped to the arms of a man. It was Chris.

They came loose from their hug and walked from the gate. He noticed that Chris looked to him lowered his sunglasses and winked to him. "She's back." He waked to them and asked them if they needed a ride. "Only, if it is by you Bond," They left the airport walking side by side wearing their face masks.

The End